THIS IS THE PLACE

Anchor

Books

Doubleday

new york

london

toronto

sydney

auckland

THIS IS THE PLACE

PETER ROCK

AN ANCHOR BOOK
PUBLISHED BY DOUBLEDAY
a division of Bantam Doubleday Dell Publishing Group, Inc.
1540 Broadway, New York, New York 10036

ANCHOR BOOKS, DOUBLEDAY, and the portrayal of an anchor are
trademarks of Doubleday, a division of Bantam Doubleday Dell
Publishing Group, Inc.

Book design by Dana Leigh Treglia

Library of Congress Cataloging-in-Publication Data
Rock, Peter, 1967–
This is the place / Peter Rock. — 1st Anchor Books ed.
p.   cm.
I. Title.
PS3568.O327T48   1997
813'.54—dc20   96-33606
                                                                CIP

ISBN 0-385-48598-0

1   3   5   7   9   10   8   6   4   2

FOR MY FAMILY

THIS IS THE PLACE

I. STATELINE

No one is satisfied where they are.
Even the angels descend slowly
through the clouds to put their feet
on the ground. Swimming delights
them; their wings shed water and,
splashing clumsily, they terrify fish.
For angels, clumsiness is a wel-
come relief—sometimes they lose
their balance, but they must practice their stumbling, trick their
grace. Yes, they drag their wings
through the desert, across the salt
flats, they gather along the border
to watch what will happen.

I am saying something like this,

going off, and Anita sits next to me at the bar, slowly shaking her head. The others are only half-listening; they look up when I pause to catch my breath. Behind them, the rows of slot machines blink and call. Nickels, quarters, dollar slots. A few desperate fools are playing, but the casino is mostly empty. The Stateline is always open, as it is easiest never to turn anything off, only to let it slow down. Out in the midst of the machines, a Cadillac sits inside velvet ropes, and we'll probably only pretend to give it away. All shiny and pathetic, on a platform, the car does not look out of place.

If only we all stumbled with such joy, I say.

Shut up, Anita says.

The sameness of these nights is the best promise of change. I am patient, I have never known despair. If it's true I've been drinking, it's only because of the coffee—in the morning I must have a few shots if I'm ever to find sleep again. I'd like to sit, but I've been standing so long that my knees are not anxious to bend.

Anita has a list of Mormon relatives as long as her left arm; she stretches out her arm and almost knocks over my drink. She says Mormon angels aren't like that, that they don't even have wings, that they look just like we do.

Watch out, says Mike the bartender. He's new, and they never last long; they always call me old, yet I see them come and go. I was tossing cards down the bar, into his tip cup, and he just took them out and stacked them there, trying not to give me the satisfaction of a response.

That's not it at all, I say. The point is that they return, that they miss it down here, that heaven doesn't satisfy them.

I've lost to better dealers, a man says, pointing at me. Smoother dealers.

No doubt, I say, sending him a drink. But tonight you got beat by the cards. He's staring at me, wearing a bolo tie made from a trilobite fossil; it's pulled tight, so his head won't slip down inside his shirt like a turtle's. Wrinkles run down his neck and his ears look strange, artificial. Behind him, most of the tables are dark, under their Naugahyde covers; only one light is on, and Sandra, who comes in to replace me, is playing solitaire, cursing and smiling to herself.

Your horse still loose? I ask Anita.

I don't even want to hear about it, she says.

You're not so hot, the turtle tells me, then turns and heads toward Sandra's table, saying something about a fresh deck. I throw a card after him, hit him in the back, but he doesn't notice. I pick up my last drink and taste it. All dealers seek a truce between what they put in their bodies—we do anything to maintain the steadiness of hands.

Maybe it's the colors that gets them, I say.

Who? says Anita, her elbows on the bar, her chin in her hands.

The angels. The view from above, through the clouds, is like windows of colors, and some are so addicted they're deaf to the music of harps.

Anita says heaven is not black and white, that there's even more colors up there, a wider spectrum, just like all the things dogs can hear.

They miss the colors down here, I say, and someone at the end of the bar cuts in to let me know that angels come down for others, not for themselves.

Maybe so, I say, but even they are a little selfish. I slide my empty glass away.

You coming over? Anita asks me. She says her boyfriend won't bother us, if I mean who she thinks, that no one will be in our way. That's all I need to know to keep me headed home.

Come on, she says.

You act like he has something to give, says Mike.

I ask him if he wants to find out and that cracks them all up. Past the machines, past the Cadillac, I work my way toward the door. Smoke has been collecting inside since the beginning of time. The voices keep on behind me, conversations that could go on forever, as if talking would keep people afloat somehow, prevent them from ever being alone.

The door closes behind me, shutting out all the noise of the machines. The air is cool, it's five in the morning, and lights reflect in the hoods of parked cars, colors surprised out of the darkness. The lights come from Wendover Will, the neon giant, sixty-four feet tall and made of metal. His gun is as big as a person, his cigarette a yard long. He is my brother. Waving and pointing to the casino, his smile is insincere, both ingratiating and contentious. You can hear him creak as he moves; with your eyes closed, you'd swear he was a windmill.

A police car passes one way, then the other. Coyotes howl somewhere, out in the desert. They are quiet when they come in close to town, so there's no reason to worry if you can hear them. Some call coyotes God's dogs, and that would explain how they became so quiet, so sneaky.

Under Wendover Will, the sign reads THIS IS THE PLACE, and he is facing east, making this claim across the salt flats, across the desert, over a hundred miles to where Brigham Young is standing atop his monument, saying the same thing. THIS IS THE PLACE. I know their argument well: in Utah you will learn morality and restraint and you will yearn for everything you deny yourself; here in Nevada, nothing is illegal, everything is permitted and encouraged and will make you feel hollow. Believe me, the states need each other to recognize themselves, to savor the knowledge that there is an unhappiness more desperate than their own. Evil likes an audience, but good can't exist without one.

Brigham is a statue. He stands in the confidence of stone, the patience of the truth. I've felt the pull of the temple in Salt Lake City, but my pride is stronger, and in the parking lot of the Stateline, most of the license plates are from Utah. Neon demands your attention. Some people see all garishness as insecurity and that's exactly why it's such an effective pose. Will shines on, waving and pointing. Stay close to me, brother. Come right in, we say, you're all more secure than we are, you're substance and not just bright surfaces. What could you have to fear?

The dispute between Will and Brigham is not for me to settle, nor would I want it settled. The words hang over the salt flats, the most forsaken stretch of earth, a terrifying expanse of sheer space, white, like another planet, hard and smooth where nothing can live. This all sounds so grim! I've known joy and I'll know it again. It's just that it takes work to get up the words to talk about love.

I keep walking, turning away from Will, toward the lights of the other casinos. It feels good to shiver and the nights are getting longer again, making it easier for me to fall asleep before sunrise. The slope down to the trailer park is full of ruts left by idiots with their four-wheel drives. All the alcohol in my body fights the caffeine. Down below, the boys' fire is almost out; a few are awake, the tips of their cigarettes glowing in the dawn, and the rest are asleep, sharing blankets.

Pyro, the boys call after me. Hey, Pyro.

There's hardly a house in Wendover—it's almost all trailers, as if putting down a foundation would be admitting something. My trailer is on the far side of the park and as I walk through the others I see the faint shadows of wings, the wooden butter-flies, a foot across or more, that people attach to the sides of their trailers. Some trailers have so many that it seems they'll be lifted right off the ground.

Behind his window, my neighbor just raises his hand from the armrest of his chair as I go by. He doesn't even show me his palm. My dog's chain lies twisted and empty in the dirt by my trailer, still attached to the stake. I reach inside the front door and take out the flashlight. There's no one in my car, no one asleep in the back seat. I rake the beam of light under the trailer, bending down to see the broken bottles, the old snake-skins, then I step inside. The trailer shifts a little beneath my weight. I check the bathroom, the shower, even the small cup-boards, every corner, to make certain I am alone.

Once the water runs hot, I soak my hands, bending my fingers, rubbing at the liver spots. If arthritis catches me now it's all over; most dealers have to retire because of their hands, if their eyes or their memories don't give out first. We'll see how much I can remember, how I can put it back together. After the water, I turn to my lotions. Yes, I'm not ashamed to admit I have more lotions than any woman, that I wear gloves to bed to spare my sheets. I squint in the light over the mirror; I am an old man, a ragged culmination, and that's an interesting thing to be. I turn out the light.

As I lie in bed I think of all the people I must tell about, how I'll parade them before you, all tricked out, and I wonder if in heaven everyone's motivations are true, if everything turns out well, just as expected. Sometimes, to find sleep, it is enough to admit that you have done and thought beautiful, terrible things.

Afternoons, I read until sunset, when I put my book down on the table, a fork in the pages to hold my place, and search for my shoes. I can't read any longer, for I work at nine and must rest my eyes. I've ironed the white shirt and put it on, then the black vest; my bow tie is in my pocket and its clips scratch my leg. There was a time when I often visited Anita before I went to work. My reasons changed, but still I would walk across town, under the highway, anxious to see what was happening in that house.

Now it is no longer a place I frequent; now there are awkward, lonely hours between sunset and the time to deal the cards.

I will begin with the spring, eight months ago; we'd seen the last snowstorm then, just as any day now we'll see the first of this new season. The nights were still cold and my dog had wound its chain all the way around the stake and was pinned there, shivering, waiting patiently for me to come and let it loose. The sun had set, and I stepped out of the trailer, down into my yard, and began to untangle the dog. It licked at my fingers, tail slapping the dust, white around its eyes, gray hairs around its muzzle. Standing, I left my dog there; it followed me to the end of its chain as I started up the slope.

A few nights before, at Anita's house, I had met Charlotte, a girl from Utah, just out of high school. She was working with a group in the Goshute Mountains, outside of town, and all they did was count the hawks flying over. They stood in the mountains and watched the sky. From this, they made predictions about the environment, filled charts with information about the state of the world.

Charlotte was Anita's niece, and we met there, mongrel dogs and inbred cats underfoot. The animals have their own door and they come and go, bringing dead voles, baby mice, children's lost clothing. I've seen it. On the walls hang posters of puppies and kittens sleeping all together, cats sitting on toilet seats. I stood watching Charlotte; nervous, I shuffled a deck of cards from one hand to the other so they filled the air like an accordion.

Any good at cards? she said. She said it like a challenge.

I told her I usually won.

It's his job, said Anita.

You probably cheat.

I can, I said, but I don't have to.

When Charlotte took down the cribbage board, Anita told her not to bother me, that I had to play cards all night.

It's no bother, I said, but Anita didn't like it. She circled the table as we got everything ready, her eyes on me. My interest

8

in Anita had faded long before. It's more complicated, of course, but part of it was that I had come to think of her as living proof of evolution; it isn't anything wild, exciting or particularly untamed about her—it has more to do with the way she walks, the way she moves among her animals, how she stands to one side and watches things happen.

Charlotte rocked back in her chair, fanning her cards, looking over the top of them and laughing at me. Her voice was smooth, polished, the opposite of shrill. Some of the kittens were so desperately inbred that they were blind, caught in corners, and Anita hurried to catch them, to set them straight, while Charlotte and I began to play. Charlotte leaned close to me when I talked, explaining some rule, and at first I wondered if she was hard of hearing; her forearms rested on the table, her hands stretched out to me. I spoke even more softly to bring her closer. She slapped my hands, accusing me of miscounting—I was trying not to stare, trying to count the freckles on the bridge of her nose. I was a marvel of restraint. I told her I never miscounted.

Perhaps it was from searching the skies, but her eyes seemed unable to focus up close, as if they looked straight through, past me—then they caught me for an instant and were gone again. In that moment I knew how things would turn between us and how they will turn; I knew it wouldn't be long before she would tell me of miracles, unbelievable stories, and I knew that I would believe them; I knew I would feel the smoothness of her skin and even her skin after the smoothness was taken. There in the beginning it was clear she had something to tell, that she had been waiting for me, and that was why I was once again anxious to get to Anita's house.

At the top of the slope I looked down, west, to the air strip and the Hide-A-Way Casino, then closer, to my trailer, dark and pathetic. My dog was already half-tangled, watching me leave him. Mac's and the Red Garter are further off; the Red Garter burned down once, but it was early, when it was under construction, and it wasn't much of a fire.

9

I turned and kept on, under Wendover Will, his neon kicking on a section at a time—one leg, then an arm, his head, hat and cigarette patient in the darkness above. Wait for me, I told him, I'm just seeking a little respite, a young face, some relief. The dry wind from the desert was raking the dusk, aging everything yet making it last. As I crossed the street, I felt someone watching me. A boy, a young man, was eating off the hood of his car, something from Taco Burger. He was wearing his belt buckle on his hip and it was so large—round and silver, an alleged rodeo trophy, one of an endless variety available in the pawnshops of Wendover—and looked so heavy I was surprised he didn't fall over sideways. I looked at him like every other person I never expect to lay eyes on again.

Want something? he said.

Who doesn't? I said. I stood still, looking at him, then turned away. Rudeness is a privilege of the old. I checked over my shoulder and he was still watching me, the hamburger in his hand caught halfway to his mouth. Anita lives on the other side of the highway; I passed under the highway, the trucks constantly disappearing above, not stopping, not even slowing down if they could help it.

The dogs hardly barked, they recognized me from a distance. I went by Anita's truck, up on blocks though she claims it runs perfectly, that all it lacks is wheels, then skirted the moonlit shadow of the haystack, the tower of bales swaying a little, just waiting to crush someone. The horses ran back and forth along the corral fence, kicking at each other; no one has ridden them, they're a terror, the only hope was they would never get loose.

Yes, Anita said, standing in the doorway.

You're not surprised to see me?

You look good.

Same as ever, I said.

No, tonight you look different. Hopeful. She stepped aside and let me in; the room was empty, but the first thing I heard was the sound of water, the shower running. The television was on in the other room, flickering on the walls. I could not understand the voices.

Anita handed me a can of beer, popping the tab first by way of hospitality. She shuffled to keep her dirty pink slippers on her feet, the animals making way and following. Some people invent personalities for their pets, but she doesn't even bother with names. The upholstery of the couch, the chairs, was shredded up and down the legs, everywhere, as if someone had unwoven every thread. I listened to the water, I watched the closed door of the bedroom.

What is it? she said. She is the queen of worried looks, trembling lips, eyes shifting side to side. She favors pantsuits and housedresses, her hair is always changing, always some shade of brown. I have never seen her sleep. She touched my arm and I pulled away.

Nothing, I said, imagining Charlotte in the shower, the water straightening her hair so it coiled on the skin of her back, along her spine, around her neck and over her shoulders. On the bookshelf lay a round orange reflector, from a roadside, its disc split into two thinner halves and connected by a string. I picked it up and set it down again, Anita watching me.

How's Charlotte doing? I asked, but she did not seem to hear me. I straightened the cribbage board, I ran my fingers along the chair where Charlotte had been sitting only nights before, where we'd sat together with our legs faintly touching under the table, almost not touching at all. She was constantly in motion, never quite still, kicking her leg a little, brushing against me. She did not pull away; she played her next card and pretended not to notice.

Anita was talking, saying something. I went around her, into the kitchen, where old onions and potatoes hung over the sink in metal baskets, new green shoots and tuberous warts growing to tangle around the coils, to hold there and not let go. Quietly, Anita came up behind and reached between my legs, trying to get ahold of me. I twisted away from her.

You are getting crotchety, she said.

11

I only shrugged; I've never been afraid to hurt her feelings. A cat lay asleep on the shelf and as I petted it the water stopped running in the shower and I closed my eyes, listening to the footsteps of bare feet. Behind the door she was standing naked for a moment, water dripping, running down her legs, as she kicked at the dirty laundry, the air cold on her wet skin, as she searched through her bag for something clean to wear.

That cat is dead, Anita said.

What? I pulled back my hand, put it in my pocket.

A rattlesnake got her.

Since when do you have rattlesnakes? I said. It was the first I'd heard of it.

Forever, Anita said. And I've been talking about it ever since you got here, for your information.

I've been listening, I said, and just then I heard the doorknob turn, I heard the hinges of the door I'd been watching so impatiently.

Where I'd expected Charlotte, a man was standing: small and wiry, barefoot, tangled wet hair hanging in his face. He was wearing a red mechanic's jumpsuit, a white and a blue stripe down one side of the torso. I could only see his straight, sharp teeth; his hair covered the rest of his face.

Feels great to be clean, he said.

Johnson, said Anita, introducing us.

He zipped up his jumpsuit when he noticed me. You the boyfriend? he said, and sat down in Charlotte's chair. He held up a comb and laughed, saying it must have been a while since I needed one.

Can't remember, I said, trying to see his eyes. From the wrinkles, the gray in his hair, I guessed he was fifty, twenty years younger than I am, but he never worried me. I never feared him.

Where you from? I said.

South.

Johnson walked here, Anita said. Hundreds of miles.

Is that a fact? I said. Now I noticed that Anita was wearing makeup, that her hair was curled. I asked if he'd walked across the gunnery range and he said he'd heard a couple shots. He preferred to walk at night, he said, because that was when the desert really came alive.

Did you see the sunglasses he made? Anita said.

I didn't even look up. As I listened to him explain about the moonflower, how it only blossomed at night, how it had hallucinogenic powers to which he could swear, I was thinking how fast I could have him on the floor with his arms twisted behind his back, how I could swing him by the ankles. That would shake out the swagger.

Tell him what you ate, she said.

Johnson had finished combing his hair and was tying a strip of rawhide around his head, to hold his bangs out of his eyes. You tell him, he said.

Lizards and snakes, Anita said. He cracks them like a whip and their heads snap right off.

The snakes are slow in the morning, he said. When it's cold and they're morbid you can sneak right up on them. They have to wait for the sun, you see. Cook them up on a stick and it's not half bad.

No thanks, said Anita.

Torpid, I said.

You going dancing? he said. That's one fine vest.

To work, Anita said. He deals blackjack at the casino.

Johnson looked at me like he expected more questions, but I wasn't going to give him the pleasure of talking about himself, not more than he already had. Finally he turned and whispered something to Anita and she said something I couldn't hear. They did not notice when I went into the other room.

I almost sat on a dog and it snapped at me as I tried to catch my balance. I bent down and rubbed a scuff from the toe of my shoe. Charlotte had made fun of my clothes the first time we met—everything I did was amusing to her and I just wanted to keep her attention. I wondered where she was, why she had gone away. Outside, the big dogs were whining; the door was too small for them to get through and they carried on as if that might change.

I called to Anita: When's Charlotte coming down again?

A man with a braid down his back came and picked her up, Anita said.

I could hear them laughing in the other room, like I couldn't see it coming. It wasn't my place to straighten them out, to warn them. On television, Grandpa Walton was sitting at the dinner table, holding forth in Spanish though his lips didn't follow; when he put down his knife and fork everyone snapped to attention. Somewhere Anita was saying her cats were allergic to smoke and Johnson was cursing them all. I heard the window forced open. Grandma Walton had the sourest face in the world, while her husband was all rustic wisdom and peace with his soft Spanish words. I watched for a while, then went back into the other room.

Johnson had started cutting corns off his feet with a paring knife; cats and dogs fought for them, rolling along the floor, under the table. He was talking about some eskimos who froze their feet and then made cuts in their insteps so they could run faster.

There was a time, I said, when I was interested in that kind of thing.

You're over it now? he said.

Long time ago.

This is a great sandwich, he said.

You didn't want one, Anita said to me. Did you?

How did you two meet? I said.

Right after I found the cat, Anita said. Out on the road. He's going to help me with the snakes. Tell him.

I can find them, he said. They mix up the energy in the ground.

The what?

The earth energy, he said.

I laughed out loud, then asked if he had any crystals to sell. He only smiled. He was slow to rise to my barbs, and I know that trick, I recognized it—it made him seem more mature. At my age maturity is never an objective.

That's why I walk barefoot, he said, to absorb some of the energy. He spoke in a contrived, wistful way, playing with the zipper of his jumpsuit. It rasped behind his words. The energy seeps right out of the earth, he explained, it makes me strong.

We have to bury the cat, Anita said.

It was almost nine; I took my tie from my pocket and clipped it on. They followed me to the door, Anita with the cat in her arms.

Later on, Johnson said.

The fresh air really hits you when you leave that house. I stretched and breathed deeply; it would have to last me all night, for the casino has few doors and no windows. I looked back at the house in the moonlight, the insulation exposed where the dogs have chewed at the wall. The horses were killing the last tree in the corral.

You promised, I heard Anita say.

Just so I don't have to touch the filthy thing, said Johnson.

They were standing with a shovel stuck in the ground between them, the dogs all around. I turned toward the Stateline, cracking my knuckles and preparing to deal. People always ask me if I do any card tricks and I say Yes. I can take your money.

The winds found no friction on
the salt flats; they came through
the sparse sage, climbed the sides
of the mountains, lifted Charlotte's
hair straight up, out of her face.
She sat still and cross-legged with
a clipboard on her lap, leaning
against a rock, her face turned
upward. She looked fiercely into
the sky, not so much taking it in
as sending her vision outward to
overpower all birds of prey. The
jacket she wore was the same color
as the mountain around her, she
was invisible, she could go hours

without moving at all. Some people fell asleep while watching, but Charlotte was never in danger of that. She was prepared to see scrolls unrolling in the clouds, see the whole firmament torn away—yet she did not miss the hawk miles above. She picked up her binoculars to bring it closer.

The raptors moved somewhere between perfection and falsehood. So rigid at times, like kites, they seemed fake and temporary, while often so fluid they seemed unreal, not bound to the earth. She had learned to appreciate this tension, and she suspected it was tied to the sadness she felt when she watched the birds, a sadness that came without warning but not without pleasure.

No one from her life before could find her or knew what she was doing; they had never understood her. Every hour she took down the weather, the wind's direction and speed. She marked the species, age and sex of the birds that passed overhead, everything she could determine. Their power and freedom impressed her, but more than anything she liked to watch the nets come down and trap it all. She had no pity for the terrified pigeons used as lures. The hawks circled above, tighter and tighter, confident, and when they were set free again, untangled from the nets, they would carry a metal band around their leg. They would be forced to carry a part of the earth.

Sweeping the binoculars out of the sky, she looked over the unbelievable white of the salt flats and beyond them, lights reflecting off the waters of the Great Salt Lake. Past it, somewhere, was Salt Lake City and even Bountiful. She had not been unhappy there, though she feared her happiness ran shallow, was of a kind that came too easily. She was anxious to be tested, she was not satisfied, she had been shown the way to her satisfaction and could not accept it. Now she sat on the mountaintop, watching for signs, hoping to be brought into contact with untold powers.

She had not expected the other people, and she resented their presence, their claims on her attention. Long-haired men with gentle voices, women who didn't shave their underarms; they liked to stand watch together, motionless and transfixed, silent for hours, binoculars glued to their eyes. They spoke as if their religion was watching birds fly over the earth, and when they held hawks to be photographed they smiled proudly, as if they had built the feathers, attached the bones, sharpened the beak and talons.

The camp was down off the peak, in the trees, out of the wind and slowing the sunrise. There was still snow in the shadows. Nights, they passed a joint in circles, around the campfire, and she just let it go by, she tried to get along with them. After a day of silence, they could not stop talking; they talked about how good it felt to be doing this job, how fulfilling, and she sat in silence. There's nothing quite like people who believe they're making a difference. Charlotte looked across the fire at the cage of pigeons, oblivious, happy as could be, no concerns for the future. A girl played the guitar, unfamiliar songs.

Someone told a joke about the difference between Jews, Catholics, and Mormons: Jews don't recognize Jesus, Catholics don't recognize Hanukkah, and Mormons don't recognize each other in the liquor store. They all laughed.

Am I the only Mormon here? Charlotte said, and a quiet descended.

It made them nervous to have her among them, as if she cared to judge, and eventually they compensated by acting out even worse than if she hadn't been there at all. They searched for a bottle of whiskey, cursed and wrestled, recalled tawdry stories from their pasts and admitted to fabricated sins. They looked sideways for her reaction, hoping to shock her. They would not admit it, but they were afraid of her, so different and so proud.

She prayed in her tent, listening to them down at the fire. She slept alone, while the sleeping arrangements of the others were in constant adjustment. Her dreams were of hawks and eagles, her prayers full of questions.

It's me, Adam said. There was a scratching at the side of her tent, then the sound of the zipper. He stuck his head inside. Is everything all right?

Fine, she said.

Just wondered what you were doing in here.

It doesn't mean anything's wrong with me if I'd rather be alone than sit around the fire. Her tongue was sharp.

Just wanted to see.

I'm praying, she said.

For us, I hope. He tried to joke.

It's not for me to worry about your souls.

Adam came a little farther, halfway into the tent. This can be a hard job, he said, not everyone can handle it. Guy last year saw more birds than anyone else, but we couldn't trust his numbers because he also documented thirty-seven UFOs; not things he couldn't identify—flat-out flying saucers.

I haven't been so lucky, Charlotte said. She stared at Adam. His beard was not filling in very well and his hands looked like a girl's. He smiled at her, leaning closer.

Goodnight, she said.

Later, as she lay in her sleeping bag she heard them whooping and shouting from the pool where they all bathed together, splashing and sliding over each other. Charlotte bathed in the morning, before anyone else was up, and the water was so cold it made her forget she was naked, all her skin open to the early morning stars. Then she remembered and she spun around, the water at her ankles, trying to cover herself with her hands. Every tree held a shadow close along its trunk.

She started early, finding new spots, hiding from the others. Watching the sky, each new bird was a surprise to her, a delight.

Have you ever seen a hawk kill a rabbit? she said. Take another bird out of the air?

No, I said. I admit I haven't. Except on Wild Kingdom, but I don't watch much television.

Raptors are at the top of the food chain, she said, so their health and numbers reflect everything. They warn us of disasters that haven't even happened yet.

If you protect them, I said, isn't that like falsifying evidence? Things could be worse than we think.

As if they really need our help—we need their help is more like it. She laughed at me. They help us by preying on the old and sick and weak.

At first I wondered if she hoped things with the world were getting better or worse; after all, for a Mormon there's nothing so fortunate, no blessing quite like an apocalypse. They are the Latter Day Saints because after the apocalypse they'll be left behind to have their fun. Yet this was not how Charlotte was thinking. It took me time to realize that all she wanted was the assurance that things were not staying the same, that they were changing. This she had learned from watching the hawks.

All desire for change arises from loneliness, and this she was still learning. She had realized she could be alone while surrounded by others; some never find this out, some find ways to help themselves forget. When you are truly lonely you are able to hear yourself, you are finally able to listen. Once, she held a bald eagle, its wingspan wider than she was tall, unwieldy but strangely light, almost weightless. Its feathers had been cleaned by the sky, its hooked beak made to crack bones; its eyes would not settle, they wanted to fight. We are never so fierce as when we're frightened, never so frightened as when we're alone.

Sometimes when you first meet someone you realize how long you've been missing them. Perhaps you have found another person you want to touch, who won't walk away when you lean against them and who feels the same way, who will lean back so you both remain standing, so you don't fall and you are not left to writhe on the ground. To break a true loneliness, any person will not do; the wrong person will lead you through hope and on into despair.

When she climbed high enough, if the light was right, she

could see the stars in the daytime, through the violet sky, the birds somewhere between. Once a falcon rocketed down into camp at a hundred miles an hour, disappearing so quickly no one could figure where it went. It was hard to believe something with hollow bones could move that fast. In the late afternoons the ridges looked like faces to her, watching with unblinking eyes, sitting in judgment, changing with the sun and shadows. She watched the cars on the salt flats, trying to set speed records. She remembered the Guinness Book of World Records in grade school, the handsome man in the leather jacket, sitting astride his bicycle out on the flats. And the cars—the Blue Flame, the Mormon Meteor. Through her binoculars she saw the roostertails of salt kicked out from the rear tires, half a mile long and longer as the cars sped up; the tails disappeared slowly, settling again. From where she sat she could hear the engines, faintly.

Who knows what kind of damage they're doing out there, Adam said.

She had not seen him come up.

It might be years, he said, before everything's back to normal.

Right, she said. You're right about that. She did not look at him, she kept the binoculars to her eyes and gazed into the sky.

I hate those cars, he said.

Why do they do it?

No idea.

For a moment, while they were talking, she was certain he was going to reach out and touch her neck, her face, but he did not touch her.

Weather's too nice today, he said. It's the bad weather that really brings them in.

She looked down at the cars again, searching the flats for the dark shadows that sometimes gave the hawks away. Those shadows were the coldest thing a rabbit could ever feel.

You going back to Bountiful when you're done here? he said.

Why?

Isn't that where you're from, where your parents are?

Yes, she said, but they don't have anything to do with what's next.

If she had a strong enough telescope, perhaps she could see her parents in Bountiful; she didn't need to see them to know what they were doing, that it was the same as ever and not that interesting. She was their only child and they had to let her go. They would be surprised to see her here, to see her joy at the snares and the nets, watching all that power tricked down to earth. Coming in! someone would shout, the silhouette expanding above. The pigeon was nervous and didn't know why, standing on one leg and then the other, eyes spinning and filming over, the neck never still. A line stretched out to hidden hands. All were silent.

Like nothing had ever happened, like nothing could be prepared, the hawk appeared only as it collided into the pigeon; feathers were everywhere, both birds rolling sideways. The hawk righted itself with a flap of wings and stood atop the pigeon, turning to dare anything that walked the earth. The silent hand swept across and the net slapped down. Soon they'd have the raptor in a metal can with both ends cut off, its head out one end, its talons out the other, its wings encircled. They would carry it upside down, its sharp beak pointed at the ground.

All this she watched, she was only a girl, and below, miles away, my dreams of her were growing so violent that I threw myself out of bed and landed on the floor of my trailer, shifting the whole thing, waking my dog in the middle of the night.

Anita called it a miracle. She was
taken in by the businesslike way
Johnson went about everything.
He started in the afternoon; first,
he stood licking his finger, waiting
for the wind to be still, then he
paced back and forth across the
yard, cursing, his mouth moving silently as if he was figuring some
arithmetic or arguing with himself.
He stood on one bare foot, then the
other, he went down on all fours
and pressed his ear to the ground.
No one would have believed what
he was doing.

It looked like rain, but he said it would hold. He didn't even have to look at the clouds to know it. She thought the way the horses were moving, their nervousness, meant rain, but he was right.

Taking a wire hanger, he bent it into a V with handles at both ends; he held it out in front of him, loose in his grip, sliding his feet as he moved, his eyes barely open. Nothing happened for half an hour. He did not seem to mind. The hanger trembled, finally, and he retraced his steps to find the spot; slowly, with hesitation, the wire seemed bent by the air. It pointed to the ground. After a moment his hands began to shake, also, and the hanger jerked sharply, insistently, like something was pulling an invisible line from underground. Then Johnson dropped the hanger and sat down where he was. He gave Anita a list of things he'd need and he lay down in the yard to wait. When the dogs ventured close to him, he kicked them away. He had to nap, he told her, he'd need all his strength, all his powers.

He put her to work when she returned; she followed him as he circled with the hanger, digging shallow holes where he pointed, pounding short metal stakes into the ground. This went on for over an hour and they did not exchange a word. Next, he took up the copper wire; he stretched the thin strands from stake to stake, winding it around them, testing its taut-ness with his fingers, pressing his cheek against it to be sure everything was straight and held no knots. He hurried back and forth, he smoked and coughed, he bent over to catch his breath. Palms flat on the ground, eyes closed, you'd think he was praying if he ever looked up. Anita asked him questions, but he did not answer. Some stretches needed one strand of copper wire, some needed three or even more. He wrapped tinfoil around the wires, patiently sliding it back and forth until he was convinced it was in the right place.

The truck did not start like she'd promised it would. They had to call Luke at the service station to come out and give it a jump; finally the old engine turned over and the truck rattled and spit exhaust from the corner of the yard, where it rested on its cinderblocks. Luke sat in his truck with the door open, his feet on the running board, watching.

Johnson used a broomhandle to prop the truck's hood open. Clamping the jumper cables back to the battery, he attached the loose ends to a longer cable, one that looked like a hose; he used electrical tape to connect this to a pliers with insulated handles. Cable trailed behind him as he walked into the yard, taking hold of one metal stake, then another. Sparks crackled at the jaws of the pliers, they ran blue along the strands of copper. The truck's engine strained, caught, kept on. It did not happen gradually, there was no first snake—rattlesnakes came out of the ground where there weren't any holes, they came right through the walls of the house. They fell up out of the ground to dance on their tails, twisting and coiling, trying to escape the earth; they came down stunned and quivering.

You electrocuted them, Charlotte said. We were sitting on the floor with the cribbage board between us, surrounded by cats. She was so close to me, both her legs out straight. Her body so limber, leaning back and forth; it made me envy her bones.

Johnson hadn't said a word; he was letting Anita tell the story. He sat smoking by the window, his legs crossed at the ankles, one thumb hooked in a pocket of his jumpsuit. The bottoms of his feet were black with dirt. He just smiled and nodded in agreement as Anita re-created the scene. She moved around the room as she talked, a tangle of cats under her feet.

It's the vibration, Johnson said, not the electricity. All energy's not electrical, you know. The ground dampens all that down.

It was a miracle, Anita said. The horses almost broke down the corral when they saw all those snakes. All the hair came up on my arms. The dogs hid under the porch.

Worthless, said Johnson.

Some of the snakes were half-awake, but he was too quick,

even they could not escape him. He pulled on a big pair of boots and walked out among them, stamping on their heads with his heavy heels, backtracking to be certain there were none he'd missed.

Why didn't you crack them like a whip? I said.

It's a goddamn menagerie in here, he said. That's what it is. All the animals that could see him were giving him a wide berth, arcing around where he sat.

The long shadows lay on the floor, cast through the window by the light above the door outside. I really would have had to see it to believe it all, yet the rattlesnakes were there, hanging from their tails, all around the eaves of the house. It was hard to deny that there had been some success.

Well, thanks, Johnson said to Anita. You made it sound a little more heroic than what it was, but then again I guess that's pretty much how things shook out.

Charlotte was drinking water from a canning jar. Her bangs were curled under to keep them out of her eyes, dark curls falling over her shoulders. I tried to touch her fingers as we played. Her shoes were set to one side and her socks were tight around her perfect ankles, the arches of her feet. Kittens gathered around her; an old dog lay sleeping with its head in her lap.

After all that, Johnson said, my whole body hurts. On the inside.

A hot bath, Anita said.

What did I ever do before I met this woman? He stood and stretched, then sat down again.

You didn't see any of this with the snakes? I said.

Missed it, Charlotte said. But you watch—without them we'll have mice everywhere now. Now the balance is off.

Snakes are a danger, Johnson said, pointing at me. You know that. They're more than a nuisance.

If you don't mess with them they'll leave you alone, she said.

Come on, he said. Wouldn't kill you to agree with me. If I was wrong, disagree all you want, fine. God! I never knew a girl to be such a snake-lover.

That's why we have the cats, Anita said. They'll handle the mice.

Eve, I said, but no one heard. There was a hawk feather in Charlotte's hair. I was watching the clock, trying to slow its hands. The game ended and we started another. On my own time, in all things, my rule is to win whenever I can; it's a deep injustice to let someone win. Charlotte told me she'd find my weakness and I encouraged her to search. Her face never stopped moving—each time I looked at her I was surprised at how completely my memory failed. It would be impossible to describe her face, but I will try.

They coil up the energy from the earth, Johnson was saying, they hoard it in their bodies, that's how I can tell where they are—that's the whole poison thing, too. Now they're stew, he said, laughing, stirring a pot with a long wooden spoon.

There's lots of things to be done, I said, problems everywhere. Now that you've conquered the snakes, I'm sure there's no end to the problems you can solve.

Next I'm going to dig a pit and put all the dogs in it, so they don't try and sleep with me at night. I'll bury them alive, he said.

They like you, Anita said.

Hard luck for them. He flicked his cigarette out the window and stared up at the ceiling. I'll tell you what I'm going to do, he said. I'm going to walk. I never walked some of the deserts around here. It's kind of an expansion of my territory.

Do you make a conquest in every town? I said. Or just piss on everything?

Listen, he said, putting down the spoon. I know you think you're some kind of badass, but I'm not going to waste my breath.

For a change, Charlotte said.

Anita leaned against the doorway, just watching; she sensed the argument coming and enjoyed it, flattered, no doubt believing it was all about her.

You must have some profound thoughts out there, I said, walking like that. Maybe you could share a few.

That's your mistake, he said. Thinking has nothing to do with it. He told us he took off his jumpsuit when he got too warm, walking, that the energy came up through the soles of his feet, how in thunderstorms he lay flat to avoid being a lightning rod. He said he was talking about the earth, not the cosmos—dirt, not stars—and that his walking wasn't really even a physical thing, but a physical manifestation of something else.

Where do you come up with this shit? I said.

I come up with this shit by keeping my eyes open, Grandpa.

It was then I knew he had quit pretending to want my friendship; I welcomed the change. Sinister as it may get, an honest dislike has a truer turn than almost anything.

One of the snakes is still alive, Charlotte said, pointing to the window. It twisted around itself and swung against its dead brothers, its head rising, falling, trying again.

Let him twist, the peckerhead. Serves him right, said Johnson.

You can kill all the snakes you want, Anita said, but if you touch my dogs. She pointed at her rifle, leaning in the corner. She'll take a shot at a coyote every now and then, on the ridge behind her house; she loses a couple cats a year.

It hurt my knees to sit on the floor, but I didn't want to show it. I shifted my weight and tried to preserve the crease in my pants. Charlotte pulled her hair back, showing the nape of her neck, enough to keep me on edge for days. She tricked me for three of a kind, then caught a pair to thirty-one.

You're staring at me, she said, and I thought she was staring back.

That's the whole reason I sleep outside, Johnson was saying.

You take naps inside, Anita said.

Just because I'm horizontal doesn't mean I'm sleeping. He laughed. You know that. All that matters is to touch the ground. A strand of hair escaped the strip of rawhide around his head; he twisted it behind his ear. That's why I could never figure on indoor churches, he said.

What would you know about church? Charlotte said.

Oh yes, you're a Mormon girl, I forgot that. Your parents are probably polygamists and all that.

Of course not, I said. That's illegal.

Poor girl, Johnson said. You'll live your whole life wearing blinders and I bet when you're an old woman you'll think the same way as you do now, that if you ever stray you'll never be able to sustain it—now you're brave, but you'll be frightened then.

You don't know me, Charlotte said.

I've known people like you; that's enough.

Impossible, I said.

Johnson turned to me. Oh yes, there are types of people. Think I haven't known others like you?

I never claimed to be unique, I said.

Everything will expand for you when you give it your attention, he said to Charlotte. Things will strain and stretch to be in your line of vision, there's nothing that doesn't want to unfold. Does that frighten you?

Seventeen, she said, ignoring him, returning to the game.

Johnson was too smooth to be trusted. I saw how Anita watched him; it's soothing to be around someone who's full of answers. He took a carton of milk from the refrigerator and drank from the spout, then lit a cigarette and explained that he'd spent half his life handling uranium; his bones were radioactive—in the right light you didn't need an x-ray machine. He laughed at the risks of smoking and it seemed he'd never stop talking.

You'll see, Charlotte said. Mice everywhere.

Vermin, I said. Staring into her eyes, I tried to let her know we'd been brought together, that I was part of what she was doing and also its end. A great enough loneliness demands its answer, calls its hot cure. She knew she deserved more than earthly instruction; she'd felt the unseen powers, the ones behind and hidden. I work close to luck, day in and out, and it's only a weak sister of the powers I've known, the ones she wanted. Yes, my mind has wheeled; my hands have been guided.

Anita kicked off her slipper and scratched at the animals with her toes; her feet looked like hands, like the feet of people who are used to climbing trees, to never wearing shoes. Next to her, all the rattles from the snakes were in a glass jar. Johnson had cut them off with a knife. He told her a necklace made from them was worth a hundred dollars, easy, that he'd give them to her for nothing. He flicked the ash from his cigarette out the window, and I wondered if there was someone there, outside, listening in the darkness.

I myself had often stood there, under that window. That was how I checked to see if Charlotte was at Anita's, hoping for her voice, sneaking back to my trailer if she was not. I would stand there, dodging the ashes, the matches Johnson threw out. I admit I sometimes just listened. I'd come at dusk, through the dark like the old fool I am, stumbling over the graves of cats, wincing and trembling each time one of the horses moved against the night. The dogs tried to defeat me, they crowded around and wanted attention, but despite my knees I've been blessed with the gift of quiet. I've learned it from working under the tireless call of the keno and slot machines, from the desert. I heard Anita's laughter, Johnson saying what a fool I was to still be capering after her when everyone knew how she felt about him. They had plenty to say about me. When you know what people think of you it gives you power over them.

Once, I heard them in there and I couldn't find anything to stand on, I couldn't pull myself up to see through the window. I hurried along the rise and in the light over the table I saw them. Johnson's jumpsuit was bunched around his ankles, the arms flailing along the floor, loose like tentacles. Cats leapt after them. The soles of Anita's orangutan feet walked in the air, like they were trying to reach the ceiling. The dogs and cats were all around them, sniffing everything, tails that would not stop.

There are hairs growing out the tops of your ears, Charlotte said.

I know it, I said, shuffling the cards.

The animals came and went through the small swinging door; tangles of dust and hair rolled across the floor each time it opened. Despite the open window, strings of smoke hung and shifted near the ceiling, above where Charlotte and I were sitting. The air we shared was clear. It was heartbreaking, the way she shuffled the cards; it was so clumsy it made me feel tenderly toward her. Over by the kitchen Johnson was tickling Anita and she was telling him to stop it, loudly enough that we could hear, in a way meant to spur him on.

What fools, Charlotte whispered to me, and I nodded, knowing no bonds set more quickly than those born of shared antipathies. There I was in the room with her, and the fact of their presence tended beyond bad luck and on into the realm of punishment. Out the side of my eye I saw Johnson's face flash in the light as he looked up, checking to be sure I was paying attention. I have more decency than that—I am a man. In my time, I locked all the animals out of the bedroom; yet even of that I am not proud.

Vermin, I said, and it made Charlotte laugh. I asked and she told me they'd be counting the hawks until November, though she doubted she'd last that long.

Planning on running off somewhere? Anita said, eavesdropping.

Not yet, Charlotte said. Not that I know of. She rolled onto her side to reach a card I'd flipped beyond her; when she stretched, her shirt slid up and I saw the pale, smooth skin of her stomach, all that I'd hoped for. I flipped another card over her head so it sliced back down to me, into the deck, as she turned to look.

The thing is, Johnson said, with those birds, is they don't need the energy from the earth so much, because they weigh so little and they can absorb it better. In fact, that's one of the main reasons they can fly, big as they are. He stood and crossed the room, closer to us. Sometimes when I'm out walking, the vultures follow me, he said. I'll pretend to stumble, I'll sit down for a while to keep them coming. I'd like to see one of them starve to death, fall out of the sky—I'd kick it ten feet in the air before I wrung its neck. Stupid birds, they don't even have voices, you know that? All they can do is hiss. Huge, though; they could take one of these cats, easy. An eagle could, too, carry it right into the sky.

Fingers outstretched, he brought his hand down on one of the blind kittens and lifted it by its head, crying and kicking, until its hind paws left the floor. I was watching Anita; she looked away. When he dropped the kitten it somehow knew to run to Charlotte. She kissed it, stroking its head.

Some say you can judge a person by how they treat animals, I said to her.

Sounds like something animals would say if they could talk, Johnson said. Which they can't. You think we got where we are through kindness? God, you're soft!

I just laughed, standing up, taking my bow tie from my pocket. I thanked Anita for the beer and turned to go.

Wait, Charlotte said. She followed me outside, then closed the door behind her. She asked me if I believed the things he'd said.

Of course not, I said.

Why?

First, because I wasn't there, I said, I didn't see it. And I don't like him and I don't trust him. Even if I did, I suspect stories like that, where things are out of the ordinary; someone's always trying to get over somehow.

Through the door came Johnson's voice, Anita shrieking with some semblance of delight.

You don't believe anything like that? Charlotte said.

Depends on lots of things, I said. Like who tells me.

I can't tell you yet, she said.

But you want to.

I don't know, she said, if I want to.

Not yet, I said.

Not yet.

There are times I feel the pressure of the endless deserts that surround this town, the tightness. I walked out past the metal stakes, the copper wires, the whole yard like a minefield or an obstacle course. Looking back, I could not see Charlotte through the window. I was further in her confidence than I had hoped; it was only a matter of time. The one snake still twisted while the rest hung limp. They would all be gone by the morning.

There are those who claim that
when you pray you must also listen. Often, if you try this, what you
hear seems suspiciously close to
your own thoughts. Are they your
own thoughts? It may not be so
easy to tell, to winnow those that
are divinely influenced from those
that are not. If you were to live
your life like a prayer, every action
a sort of prayer, it would be easy to
believe that all your thoughts were
the words of God. Perhaps they
would be.

There's no fear of that here —

these words are mine. The difference is that I know my own thoughts when they come to me; I recognize them.

Charlotte was praying. She'd gone to the service at the Mormon church on the Utah side of town. It might seem that the Utah side would be more pious; in fact, it's only poorer, it lacks the gambling revenue we enjoy across the border. Any Mormon will tell you that the rich man is enjoying God's grace and favor; the poor have no corner on piety. On the Utah side, the church is surrounded by trailers, like boats moored around an island. You can see, from the parking lot, the huge head of Wendover Will as he looks down over the rooftops. He looms, smoking and smiling, keeping his eye on everything, both secular and sacred, in his long shadow.

It was a mistake to sit in the front. She felt all the eyes on her, someone new, and it would make her escape more difficult. Babies were crying, like they always did in church, as if they knew better. The announcements—relief society, Boy Scouts, primary and firesides—made Charlotte feel at home, not comfortable. It was all too familiar. She did not want to meet anyone, she only wanted to come to the sacrament meeting, to keep up her strength, to remind herself what she was doing and why.

She wore the only dress she'd brought along, one she'd sewn the year before. It was long, with yellow flowers, lace around the neck, cuffs and hem. The straps of her white sandals were as stiff and sharp as metal when she flexed her toes. Praying, she paid no attention to the service. She asked to know if she could trust the things she saw, she prayed to be called, to be singled out, she prayed not to end up like the women sitting behind her—weary, self-sacrificing, struggling to quiet their children. Charlotte trusted herself, but still she asked questions and tried to hear the answers. She dared the spirits to stop her, to tell her not to follow, to disbelieve the things she'd seen. If she only listened right, she feared, she would truly believe and she would not feel such dissatisfaction, such ambition. The words would wear away her uneasiness, calm her down, leave her cool and smooth.

It was hot in the church. Now people were bearing their testimonies, standing to say I know this church is true and then the endless reasons why, the unexpected strengths found to deal with all the little things that weren't predicted, the mundane surprises that make up a life. Charlotte waited it out. Despite the heat, the hard wood of the pew seemed to turn colder and colder, freezing the backs of her legs.

After the service, the whole congregation gathered outside the door. Children chased each other, women talked, men licked their lips and looked into the sky. It was clear all the men had bought their suits at the same place. Charlotte watched them through the glass door, then turned and went down a hallway, through the kitchen and across the dark basketball court. Her bicycle was waiting out the side door.

She pulled her skirts back between her legs, then climbed on and began to pedal. Her hair blew out straight, the wind filled her ears. Rather than turning into town, toward Anita's, she went the other direction, toward the Speedway.

Johnson had helped her piece the bike together, using the pieces of a couple wrecks, but she didn't let that change the way she felt, she listened to me, she didn't start to trust him. Standing on the pedals, she moved faster, coasting down toward the edge of town. The sky was almost pure white, hardly blue at all. She felt the sweat on her skin, under the fabric of her dress, and she liked it. She was still praying, she was still listening. As she passed over the bridge, semi-trailers passed below; the skirt of her dress went sideways and, one-handed, she gathered it in.

The whiteness of the flats lifted the mountains, miles away, from all contact with the earth. She rode on, squinting into the sun, toward the line of cars, the canopies and the people moving slowly, sunbathing. The sound of the engines rose as she came closer, the tails of dust visible against the sky as she descended to the level of the flats.

She walked her bike past piles of oil cans, stacks of tires. There was no organization, no buildings; no one seemed to be in charge. Finally she found a shack, small enough to fit in the back of a pickup truck, but no one was inside. A list of names and speeds hung from one wall; on the other side hung a poster, a grid of tiny photographs under the words THE 200 CLUB. When she leaned close to look at the faces she knew she was in the right place. Dirty and skinny and pale, they were like people from another planet. The few women on the poster looked cruel and desperate, with eyes like they had never slept.

Fumes filled the air. Everywhere people were smoking cigarettes. Charlotte expected the explosion at any moment. Turning, she pushed her bike past the line of cars. They shone in all colors and blinding chrome; heat rose from their hoods, it shivered and twisted the air. Men looked up, holding wrenches in their hands, reaching into styrofoam coolers and pulling out cans of beer. Women in tube tops watched her pass, then looked at each other.

Hey Cinderella, they called. Hey there, precious.

She kept walking, not slowing down. The cars were painted with words and numbers, speeds and girls' names. The bumper of one said PRAISE THE LORD. Pieces of ice fell around her feet, but she did not turn to see who had thrown them. Some people had brought tents, canopies, picnic tables. An enormous man and woman sat in a wading pool on a square of AstroTurf; they did not even turn their heads to watch her pass. Their eyes went from left to right. Suntan oil spun on the surface of the water.

Charlotte headed for the last car, set a little apart from the others. She was afraid, but fear kept her there. The car did not shine like the others she'd passed; there was rust along the hood, cracks in the windshield, handprints of grease along the roof. One door was red, while the rest of the car was a pale shade of orange. It was jacked up along one side and a pair of cowboy boots stuck out from underneath it. Their sharp toes pointed at the sky.

Hey, she said.

After a moment, the heels of the boots kicked at the ground and the man pulled himself out. The cuffs of his corduroys were ragged, the knees worn slick. His arms were covered in grease from the tips of his fingers to his elbows. She was surprised how tall he was when he finally stood, and thin, his sideburns red. He grabbed his shirt at the shoulders and shook the sand and salt from his back. He looked at her.

Your belt's on sideways, she said.

He ran his finger down inside his lip, then threw a black wad of tobacco away, past her. There's a good reason for that, he said. So I don't get hung up on the bottom of the car.

Do you live here? she said.

What?

Do you sleep out here?

Right here, he said. Who are you?

Charlotte was thirsty, the dry air sharp in her throat. She wondered if this was how the ocean smelled. Looking toward the mountains, she tried to figure out where she usually sat to watch the hawks; it was possible someone with a telescope was watching her now, that tomorrow they would ask her what she was doing down at the Speedway. She looked across the long stretch of the flats, then back to the other cars. The people she'd passed made her even more certain that she was right, that he was the one.

Do you always dress like that? he said.

It's Sunday, she said. She decided he must be almost her age, at most a couple years older. He could not look her in the face, so she tried to catch his eye.

Where you from? he said.

I work around here.

But you're not from here.

I'm from Bountiful, she said. North of Salt Lake.

This here's the furthest east I've been, he said. My name's Keith.

Keith, she said. Your car does not look too good.

Salt's hard on a car.

How long you been out here?

Couple weeks.

You ever just drive out on the flats and fool around with things? she said.

What?

Forget it. Are you a member of the 200 Club? She saw from his face that this was the right question. He just shook his head.

What's Bountiful like? he said.

It's not like anything, she said. How come you can't get this thing to go two hundred?

I will.

Why?

Why what? he said.

Why do you want to go so fast? It's not like you're going anywhere.

It stands for something, he said. Other people have done it.

That's the backward reason most people have for doing things, Charlotte said.

How's that?

Because something hasn't been done before, she said.

But it has been done before, said Keith.

Charlotte just kept looking at his car, thinking about the faces on the poster and wondering why someone would feel compelled or inspired to join their number. I've seen hundreds like Keith, boys who believe their jacked-up Dusters are faster than they are. The radar guns make liars of everyone's speedometers.

I just like driving fast, he said.

Why? she said.

How fast did you ever go?

I don't know.

You want to try it?

You say that, she said, like you know I won't.

I just asked if you wanted to, he said. I didn't ask it any special way.

I do, Charlotte said.

She watched him turn the ratchets backward, lower the car, then throw the jacks to one side. He opened the door for her and she climbed in. It was hot and dusty inside the car. She began to roll down the window and he told her she wouldn't want to do that. He started the engine and they lurched forward. In front of them, two men packed a parachute into the back of another car.

He told her that was to slow it down; he didn't have one because he didn't need one. The Speedway is ten miles long, he said, but only eighty feet wide, so you're screwed if you can't stay straight. The tape's over the speedometer because I don't want to see it. They'll time us with the gun.

I'm not afraid, Charlotte said.

Everything was smooth through the lower gears and then the horizon leapt up toward them. She looked back and could see nothing, as if the earth were falling away behind; when she turned around the horizon was also lost. She felt her spine held tight against the back of the seat. Wind whistled along the hood, then the edges of the doors, and suddenly it was silent, the inside of the car sealed tight. She watched the cracks in the windshield, ready to feel the glass come inside and cut the skin of her face, and then all friction was lost and everything seemed to spray and slide out from under them. She reached across and took hold of his arm. For a moment she forgot where she was, she only knew she had to go farther. The hem of her dress jumped and slid along her thighs. When Keith hit the brakes the rear end of the car swung back and forth, swooping smoothly as if they were on water, as if the car were a boat.

You can let go of me now, he said. They turned and started slowly back, their roostertail of sand, salt and dust still settling around them.

Think we're in the club? she said. She waited for him to say something, but he was silent, looking out the side window and then straight ahead again. As they passed the other cars, the people's upturned faces moved from side to side. A man held up a blackboard with the number 136 on it. He was laughing as he waved them on.

He could be lying, Charlotte said. Her teeth were sore from clenching her jaw.

He's not lying, said Keith. He parked the car, got out, then leaned against it, staring across the flats.

How fast did anyone ever go? she said.

They go over six hundred.

She laughed.

You liked it, he said. I saw how you liked it.

What's the point of trying to go two hundred, she said, when someone's already gone six?

That's for rich people, he said. Rocket cars. Two hundred is for regular people, in their own cars that they work on themselves.

It's still pretty funny, Charlotte said. Why don't you just borrow one of your friends' cars?

That wouldn't mean anything, he said. And those aren't my friends. He spat, kicked at the ground, then looked over at her. Why are you here? he said.

I work on the mountain, she said. I count the hawks that fly over, the migration.

You count birds.

Yes.

And you think racing cars is stupid?

There's good reason for it, she said. What I do. But it's not worth my time to explain it to you.

Thanks, he said. What I meant was why did you come down here, to the Speedway.

I don't know.

You had to have a reason.

Why? she said. I just wanted to see it up close.

41

It was a dare, he said. Someone put you up to it, that's what it was. What's your name again?

Charlotte picked up her bike. He watched her bunch up her dress, keeping it from the spokes and chain.

See you again? he said.

I don't know.

He searched for his can of chew as he watched her go. She pedaled off, in a long arc; stopping once, she stood on tiptoes, looking over the flats. She looked back at him, but did not wave. He watched for a long time as she pedaled toward Wendover.

I sleep in the mornings and have my breakfast at two in the afternoon. One day my dog woke me early; first it whined awhile, before letting out a bark, so I knew whoever was coming was some distance away. My legs are shot after a night at the casino—the weight of eight hours, blood draining into my feet—and I keep my trailer hooked to my car and sleep on an incline. When I wake, my hands are soft, from absorbing all the lotion. I sat up and took off my gloves; I waited for the blood to return to my legs, so I could stand and not stagger.

Once I could feel my toes, I pulled on my shoes and went to the door. I could see him coming across the desert, aimed straight at my trailer. I climbed down, waiting to speak until he was close.

Been hunting jackalope? I said.

Funny, Johnson said. Did I wake you?

Yes.

Sorry. Was just coming to say hello to your dog. It looked lonely. Weren't you there, pooch?

It's used to the loneliness, I said.

Hot, he said, zipping up his coveralls. I'd prefer walking at night, but I've been otherwise occupied. He laughed. And the flies over at Anita's—they've multiplied with the heat. It's those damn horses.

I nodded. At the slightest sign of thaw the flies crawl out from behind the wood paneling; I'd seen how they avoided Johnson, though, how they did not dare land on him. He'd light a cigarette, claim it was the smoke that kept them away. Now I watched him as he carefully looked over my old dog; he checked its mouth, its teeth, its feet, as if he'd never seen a dog before and was considering making an offer. The stupid animal wagged its tail.

I notice you're not coming around much lately, he said. Hope that means you know when you're whipped.

What? I said.

Anita doesn't care for you anymore.

That really doesn't bother me, I said. I didn't know what it was he wanted—perhaps it was simply attention, an audience for his pathetic doings.

He turned over my dog's collar, reading my name on the tag. My neighbors stood behind windows, watching us, in half-open doorways and through the dark slashes between curtains. It infuriated me that he acted as if he'd gotten the better of me, as if he had something I wanted, and it would be impossible to get away with strangling him in my front yard.

You can sing that song all day, he said. Won't make it true. But I'm too much of a man to ask how you feel about it.

I see that, I said. I felt so gangly standing above him, looking at my untied shoes, his bare feet covered in dust.

Must be frustrating walking around here, I said. Always returning to the same place.

Do you think a person can ever actually return to the same place? he said.

Save it, I said, and he just crouched there, grinning at me.

You spend more than half your life indoors, he said. Your skin doesn't even look real. That must, it just must shrink your soul.

The temperature's steadier inside, I said. That's what I like. I'm not so sure I can speak for my soul.

Exactly, he said.

You own a borax mine? I said.

Uranium. Nice try.

I thought you said borax before.

No such thing, he said. You trying to trip me up? Jesus.

Uranium, then, I said.

I never found it until I threw the radiometer away and started trusting myself. Johnson stretched one leg out straight and looked up at me. Listening to my body, you know.

That cord around your head, I said. Did you ever think it's a little tight?

You're not a very happy man, he said. And you're afraid of me.

I'm afraid of you, I said. Right.

That's not clear to you? He scratched around my dog's head, behind its ears. Ah, he said. Your master's afraid of me.

I could hear a wind somewhere and wanted to feel it on my skin. The breeze did not come. I listened to Johnson talk, the tone of his voice leading me to believe we were closer to the time when he would try to hurt me. He moved quickly sideways and I flinched before he went right by; he reached under my trailer and pulled out one of the boards on which a snake-skin was stretched.

You may have some misbegotten reputation around here, he said, but I'm not a person to fuck with.

He handed me the board, the edges of the snakeskin held down with tacks, zigzagging in and out, the dark diamonds in the middle, the head crushed and the eyes long gone, the rattle on a string around Anita's neck. I looked up and Johnson was already a hundred yards away, stalking off without looking back. I wished I could summon a real anger and not merely disdain for the fool he was.

Traitor, I said, then reached down to pet my dog, to kiss its head.

It was the boys who brought them, showing up one night, standing in the squares of light outside my windows with the snakes in their hands, tails dragging along the ground. The boys did not know how to skin them and the snakes did not look good, their heads smashed and flat, fangs showing where they pierced the bottoms of mouths, forked tongues dry and sharp and brittle. We found some old pieces of wood, some tacks, we used rocks for hammers. They told me he killed them all barehanded and I said that was ridiculous, that they ate some poison, had some kind of disease. Look how their rattles fell off, I said. Now that's a sign of a sick snake.

I threw the board back under the trailer, where the rest of the skins were drying. I went back inside, searched for my book, then made a couple slices of toast, broke the ice cubes into the pitcher and filled the trays with water again. Sitting here, reading, I drink pitcher after pitcher; I've lived in the desert so long I've got sand in my gizzard, a thirst that can't be quenched or slaked. On my nights off I stay up late, reading, keeping the same schedule as when I work. Sometimes that's when the boys come to visit, when they see my light on. I enjoy them; they're a different kind of entertainment altogether.

They come to my trailer with mini-bottles they've stolen from somewhere, telling tales of their young bravery. I come up with stories that quiet them, that make them shift in their chairs to hear more clearly. I tell them I once took on three men with a bullwhip outside of Fallon, that I know women who wrestle in oil for a living, how I blinded a man from thirty feet with the six of hearts. Once the boys smoked banana peels, they ate nutmeg to see what would happen, but now they are getting older; soon, as soon as they can, they'll get out of Wendover, like their brothers before them. I tell them to stay in school, to get an education, and we all have a good laugh. Their parents work all night in the casinos, they don't know where they are, and the boys sleep together, under blankets around campfires, laughing in Spanish. Most of them hardly speak English, though most people who do don't make sense to me. Hell, I'd be happier if the whole world spoke Spanish; at least then I wouldn't feel as if I should understand what people are talking about.

Some nights off I drop by the Hide-A-Way and have a few drinks with the oldtimers there, act all spent and despairing. Mostly I sit and think. I read. I am sick with love, extending my afternoons on into my nights. The library, such as it is, is down by the Hide-A-Way, and the bookmobile brings me new titles every week, books from Salt Lake City. I read all afternoon, westerns and romances, sometimes something heavier, even poetry if the weather isn't too bleak. The driver of the bookmobile saves me the new ones. Bodice rippers? Yes, I read them, and so what? A little cleavage on the cover is a promise of something.

That afternoon I was reading about stable boys, aristocrats, love-crossed cousins. I looked out the window to be sure Johnson was gone and I saw my neighbor dragging a piece of cardboard, adding it to a pile of wooden shingles, broken pallets. He acts like he's always cold, sweating in down jackets and snowmobile boots. A dirty lock of hair escaped his stocking cap. He's a fool, but I do like to watch the flames.

Somewhere there were gunshots, the sound of broken glass, birds singing. My neighbor has a birdhouse on a post, popular for lack of trees, and the singing cuts in and out of the books I read. I sat drinking water, simply trying not to think of her, and I looked up from the page and Charlotte's face, a vision, floated smoothly past the window. I am familiar with this kind of thing; I just watched the flames starting in the oil drum as my neighbor fed cardboard to his fire.

There was a knock at the door. It did not seem possible. When I opened the door I could not find my voice. She was there, beautiful astride her bicycle, sweat on her forehead and bugs in her hair. She rested her elbows on the handlebars. She had come to see me. She had read my mind. Her lips were thin, her teeth crooked when she smiled. Her calves round, a handful, her thighs thin as bones above her knees. My dog strained at the end of its chain to be close to her.

It's no mistake, I finally said. I know why you're here.

You do? I wanted to ask you a favor.

Come in, I said. Cool off. I heard my voice shake. I wanted to delay her asking the favor, believing I might somehow influence its nature. At least, at last I had her in my trailer. Her presence gave me new trust in my powers, but I did not know what to do next. She circled the trailer, laughing at my uniforms hung together, all my clothes the same. I could not let her see how nervous I was. She pulled back the curtain, stepped into my shower.

You fit in here? she said.

I have to bend down.

How long have you lived like this?

I can't remember.

A long time, she said.

Yes.

I tried to hide the book I'd been reading, but she saw that and took it. She laughed at me, then tried to copy the pose of the woman on the cover. She unbuttoned the neck of her blouse, threw her hair back and closed her eyes. I did not know what to say. Yes, I'm old enough to be her grandfather; her great-grandfather, if someone was promiscuous early, if no one hesitated. Her people do breed young—after all, it is the duty of every righteous man and woman to prepare tabernacles for all the spirits they can. I just smiled at Charlotte.

Your car, she said.

What?

I need to borrow your car, she said.

That's the favor, I said. Are you taking it to the city?

No.

I told her that would have made more sense to me, then I teased her about visiting her boyfriend. She said she didn't have a boyfriend, that she couldn't tell me, not yet, why she needed the car. She sat down at the table, opening and closing the pages of the book.

I'll pay for the gas, she said, and for some reason that started me laughing.

I led her back outside, around to the car. She checked the sky, then watched me undo the hitch. I always keep everything hooked up, because otherwise you're at the mercy of the world; anyone can come hitch up to you while you're asleep, take you wherever they want. Happened to a woman up around Winnemucca—couple guys took her out in the desert and did terrible things to her. I watched Charlotte's reaction when I told her this, but she didn't seem to be listening, her eyes astray.

A couple hours, she said. I think that's all I'll need.

Promise you're coming back, I said.

Back inside, I hurried to sit in the chair where she'd rested. Now I felt things turning, invitations further into her secrets. I had been so frustrated, so infrequently at Anita's, and now, finally, Charlotte had come to me. The last time I'd seen her we'd been interrupted, we'd hardly had the chance to talk. I sat at my table trying to feel the warmth of her body, and then I suddenly remembered her bicycle and I leapt to my feet, stumbling back outside. Salt covered the tires, dried white, crystallized on the spokes and chain. I sat down on the seat, let it feel my weight, then climbed off again, to unclip my dog. We set out.

My hands trembled, the front wheel shook, people locked their doors when they saw me coming. It had been a long while since I'd been through the park like that; none of the faces are even familiar and I don't like being reminded that I live my life surrounded by fools. There were gunshots again and I pedaled harder, my vision like a scythe, cutting them all down. Past yards full of antlers, pinwheels on fenceposts, those ridiculous butterflies; most of the trailers are on blocks, aluminum skirts hiding their wheels, landlocked. One time, years ago, my dog jumped out the car window and broke its pelvis. The dog ran behind the bicycle, trying to keep up, back legs out to the side as if they might catch up or go over its body and twist it in two.

I was floating, the bicycle's tires hardly touching the ground because of the certainty of her return, that Charlotte had to come back and I would see her soon, that we would talk, perhaps even touch. As I rode I thought of the last night I'd seen Charlotte, at Anita's. We'd just taken down the cribbage board, I was shuffling the cards when Anita screamed.

She said she'd seen a face at the window. There was a clatter outside, and the dogs were barking far away; they were so frightened they'd gone out to the road.

I'm the one to handle this, Johnson said.

He went out onto the porch and we heard him shouting. After a couple minutes it was silent, and then he returned, holding the boy by the arm. Johnson let him loose and he just stood there, a tall young man looking at the floor, silent, stealing glances in Charlotte's direction. She was watching him, but she did not speak.

What were you doing? Anita said.

Just walking by, he said. There were black lines between his teeth, a few red whiskers on his chin. His dirty flannel shirt hung halfway to his knees.

You were spying through the window, Anita said.

Plains Indians wore their umbilical cords around their necks, Johnson said. That's how it is, some kind of pull. He acts like he's not happy to see me, but, take my word for it, he is.

You know him? Anita said.

Know him? That's my boy. That's Keith.

He introduced us all, exclaiming at the coincidence that they both found themselves in Wendover. Coincidence has never seemed a compelling or surprising concept to me. Keith just stood there, his eyes cast down, leaning toward the door like he was anxious to escape. I was sizing him up, sweet boy, trying to see his future and how long we'd cross each other.

He stays out on the salt flats because he knows I won't go out there, Johnson said. The salt kills the energy out there.

Like a snail, I said. He ignored me.

And those cars travel so fast over the flats they tear it all up, they scramble it—it's always a mistake to put a machine between yourself and the earth. That's what my boy does, that's right. The cheetah's the fastest animal on the earth, but he's got no endurance, it's all or nothing, the tortoise and the hare all over again. Speed's just another word for not paying attention.

I wasn't going so fast on the bicycle, coasting, leaning in to swoop around a corner. I didn't see the hedge—I almost crashed, but came out the other side still upright. My dog trailed behind, it could not keep up, moving like a crab. Up ahead, boys played ball with their shirts off—I saw their ribs, their tiny dark nipples—and I shouted for them to get out of my way, that I'd run them right over. I coasted back to my trailer, panting; I tried to remember how Charlotte had left the bicycle, so she would not notice it had been moved.

Inside, I poured myself a glass of water and tried to let the time pass. My neighbor's fire was coming along nicely, both soothing and exciting me, the flames reaching everything they could. Red, yellow, orange and blue, I watched it, I tried to watch the road for my car. They kept me warm; she would end my loneliness, light the change.

The hood of my neighbor's parka was inside out and sat on

his back like a hump. Once he threw an aerosol can into the bin and it exploded, put a hole in the side of his trailer. I've never really talked to him, there's no reason; I'm not curious why he lights the fires, why he cannot feel the heat of the sun.

Watching the flames, I thought back to the Red Garter. I was simply there first, that was all, though they took me in for questioning. As if it's a crime to walk at night, to watch a fire. As if I'd burn down a place I might want to work someday, a potential employer; there are enough fools to support ten more casinos in Wendover.

The boys have a healthy adolescent love of fire. They're always asking me about arson. Fire, I tell them, is the weapon of cowards. What else do you have? they say, they call me old. I tell them if I had a phone I'd have a phonebook and I'd tear it in half to show them how old I am. I throw cards at the dartboard, saying they could draw blood. I tell the boys I bit off a man's finger in a fight in Tonopah, swallowed it; I show them what I say is a scar from a bullet, in the muscle of my arm.

I was so deep in the flames I did not hear Charlotte return. She skidded to a stop outside; my car sounded on the verge of overheating. When I opened the door she was halfway to the trailer.

How fast did you get it going? I said.

What?

I thought you took it out to the Speedway.

No, she said. That's not where I was.

I saw the salt along her arms, white on the soles of her shoes. She didn't look at me. She just reached for the bicycle, as if she was leaving.

Wait, I said. You owe me.

What do you want? she said, and I saw then she was shaken up somehow, tentative and trembling.

Is something the matter? I said.

No. Nothing.

I thought we could play a game of cribbage, I said. That would pay me back.

She came inside and sat down at the table. There was red around the rims of her eyes, as if she'd been crying or had been up for days. I had not noticed this before, I had not noticed that she wore a CTR ring on her thin finger. She twisted her hair, watching the cards. Unclipping her barrette, she laid it on the table. The birds were fighting each other, trying to look at her through the window.

These cards I know are crooked, she said.

If I had to mark the cards to beat you, I said, I would.

We played a few hands, but she was not paying attention. She turned, looking around the trailer, turning the books to read their spines.

Don't you ever want to leave here? she said.

You're here, I said, but she did not understand.

I just got here, she said, and I know I'm not planning to stay.

The day may come, I said.

When I stay or when you leave?

I thought only little Mormon girls wore CTR rings, I said.

She smiled, at last. Is a person ever too old to choose the right? she said.

What was it you saw out there? I said.

Out where?

On the flats.

I can't tell you, she said. I'm not sure I can.

You have a boyfriend out there, I said.

No I don't.

That's not it, then.

No. She smiled like she had seen her way free. I had a boyfriend once, she said. He went away on a mission.

A secret mission? I said.

You know what I mean. A church mission.

Did he try your virtue?

Please.

We kept playing, silent for a time. I touched her hand. The birds were singing to us. She looked away and I palmed her barrette, put it in my pocket.

You changed the subject, I said.

Did I?

You can trust me, I said.

She looked at her cards a long time before she spoke again. I poured her a glass of water. My trailer felt small with another body in it and I silently thanked the walls for closing in, for bringing her nearer to me.

Someone's sending me messages, she said.

On the flats.

Yes.

What do they say?

It started with my name, she said.

I knew it, I said.

Did you?

I know you won't lie to me, I said. You have to have some-one to tell; you can't hold it all in.

The messages are for me, she said. Not anyone else.

You can tell me.

Maybe, she said.

I'm not going anywhere, I said.

She was anxious to leave and I saw this and considered losing on purpose; the loser always has the right to challenge, to play again, to keep the winner from escaping. Instead, I won and she did not challenge me. She left me there alone.

I remember the night. Believe me, I remember it well. It was my night off and I was reading past dark, the western about the headstrong Mormon girl who thought her black horses were the fastest things on the sage. After I was finished I didn't want to read anymore, didn't want to go to the Hide-A-Way, didn't want to wait to see if the boys would come listen to my stories. I never said I wasn't a lonely man; everyone needs their motivations.

The sun was down but had left

some of its light behind. The moon was open wide. My dog wanted to come with me that night, but I told it it was too arthritic to cover all contingencies, too toothless. I fed the dog and told it to watch the place, giving what encouragement I could as I started up the slope. The days were longer, hotter, and the nights were bringing less and less relief. There was enough light in the sky that I could see all the painting on the cliff above Wendover. Someone had painted SLEIGHT OF HAND, and others had left modern hieroglyphs, numbers that were either speeds or lucky strikes on keno or the roulette wheel; perhaps they were some sign to the powers above, hints or prayers.

Somehow I'd let myself court impatience. It had been over a week since I'd seen Charlotte and I thought it was time she came down from the mountain. I missed her so much it seemed impossible she didn't also miss me. Feelings as strong as mine demand reciprocation, they earn it. Once I'd come home from the library to a note on my door; it wrecked me to miss her and I wished she'd just taken the car—she knows the keys to the door are hidden in the car, that the car keys hang on the cupboard.

Will was waving to me, pointing at the casino; I felt a little less anxious in the glow of his lights. I could go into the Stateline, grab a free meal, read the paper, but I try to stay out of there on my nights off. Besides, I was wearing my uniform, something I'm not supposed to do off-shift, and if someone had called in sick they wouldn't hesitate to press me into service.

Headlights kept passing out on the interstate, cars moving as fast as they could. I hated to go to Anita's; I debased myself, listening under the window, playing the voyeur, and I had vowed to give it up. That night I was so lonely for Charlotte I was willing to risk watching Johnson and Anita, to stand quietly behind the window's reflection as they fornicated on the table, rolled on the floor among the animals. There was always the chance that she would be there. I stood under Will, right on the border between Utah and Nevada, thinking, trying to decide. The border is an edge though the world is still round. A rift, it keeps out and it keeps in.

At first I could not see where she was, I could only tell she was coming closer. She was singing to herself, I heard her voice; she swooped out of the darkness with a flashlight in one hand, coasting, her bicycle's tires hissing along the street. I raised my arms, but she did not see me, she kept moving past.

Turning, I left Will behind, I ran under the cowboy clown on the pawnshop's roof, past the Taco Burger and all the downscale motels on the Utah side. I was struggling to find all the air I needed. I kept her in sight though she was pulling away. I feared I would faint but I kept running. Stray dogs, crying babies were left in my wake; someone laughed and I cursed them all as I shuffled past.

I kept on, east of town, across the interstate. I saw where she was going now, I had suspected it. It's not so much mountains along the flats as pieces of gnarled rock forced up from underground, all the salt and sand blown away to expose them. Ahead, she was pushing her bicycle and I was gaining a little ground as we left the road. I had to be careful in the darkness, in the night shadows; a fall could ruin me—I must protect my hands like a surgeon, like a pianist, like the artist I am.

She looked back once but she did not see me. The sage grew more sparse, salt-encrusted along bottom branches, on the sides away from the wind. I stayed out of sight, my breathing slower, my recovery faster than I had hoped. Behind me I heard planes taking off, landing at the airstrip; the Enola Gay practiced here, then dropped bombs that killed a quarter of a million people, took many straight to ashes.

I moved in the shadows of the rocks, closer to where the bonfire was burning. Bottles were upturned and the music was loud, people leaping over and through the fire, throwing oil and gasoline just to watch the explosions. I closed my eyes and still I saw the fire, though I lost the music and the voices. I saw cards spinning in the night sky.

Yes, there are bad boys out on the flats, loaded on amphetamines and unable to stop talking; they come into the casino sometimes with their unblinking eyes, smelling of gasoline, leaving the cards so dirty and smudged I'd think they were marking them if they didn't always lose. Pieces of the fire blew loose, rising on hot updrafts and rolling wild, spending themselves on the flats. There were naked bodies in the firelight, but Charlotte was not among them.

I moved closer. No one saw me, no one was looking for me. Finally I noticed the other fire, smaller and off to one side, and I moved in that direction. There was less to hide behind; I crawled on my stomach, toward her face—it stretched and twisted, pieces breaking off and then returning—in the heat above the flames. Keith was there and I watched the skin of her arm flickering, reaching out to him. I crept closer, on my hands and knees, to the edge of the firelight, afraid my eyes would reflect like a coyote's. More like a jackal or hyena, I shuffled backward, I lay flat when they turned my way.

What are you doing? she said the first time he touched her.

Nothing, he said.

I didn't mean you had to stop, she said.

If things had gone too far I would have created a disturbance, perhaps, but I knew Charlotte better than that. Yes, I watched them kiss, I saw his hands beneath the back of her shirt. Every move of one surprised the other, everything was so wonderful and unfamiliar. They were floating together above the fire and I forgot my own body, the vertebrae that had been a stack of sharp and mismatched teeth, the ankles recently unbalanced by their load.

When Keith went to fetch wood he walked right by me. She had him talking to himself; some would say she wasn't the prettiest, Charlotte, but she's a church girl, clean and chaste, and there's plenty of hook in that, there's nothing better in bed than a believer. While he was gone I watched her, looking into the fire, and the whole time I was planning—schemes like the million I've never acted on, the few I have—trying to figure how to use the messages, how to bring her to me so she would

58

believe and not suspect. Down at the other fire they were throwing Molotov cocktails, and someone was bound to be blinded before the night was out, to lose a hand or at least some fingers.

I stayed close to the fire, out of sight. I listened to their conversations and they left me with nothing to fear—young love, infatuation, whatever you want to call it, it has no teeth. It might seem I'm holding back, that there's something here I don't want to tell, that perhaps Charlotte was not so chaste that night. She was. We'll see how much I hold back, how little shame I have.

Keith did not want her to go, and I admit she was reluctant to leave. Of course she was, but she did leave, pushing her bicycle away from the fire, toward the lights of Wendover. I stayed low in the shadows, so close to her as she went past. I waited, giving her time so she would not guess where I'd been if she circled back, she would not guess what I'd been doing.

I went far out of my way to keep from running into her; through the cemetery, I walked across graves, I stepped on the flat tombstones of babies to hear the sound. People don't die, I've suspected, so much as they move around—at least that's what I plan to do. Police cars went back and forth between the casinos, in and out of the lights. A voice shouted; there was no answer.

Long before I reached my trailer I could tell something was wrong. The night was too still. As I came closer, I saw my dog, on its side, half underneath the trailer. I had expected something like this. All the dirt around it was scratched and worn down, as if the dog had been running circles on its side. The fur was matted and wet with tears all around the eyes. The legs were stiff, the body swollen.

I turned on the light over the door of my trailer and suddenly I knew I was being watched. Turning it off again, I stood for a long time in the darkness. All I heard was the wind and the coyotes, flowers blooming, the moon turning pale as it tightened itself down. Finally I gathered the dog in my arms and carried it across town, through hopeless gamblers, endless fools, to the house of the veterinarian. I banged on the door until he got out of bed, I made him do an autopsy on his front porch. He said it was rattlesnake venom, much more than one snake could muster, that usually the bite was easy to see, all puffed up and inflamed where the fangs went in. He could find nothing like that, nothing at all.

Charlotte was looking for the first
sign when it came to her. It was no
surprise, no coincidence. The cars
drew her attention down from the
sky, true, she searched the white
surface for the shadows of
hawks—yet from the beginning she
had suspected the sign would come
from the salt flats, all that blank
space spread out before her. She
found it with her binoculars, then
with her bare eye, squinting over
miles. It seemed to be a giant, im-
perfect circle, stones spread out to
inscribe it, but it was not irregular

at all, there was really only one gap. It had to be a C, calling her down; she was certain there was more, more that could not be seen from a distance.

She began to take the bus back and forth between Salt Lake City and Wendover, round-trip tickets, looking out the window the whole way, searching. In Salt Lake she would walk to the end of the block until she could see the temple through the buildings; she waved to the gold angel on top, Moroni, then turned and caught the next bus back. Other passengers tried to strike up conversations with her, but she shut them out. Going gambling? they said. Myself, I just keep straight how much I can afford to lose. Kneeling on her seat, she did not turn around. She pressed her binoculars against the window, hints of a black eye at every bump.

All along the flats, signs said KEEP OUT. There were words in the desert close to Salt Lake, made out of stones, glass, bottles stuck by their necks into the mud. They were not messages for her. They were only hearts and initials, obscene invitations and bold claims. Further, there were shadowy words in shallow pools and puddles, almost decipherable, the stones like fish beneath the surface, holding still to keep the words intact. They did not interest her, they did not feel right.

She saw her name on the roadside. CHARLOTTE. Her initials, also, yet either one of these things could belong to someone else, someone else held trapped inside a heart. Thoughts were turning over in her head, people and things she could not shake; she wanted to stop thinking, to do something—she wanted to surprise herself. The bus passed a mountain of salt, buildings and the huge sign showing the girl in her raincoat, her dog trying to draw her attention to the salt spilled behind. Above her umbrella, black smoke rose up, coughed from a hidden stack.

It was only later that she knew. She read her name spelled backward, east to west, stretching out, the letters separated by miles, all in the same black stones. No one else could have seen her name there, no one else could have found it. She was being called.

The bus crossed the flats, then climbed a little into the desert. It raced the train along the shore of the Great Salt Lake, past Saltair, and on. The Mormons built Saltair at the turn of the century, as a place of wholesome recreation. Its dome is a reminder of the tabernacle, gold spires like India—or even Atlantis, now that the great building is underwater, so flooded you can row a boat through its vaulted rooms. Once people came to take the cure on the Salt Lake, to float there, unable to sink—as if there could be thrill in swimming without the threat of drowning. Twice the building has burned down and now the water wants it, surrounding it like a hungry moat. Charlotte looked right through it. Once a rollercoaster, the Racer, went up in flames; scaffolding folded in on itself and the heavy tracks collapsed, hot metal through the smoke. The last time Saltair burned, in 1970, it had already been abandoned. Someone must have lit that fire just to watch it go.

The bus driver would not let her out on the flats, he could not be persuaded to break the rules. All she could do was watch the land roll past, lost and kept hidden behind her. The signs along the interstate say EMERGENCY STOPPING ONLY, but they did not discourage her. When she borrowed my car she left it to the fates; it would be towed if that was meant to be.

Hawks rose in the foothills, but she did not watch them long. She tried to get her bearings, to figure where she was in relation to where she had sat on the mountain, which direction would take her to the letter C and the other messages she was certain lay nearby. The surface of the flats cracked beneath her feet, then hardened again, baked by the sun. She walked circles, sideways, back and forth. The land was barren and it was bare, white, smoother and cleaner the deeper she went. She could not find the C, and she sat down, closed her eyes and waited to see what came. The wind smelled like fish; it could not sustain itself. The sun reflected in the darkness, turned to heat, and the flats burned the palms of her hands.

Taking off her shoes, she stood and began to run, as fast as she could, in a perfectly straight line, lengthening her strides until she could find no more air. She doubled over, panting, then knelt down, rolled onto her back and looked into the sky as it wheeled past. When she turned her head sideways she saw her name spelled in tiny pebbles, the whole thing smaller than her hand. She was frightened and she treasured her fear. She walked a spiral out from her name, and ten feet away she found the word LISTEN, its letters made of broken glass.

I'm so relieved to be telling someone, she kept saying to me. I've been holding it in for so long.

She had been walking around my trailer as she talked, picking up my things, laughing at my books, the tilt of my bed, my bow ties hanging like bats, clipped to my closet door. It was late afternoon, she had just returned my car, we had pushed the cribbage board to one side. Outside the window, my neighbor was carrying old fence pickets over his shoulder, adding them to his pile of things to burn. The fan dried the sweat on one side of my body, its face jerking left, then right. I cannot doubt that Charlotte knew how things were turning between us.

Are they out there now? I said.

Somewhere, she said. There are new ones. But after I read them I take the letters apart; if I left them it would confuse people—or it would warn them what I might do next.

Show me, I said.

You'll see it.

No, I said. Not what you're going to do. The messages.

That might change things, she said. And they're really only for me.

You haven't told anyone else? I said. Not Anita? I was afraid she'd said something in front of Johnson, maybe even Keith. I wanted to be the only one.

Only you, she said, and you're sworn to silence.

What will you do if I tell?

Do you hear something? she said.

No. I was watching her, sitting across the table from me. She looked away from my eyes. Do you get the feeling, I said, that someone's trying to set you up?

Why would they?

A million reasons, I said.

It's nothing like that. I'd know if it was like that.

Like what?

No one's trying to trick me, she said. No one could. I found my name a mile from the interstate, in tiny, tiny pebbles; it was smaller than my hand, miles from anywhere. How could I come across that? Who could set it up?

I admit it's strange, I said. Especially if you're telling the truth.

You know I am. She was leaning across the table, her hands flat on its surface, pressing down as if she was about to stand.

I believe you, I said, I just wanted to see what you'd say. And I wanted to watch her. When I first met her she seemed to hold so much energy in thrall and now I was seeing it, a tension easing, slowly being brought to bear. Dark freckles ran along her cheekbones, along her chest but stopping before her smooth throat. She had raised her voice to me. Looking at her, being so close, I had trouble listening to what she was saying but still I understood perfectly. Words smoldered between us, marking our future and assuring it. We would be changed; I knew it all then, beyond purified. It was not for us to speak things, only to follow them through.

I hear someone, she said.

What?

There's someone under the trailer, she said.

I knew who it was, who it had to be, listening to us. I stood, I took the length of pipe in my hand. I swung the door open so it slapped the side of the trailer. For a moment everything was silent; then the boys ran, scattering, only a few brave enough to stand their ground. I laughed as I stepped down, yet still I looked under the trailer to make certain. The boys stood holding the boards with the snakeskins, arguing about which was which.

They're still drying, I said. Put them back. They're not ready yet.

The boys who had dispersed now came closer; they kept some distance, though, as if I might suddenly grab hold of them or lash out with the pipe. Charlotte drew them—she had come out behind me—but they were afraid of her, also, they did not know what to do. My neighbor stood watching with a box of matches in his hand. It was eighty degrees and he was wearing a scarf, that same stocking cap.

Johnny, Enrique, Christopher, I said, and if I was mistaken they had the good manners or fear not to correct me in front of Charlotte. Slowly, they put the snakeskins back under the trailer and set off through the park, along the edge of the desert.

Two weeks, I called after them. At least two.

What's going on with the snakes? Charlotte said.

Nothing. I took a few steps and kicked my dog's chain. Anyone can walk right up here now.

I'm sorry, she said.

I'm not sentimental, I said. It was an old dog.

Still, she said.

Some people say pets are a cure for loneliness, and to some extent that's true; mostly they're a reminder that there is no person who will spend that much time with you.

When we sat back down at the table I saw her eyes and I knew I could turn her my way, to get her talking.

You believe it all, I said.

I prayed for it, she said. I know it's true, I can feel it's true, and the messages are for me.

Tell me some, I said.

You wouldn't understand them if I did. She laughed. Sweat shone on the curl of her upper lip. Sometimes, she said, the words are misspelled, letters are left out or even whole words missing in sentences.

Like shorthand, I said, or a mistake?

I don't know.

But it helps you to run barefoot.

Yes.

Sounds like earth energy, I said. Simple.

That's not it.

Do they tell you to do things you haven't done before? I said.

That can't be helped, can it?

Do they tell you to sin?

What do you know about the messages? she said.

Only what you tell me.

No one needs to be told to sin, she said. It's the other way around.

Slippery, I said, but safe.

She knew what I was thinking. Often I'd plan far ahead of time what to say to her, even guess at her responses and prepare for them. It was as if she anticipated even this. The birds outside were screaming their heads off. Her eyes, they are brown, they are hazel; if she were standing in a field of alfalfa her eyes would be green. I was holding her hand and she seemed not to notice. Sparks gathered between us, called through friction. Her fingers were smooth and her mouth small, her eyelashes long, her teeth crooked. I could not remember if she had always flirted with me like this.

No, she said. Safe would be staying in Bountiful, marrying my missionary, playing hymns on the piano, waiting for my girl's hair to grow long enough so I could braid it. This is not safe.

Here you are, I said, come out among the heathens, lepers and moneylenders.

No, she said.

What, then?

I have to go farther than where I've been.

Farther into what? I said.

I don't know. I'm telling you too much.

You can never tell me too much, I said, and the words seemed false and contrived as I spoke them. I tried to laugh, but coughed instead. She slid my glass of water across the table.

I have to think about what they mean, she said.

You haven't told anyone else? I said.

No.

Don't let your hormones lead you astray, I said. I know even you Mormon girls have hormones somewhere.

Are you a dirty old man? she said.

Neither.

She smiled and I knew everything was going to be all right.

Sweetheart, I said, though she didn't seem to hear.

She had told me enough, the very fact that she told me proved she knew I was involved, that she needed me to go farther, wherever that was. She must have seen that—that's what brought her to me in the beginning. I wanted to lead her.

There's not a favor I wouldn't grant you, I said.

I wondered what I might resort to to keep her from leaving; once she left I knew I would be very tired, and I could tell it was going to be a longer night than usual at the blackjack table. Charlotte watched me like she was waiting for me to speak. Looking back, I have to praise my patience, my restraint. I could have had her there and then.

I always burn a few cards off the
top of the deck, to earn the players'
confidence. My chips are lined up
in front of me, five, ten and twenty,
and I trade them for bills across the
green felt. Some dealers wear rings
on their fingers, they need those
distractions; I do not. Speed gives
rise to distrust—I've learned not to
go too fast, to slow it down and
take the money deliberately, as if
anything could be fair.

I looked across the table at the
man, his sunglasses, his visor, his
t-shirt with the name of some lost

city. Behind him, others stood watching, the real players checking to see if I showed any kindness, any weakness they might exploit. I dislike the summer because the people, the old people, come in wearing their summer costumes, showing more skin. There isn't a sixty-year-old woman alive who should be allowed to wear shorts, and the men aren't much better.

I've gambled all over the world, the man said. Legal, illegal, you name it.

Well now, I said, you've hit the bottom. Wendover, some call it Bendover. I took his money, sold him more chips.

They deal backwards in Australia, he said. Like water down the drain. Nah, I'm just pulling your leg.

The thing about jokes, I said, is they're supposed to be funny.

It was hard to say how drunk he was, but it was certain he wasn't sober. I hate it when people talk in the middle of a hand, as if, given time, the cards might change, as if my control is tied to quickness. I left him at eighteen, took twenty for myself. Some people ask for the rules and then act as if I made them up, others saunter up to the table bantering around terms of no known origin. They're always trying to buy me drinks, they pretend they're loaded. Coffee, I say, coffee will do me just fine, and I let them buy it though I get it free.

You have to stand at seventeen, he said.

You're thinking of some other casino, I said, I can take it as far as I want. As far as I can.

Deal, he said.

Drunks invariably lose track of what's happening and then accuse me of cheating. I make them pay. I know the cards without marking them; the weight of the ink, the difference it makes in the suits and numbers. I can tell five hearts from five diamonds and I could win every hand if I wanted, yet chance is more interesting and I've been following it for so many years. I could have retired long ago, but I fear the nights would turn endless—and, in chance, I straddle a border and feel the movement between things. It keeps me sharp.

The man bought more chips, then spent some time stacking them. When I was in Australia, he said, I saw a woman dancing. She was dancing underwater, naked, in a giant aquarium that was all lighted up inside. Somersaults and everything, just like a mermaid with legs—she came up for air but she didn't need to. What a set of lungs she had!

I wasn't really listening. I winked at the waitresses in the casino's restaurant and I shuffled the cards slowly, deliberately. All the way over by the door I saw him, coming through the slot machines, around the roulette wheel, his head turning from side to side. Keith was searching for me. I'd seen him on my last break, as I stood outside, his car cruising slowly back and forth, passing and returning.

Now he stood there, waiting for me to finish the hand. He looked bewildered and confused, as if all his nerves had been tightened, shortened. The boy stood watching me, the dealt cards, tossed chips settling on the felt. His patience was endearing.

Want to play? I said, knowing that was not what he wanted.

Do you know where Charlotte is? he said.

You don't know?

Have you seen her? he said.

That I haven't, I said. No idea. You in or out?

He turned slowly and navigated back through the machines, still searching.

That your son? the man said.

That was a fool, I said.

He was looking for your daughter, then.

I'm sorry for the interruption, I said. Are you in? I get paid to turn over cards, not to talk.

Save the good ones for me, he said. I'll be back. Have to drain the main vein.

I hear it all, believe me, and I smile as if I understand, as if these people and I are in on something together, as if we share a world. Still, I lean forward to try to understand the mumbling of drunks, to pretend to make sense of the words of the sober. No doubt I'd love them less if I could understand them.

I had lied about Charlotte. I knew where she was. I thought of her as I looked over the machines, deaf to their incessant calling. Once it was merely the dealers' voices, the mechanical slots; now I'm hoarse at the end of every shift, rasping away, shouting to be heard over the din. Young dealers come through here, trying to make their way up to Reno or Vegas, and I have to disabuse them, to let them know this is not a stop on that line. People try to sneak in cameras, they press tape recorders along the sides of slot machines. Yes, there was gambling for the robe at the foot of the cross, and there's no reason to believe it was less tawdry than this. The buses never stop, busload after busload of the old, retired. This is not really a place for the young, nor a place for the rich, the hopeful, or even those who like risk; this is a place for killing time, praying the hands of the clock will keep moving when we look away.

The security guards circle on their silent shoes—they are not allowed to talk to other employees or to relax their vigilance in any way. The sweep of the second hand, the slow needle, is a killing and also a cleaning. As I watch it, willing it along, the waitresses in the restaurant make fun of me in Spanish, pointing and laughing, mothers and daughters working together. Theirs is a world I share; they tease me and I know they are saints, they save me, saints as people can only be if you'll never know them well.

Anita and Johnson came in and sat down at the bar. He winked and shot at me, his finger like a gun, his thumb the hammer coming down. Now he was dressed in the clothes of Anita's husband—a sky blue silk shirt, a dark brown denim suit with white stitching. I had seen the clothes before, filling the whole closet, but I had never agreed to try them on. This was only the second time he'd come into the Stateline. The first time I told him I didn't deal to people I know. If I win I feel bad, if I lose I look bad. I pointed to the camera and he waved, blew a kiss. Lord knows the slim chance that someone's watching, that there's actually tape in the stupid thing.

Dog killer. The killer of dogs. He sat at the bar and watched me through the smoke and noise, through the colored lights. When you've lived enough years, you begin to see the movement of things, you learn to know and expect how things will unfold and where they'll tangle. I am neither stupid nor modest. There is a lot of discretion in the desert, much more than valor. The waiting overpowers all action, the restraint breaks men down.

It was midnight, so I closed my table for fifteen minutes. As I passed I saw the man who had gambled in Australia; he pointed at his watch, held up five fingers, then headed for the bar. I went through the side door, out into the air, paying my respects to Wendover Will. The boys were out there smoking cigarette butts, wasting time. When they were younger they'd try to sneak into the casino to play the slots, though the gambling itself held no thrill. Children are born on the other side of the con and they must be taught the pleasure of being fooled.

Another bus pulled up out front, wheelchairs and walkers being unloaded, old people whose pants were falling down, their pockets so heavy with change. I watched the road, cars slowly passing. Charlotte was out there, somewhere; she'd borrowed my car to see what she could find at night. The moon was full, spilling over the salt flats. Don't take your eyes off the road, I warned her; no matter what don't get out of the car.

Keith's car passed several times while I was taking my break. I don't think she really knew what to do with him, she never knew, though she had hopes for him—certainly no one could cast aspersions on his tenderness.

Pyro, the boys called, looking in my direction. They had not been by for a while, and once I'd seen them early in the morning, following Johnson across the desert. At first I thought they were coyotes. He did not see them. The sun was just rising. He killed all the snakes, they told me, he did it with his bare hands, too, and I said at least I don't wear a shoelace around my head, at least I don't walk circles with my clothes off. They found the thought of this hilarious.

Hours passed, I never sat down, I only lost when the cards showed their independence, I raked in money for my employer. At five o'clock I threw a card at the bartender, so she would call Sandra; Sandra is not always on time, and I wanted to get out of there. Sleepy-eyed, she came up behind me and took the cards from my hand. She fanned them over the felt, her fingers covered with rings. I was free.

I wanted to go out the side door but I also didn't want to give Johnson the wrong idea, that he could cause me to harbor fear. I nodded as I went by, hoping that would be sufficient, but he caught me by the arm. He asked me what I'd have to drink and I told him I was just headed home.

What? he said. You got something going on? You expect us to believe that?

I've been working since nine last night, I said.

Have one, Anita said. Just one.

Your son came in tonight, I said to Johnson.

He's out wildcatting around, that boy. Johnson laughed. It's reassuring to me, you know, that he's out hunting a little tail, that he takes after me. People like you, you live in your head, only in your head, but I live in my body. Do I ever.

Thanks, I said to the bartender. I can't remember that girl's name; she hardly lasted six months.

Haven't replaced your dog yet, Johnson said. I liked that dog.

He was old, I said. Heart attack or something. I noticed that Anita paid for the drinks, that Johnson was freeloading. I never believed his story about the uranium mine.

Sit down, he said.

Can't do it, I said.

In the mirror I saw them sitting there and myself, standing, looking awkward, perplexed and old. Johnson was still talking and Anita's eyes were telling me there was no reason she

74

shouldn't have her pleasure, that she'd take it where she could find it. I had to escape, I had to find Charlotte. Johnson told Anita to pull up her pants, that half her ass was showing.

No one complained, she said.

My boy, Johnson was saying. He's the apple and I'm the tree. He takes after me, chasing the ladies. Can't imagine what it would be like having a fairy for a son.

Better than none at all, I said.

You'd know about that, he said.

This man, I said, has gambled in Australia. I took him by the shoulder and turned him to face Johnson, introducing him.

You're wearing sunglasses inside, Johnson said.

I'm a gambler, said the man.

He's a walker, I said, pointing to Johnson. A great walker.

In Australia, the man said, the aborigines walk for days, you know. He began to tell of the songs they sang instead of maps, how they covered miles and miles, kilometers and kilometers across the outback and never got lost. Of course Johnson was an expert on the songlines and he wouldn't give the man the satisfaction or authority of talking about them. I managed to slip away.

Once outside, turning from the casino is like walking out of a matinee movie into the bright afternoon sun, only the reverse. I limped into the darkness, trying to trick my circulation. Once someone recommended support hose, but it did not feel right, it took my concentration from the cards. The boys looked up as I passed, but they did not follow. There was a card in the gutter. Five of hearts. I headed under the overpass, toward Anita's.

The horses were chasing each other up and down the corral and the sun was rising. The horses kicked out with their sharp hooves, slashed with their yellow teeth. The metal stakes were still spread across the yard, the copper wire tight between them in some places, in others strewn frayed and tangled.

Either the house was empty or Charlotte was inside. She might be sleeping, she might be waiting for me. When I opened the door I interrupted a dog and cat trying to start a new species; the cat shot away and the dog's pelvis was still going as it tried to walk. There was shame in its eyes.

I called her name and it sent all the animals to a new level of agitation. They came out of their hiding places, they collided, they lifted their heads from where they'd been sleeping. There was no answer. I felt my heart strain against my ribs, grown too large for its cage to hold. A photograph of Charlotte stood on the table, in a small frame; it had to be several years old— she was wearing braces and her hair was much shorter, the curls cut out. I put the photograph in my pocket and went back outside.

She must be waiting at my trailer, I was thinking, to tell me what she'd found. I covered the distance as fast as I could. She knew where I hide the key—that hasn't changed. From the road, up the slope, I could see my car was back, parked next to my trailer. Out of breath, I found the door locked, struggled with my key, finally got it open. The trailer was empty. She had hung up the keys, she had been inside. I searched for a note. I sniffed the air.

Time would not pass. I could not read. Sleep was out of the question. I took out the photograph, hid it in the cupboard, then kept getting it out again. If this was a simple love story, a romance, we'd be halfway there by now. Instead, I sat waiting, fretting, hating the idea of wherever she was. I could not bear it.

I took down the keys. The car was empty, she was not there, and I started it and headed out. First I stopped at the Speedway. I knew she would not be there, but still I checked; I drove off the road, past a few cars, people cooking breakfast outside their tents. Keith's car was at the end of the line. He was asleep in the back seat, alone, a blanket twisted around him, exhausted after a night of unsuccessful searching. Quietly, I left him there.

Out on the interstate, I headed east, toward Salt Lake City. It seemed strange she'd be out on the flats without a car, but I'd learned not to underestimate her. The cold metal frame of the photograph pressed against my skin, inside my shirt. I propped it on the dashboard. She watched me, and ahead a semi carried a house trailer, plastic over the windows, a sign reading WIDE LOAD. Someone would live in there, some day soon and in some other place, and they would have their own problems.

No matter how fast you go it seems slow on that highway. The asphalt was stained red and I could see no roadkill, find no corpse before it went black again beneath me. I tried to see in all directions, I tried to keep my eye on the road. Something could have happened to her or perhaps she'd tricked me, doublecrossed me somehow. That did not seem possible, yet I was angry, I was worried, I could not settle.

Long sloughs of water ran alongside the road, below it, and the tops of fenceposts were just visible above the surface; clouds slid in the water, torn and pulled apart, and as I was wondering what those pens held there, underwater, the road turned white, white with salt. I turned around at Tooele, at the edge of the Great Salt Lake, and started back.

I slowed down once I hit the flats again, searching the horizon for the shape of her. Something moved, and then I saw it was a shining, lights a hundred yards from the road. I parked the car, climbed out, and all at once the heat caught me up. I unclipped my tie, unbuttoned my collar, then threw my vest in the car as I slammed the door. Pieces of dead seagull lay by the side of the road, no doubt cleaner dead than alive; farther along, there was one rubber boot, dirty and twisted clothing, children's clothing, and tangled black ribbons of cassette tape.

People die of thirst in the desert. Imagine a desert made of salt. I was halfway to the shining when a horn started honking; looking back, I saw the Bookmobile parked behind my car. Ray, the driver, was shouting something that wasn't reaching me. I walked back until I could make it out.

It's illegal! he said.

What?

You'll get arrested for being out there.

That's all right, I said. When they ask I'll tell them you warned me.

What? We were fifty feet apart and he wouldn't take a step toward me.

Save me some good books! I said, and watched him turn away.

The Bookmobile was levitating now, a foot off the road, held by the heat. The mind is used to straight rays of light, but the eyes also follow those which are bent; the two will not be reconciled. I've seen coyotes swim through mirages, I've seen the sun lift mountains and tip them. Cities can be pulled loose from the earth. They can loom in the sky.

From twenty feet I saw it was broken glass reflecting the sun. At least a hundred bottles had been smashed together there, scattered in a circle. I looked at it for a long time. One end was a little pointed, almost like an arrow, and I set off in that direction. Once, I looked back at my car—farther away now, bound to be towed—and I cursed myself for not thinking of bringing water along. I kept walking, certain Charlotte was out there, that when we found each other we could finally talk and not just dance around what we wanted to say.

A wind rose up behind me all at once, sharp sand pulled across the surface and the sound followed, the clatter of some infernal machine; I looked up and the jet was almost out of sight, just a hundred feet up. They test all sorts of things out there, things they don't tell us about, and I could care less; they crash all the time, too, but they close down the area and collect all the evidence before some fool stumbles across it. That's the kind of thing that gets the UFO freaks talking every time.

When everything settled, when I opened my eyes, I saw the first letter, a W, five feet high and made out of white stones, hard to see against the flats. Thirty feet away I found the O, ten feet across, all dark stones; just off to the left was the L, the top cut off so it could have been part of an H or even an E. That's all I could find. LOW or HOW. I walked around them, thinking, wondering if maybe she had left them for me, if they were only part of a word, a word like FOLLOW. Perhaps the words ran laterally, vertically, even horizontally. A stepladder would have saved me, any elevation, but there was only perfect flatness, the curve of the earth no doubt hiding things from me.

I had been awake for twenty-four hours and I mistrusted myself. The only footprints around the letters were mine, as if the stones had been dropped from above. It was possible, even, that they had been pushed up from below—listening to Johnson made me think like that. I scattered the stones, kicked the letters apart, and kept moving.

Out on the flats it's as if something is not right with the land, a low, unbalanced chuckling that keeps everything level. In the winter they're flooded over, and I wondered if the stones could have been left the year before, the footprints washed away; most likely they would be covered over, then, buried in the silt and sand. Now the flats were baked dry. Nothing can live out there, nothing at all. In the spring and fall they look dry, but they are not; the Donner Party got slowed down that way, had to abandon wagons to the mud and salt. The flats turned them from pioneers straight to cannibals.

I came to a place where there were more stones, spread into disorder, scattered. I found her footprints everywhere, her bare feet, and I knelt down and followed the edge with my finger, I put my hand inside. If only I were a tracker I could bring the earth to my nose and smell her, to my lips and taste her—this would tell me how far ahead she was, which direction she had taken.

I admit I wanted to solve the messages to impress her, I wanted to learn enough to manipulate them for my advantage, even tried to convince her I knew more than I did. I tried to toss stones from a distance, to build letters and words that way, but it was impossible.

I was lost, confused and in the middle of nowhere when I found the rectangle of stones, a J in one corner and a kind of

cloverleaf. A jack of clubs, a black jack, and then I knew I had
been expected there, somehow. The sun baked moisture from
my body, hawks circled miles above. My last doubts had been
removed; Charlotte would never lie to me, and there is nothing
like sharing a secret with someone to bring them closer.

This was the last night I watched
Charlotte and Keith. Their fire was
low, mostly embers and ashes, and
I was able to get close, flat on my
stomach, only fifteen, twenty feet
away. I listened to them talk as
the thunder broke above. We often
hear the thunder, yet rarely get the
rain. When we do get the rain it
tastes salty; it dries white on the
sidewalk and leaves lines in the
gutters.

There was no other fire—it was
the middle of the week and the flats
were deserted. A dog came out of

the darkness and found me, put its snout in my face, its rotting teeth, and I tried to get it to lie down, to quiet it. Somewhere above there was the sound of wings. The dog growled low.

Get out of here, Keith said, throwing a stone that just missed me. The dog leapt away into the night, the perfect flatness that spread out behind me for miles and miles, that hid letters and words, new clues all the time.

I don't see how you can believe all that, Keith said.

At first I was afraid she had told him, let him in on our secret, but then I realized they were talking about religion, that there was no danger.

It doesn't stay the same, Charlotte was saying. Faith can't grow unless it's tested.

Temptation, said Keith.

Not exactly, she said. It's more like a sharpening.

You want me to tempt you. That's what it is.

I don't know if you could tempt me. Not like you think, probably.

You don't know what I think, he said.

They were circling, but I had no fear they would ever arrive. At least we were in the desert, out in the barren waste, the right place to talk about temptation. Charlotte was a great distance from where she had started and now that distance could only grow. It was hard to say how far she would fall, if gravity could claim her, who or what would catch her, if she would ever be set gently down. I liked what I saw. I've never seen a temptation I did not like, that I didn't follow or could not satisfy.

You're not listening, Keith said.

I am.

You don't have to agree, he said, you just have to listen.

Well, she said, you don't have to listen to me, you just have to agree.

I lost words to the thunder, but I could guess at them. No doubt Keith had never met a girl who talked to him the way Charlotte did. That was part of the attraction.

Where you going next? she said.

Don't know.

But away from here.

Probably, he said.

You could go to Salt Lake, she said. I could go.

I'll figure it out once I start driving.

It's not as simple as that, she said.

You say that, he said, like there's something good about complication.

I watched the fire, afraid they would forget and let it go out. It needed attention, like everything else. No one was satisfied. Charlotte was unhappy counting hawks on the mountain, I knew; she didn't like the people and her efficiency had declined—she spent too much time watching the flats. I expected she would move, I trusted her to return.

I had also talked with Keith about his plans. One night I had gone to watch them, pathetic as I am, and Charlotte was not there. There was no fire near Keith's car, only the larger bonfire, further on. I knocked on his window until he woke up and he told me to go away, he said he had a knife. Finally, he opened the door and climbed out.

It's you, he said. What are you doing out here?

Stretching my legs, I said.

I don't even want to know.

He searched for and found his can of chew, took a dip, then offered me one. I declined. I was trying to see around him, into his car, to reassure myself it was empty. I walked to the other side, rested my hands on the hood.

How fast is she running these days? I said. Any closer?

Some things, he said. Sometimes some things are not meant to be—you have to accept that.

I agreed with him, but I recognized this as the reasoning of a loser, one too weak to change the course of events, to influence fate. Still, as we spoke I felt an empathy for Keith; I understood his problem—perhaps he even understood some fraction of mine, though he'd never have the equipment to sound its depths. The more I saw of him, in fact, the more I commended Charlotte on the subtlety of her judgment. He was not the worst in any obvious way, he was only shiftless, with the confidence of the little informed. His slow certainty was seductive and it's true he was handsome in a way. No doubt she had never seen anything like him in Utah. And, in the end, his patience with her, his constancy must be praised—though of course her time was ample recompense.

What are you going to do? I asked him.

Thinking of working as a mechanic, he said.

Not much call around here. Everyone in Wendover thinks they're a mechanic, you know that. Anyway, I guess you'd like to get away from your father. It wasn't much of a guess. The quickest way to find sympathy for someone is to become familiar with his father.

Maybe, Keith said. It doesn't bother me either way.

Your father killed my dog, I said.

He never liked animals.

They remind us too much of ourselves, I said.

Speak for yourself, said Keith.

I see it runs in the family.

What?

Forget it, I said. That's not true. What about Charlotte?

What about her? he said. Don't see what it has to do with you.

Right, I said.

Later, I walked over to the bonfire, leaving Keith to dream of her. The people there were startled at my appearance, they hurried to the other side and shouted across the flames. They were a little spooked to see a man my age walk out of the night way out there, wearing my bow tie, my black vest. I told them I only wanted to watch their fire, to share it. After a while they left me alone.

At last, that last night, Keith put on more wood and the flames returned. I could see their faces again, their lips moving—this made them easier to understand, though their words

84

were empty, weightless. I share hooks with Charlotte that Keith did not, that he never will.

I had told her about the messages I'd found. I talked until she had to believe me, until she could not deny I was on the inside.

The letters are all different sizes, I said. That surprised me. You never told me that.

That's right, she said.

It was late at night when I told her, dark outside the windows of my trailer. I turned out the lights so no one could look in.

What are you doing? she said.

Nothing. I turned them back on.

Were you looking for them? she said.

At first I was only looking for you.

What did you find?

I told her about the black jack, the word LOW or HOW in different-colored stones. Then I told her I had found our names together, the letters of broken glass, encircled by a heart of pebbles.

You're lying, she said. You're making it up.

Why would I lie?

A million reasons, she said, smiling at her cleverness. See? You were so sure I made it all up and now you tell your own stories about the words out there. I was right all along.

What if I am lying? I said.

She looked into my eyes and neither one of us dared look away. She didn't know what to believe, though it was certainly all or nothing. I told her the same thing over and over, holding her gaze, wearing her down.

I did not expect more from her then, I did not believe she would collapse into my arms. My recollection would not do it, talk was not sufficient. She had to be shown, I had to show her, I needed her alone out on the flats. I had gone out twice more after the first time and I had found nothing, not even a sign of her. I wandered, praying she knew how to find me.

85

That last night, they just sat in each other's arms, staring into the fire. That made me more nervous than any amount of kissing or wrestling. A cloud passed over the moon. I wanted to show her, at least to find her doubts, her places of least resistance. She whispered ridiculous promises I could not hear. I did hear the boys, somewhere close by, calling back and forth, but I could not see them. It was strange that they were so far from town.

I crawled backward, a safe distance, before I stood up. I could still see them in the circle of the fire, Charlotte standing, getting ready to leave. Turning, I shuffled off in the darkness, back to the outcroppings of rock, to the gap she always went through. She climbed onto her bicycle, then her tires hit a soft spot and she got down to push again. I lay in wait.

I called her name, twice, as she passed, so softly that only she could hear it. She stopped walking, still holding her bicycle, looking around her.

Hello? she said.

It's me. I stepped out so she could see me. Twisted my ankle, I said, then faked a few gimpy steps, hobbling close to her. She laid her bicycle down. Past her, I saw Keith so far away, his back turned toward us.

What are you doing out here? she said.

What are you doing? I said. It's dangerous out here.

You're the one who's hurt, she said.

I could smell her in the darkness—her curls, the cleanness of her skin.

Where are you going? I said. Where are you coming from? A man finds you out here, who knows what he'd try. I put my arm around her shoulders. Something like this, maybe, perhaps more like this. My hand was on her bare skin of her back, its curve, every vertebra. My other hand held the front of her belt, my knuckles against her belly. I had my hold.

This is difficult, it's hard to tell it right. Even she would admit it, she knows the truth. This was how it had to happen. She did not cry out, she did not fight my hands. I kissed her neck; I tore her shirt; I tripped her and landed on top and tried to force my knee between hers; I let go of her belt, straightened my fingers, slid them down further. She never cried out at all, she gave no warning before she bit me, caught the skin of my face in her sharp teeth. She recovered her ferocity and fought her way loose. She knocked me down into the darkness.

II. CITIES WITH NO CLOCKS

Charlotte stepped down on the gas
pedal and she felt like no one, like
nothing could catch her. Floating
shapes, pools of water, rose up and
disappeared on the highway; she
had to keep reminding herself not
to slow down. If you hit something
doing fifty, Keith had told her, you
might as well be going eighty. Still,
she was glad there were no other
cars, that she didn't have to pass
them—she did not trust the way
the light was working, she was not
sure what might jump out of the
false water ahead.

There were no other paved roads, only this one, as if there could be no choosing. The desert spread out on all sides, full of lizards and snakes, everything hidden and blending in, the same colors, hiding from her and from the sun. Clusters of swallows swooped close in front of her; she did not believe they had space or time to escape. She drove faster and faster and the hot air snaked from window to window, it pulled strands of hair loose from her ponytail and whipped them back and forth in front of her eyes. Next to her, Keith was sleeping, his face half in the sunlight, half in shadow, his legs folded against the dashboard. Yes, now everything was really starting. All the things she'd need were in the trunk of the car, with Keith's tools and the few clothes he kept in a garbage bag. She swerved at the ravens on the side of the road; they were eating from a corpse that could no longer be identified.

At first it had made her anxious when Keith fell asleep. She checked the oil pressure, the temperature and gas gauge, then added, subtracted and multiplied the numbers. The woman singing on the radio could not enunciate above the wind, but she kept Charlotte company. Now things were really beginning. She looked at Keith, watched him sleep, and wondered where she would take him.

The reasons they left, I don't know them all; for a long time I did not even know where they had gone—I could only develop my suspicions, my certitude that she was not through with me, that she never could be. I could say my attention lapsed—I had Johnson to worry about, another dealer got fired at the Stateline, I was working double shifts, murderous hours—but that is really beside the point. I let them go. It hurt me, yes, but I am patient.

Charlotte ran her fingers down Keith's arm, but it did not wake him. A few red whiskers grew sharp under his chin, there was razor burn along his throat, he slept with his mouth half open. Shifting, he drew a long, rasping breath, and was quiet again. His hands rested with palms upturned in his lap, as if he was about to receive something or had just given it away.

Before they left Wendover, she had stood outside the car saying a prayer; he had sat waiting, letting the engine idle.

I won't pray with you, he said.

I know, I know, she said. You're not religious.

They stole glances at each other, sharing the exhilaration of an escape. Under Wendover Will, past the Stateline and the trailer park, they looked like they were only going for a drive, perhaps running an errand. Their fear reassured them, it held them together. Charlotte looked out the back window and tried to believe they were leaving it all behind.

What are we doing? Keith said.

Let's find out, she said.

He drove through the mountains, the winding roads. The sun burned mist from the ridges. Antelope leapt fences, turned to watch, then disappeared in the heat.

I told you, Keith said, that if you came along it was to be with me, not try and change me around.

I remember, she said, I know I said that. Even then she had known it was a kind of lie, that the two were not so easily separated, that when people met they changed each other. She leaned against him as they coasted down out of the mountains, until the road leveled and straightened out. They switched places without stopping; she climbed over, almost into his lap, and he slid sideways beneath her. He adjusted the seat so she could reach the pedals.

Speed, he said. This car hates to go slow.

The air was bent all above the highway. Birds shot by, the radio played somewhere, cacti jumped and flickered, the wind could not slow them down.

I am too religious, he said.

How's that?

I was baptized and everything. When I was a baby.

Charlotte laughed. That head-sprinkling doesn't count, she said. You have to go under the waters.

That some kind of Mormon thing?

Yes, she said. It sure is. So what?

Remember, he said. This is Nevada. Everyone knows there's no speed limit in Nevada.

That was the last thing he said before he fell asleep. She drove faster and faster, first anxiously watching the numbers, then blasting straight ahead, trying to reach the water before it disappeared. Telephone poles separated as she ran them down, then they thickened again behind her.

She hit the edge of the town doing ninety and stood on the brake, one arm out to keep Keith from going through the windshield. Slowly now, she coasted, wondering how a ticket for fifty miles over the limit might look. There were no sirens.

Keith stretched his arms, but he did not open his eyes. The town was almost empty; a woman pushed a stroller down the sidewalk, followed by a mailman wearing a pith helmet. All the signs were so faded it seemed twenty years had passed since anyone had stopped or gone inside the buildings. No doubt there were cobwebs in there, broken glass and skeletons.

I know this place, Keith said, sitting up and looking around. Keep driving.

In the park all the trees were dead, leafless. They were surrounded by their own broken branches, which lay all over the ground, across paths, over benches. People watched the car pass. Three boys ran out into the street behind and shot after them, cocking their toy rifles and firing at will.

How long was I under? Keith said.

Over an hour.

Sorry.

I don't care, she said. Sleep some more if you want.

He opened his eyes wide, rubbed his face, then leaned over and kissed her cheek. Looking back, he read the distance from Wendover and laughed.

We're moving, he said.

You're in a good mood, she said.

The edges of the town slipped away, broken-down houses at longer and longer intervals. Keith climbed halfway over the seat, trying to straighten his legs, and Charlotte barely avoided being kicked in the head. He stretched until his boots lay on the shelf behind the back seat, his stomach across the top of the front seat and his head halfway out the window. As they passed a pen of dairy calves he called out to them, he named them.

Hey Precious, hey Loner, hey Wagtail, hey Gimp.

Now we're going to have an accident, Charlotte said.

Hey Beautiful, hey Blackeye, hey Friendless.

They drove on, talking, unfolding the map and considering all the possibilities. Charlotte watched a hawk circle high above, then lost sight of it and could not find it again. Keith rubbed the back of her neck as she drove. He began to laugh, and when she asked he said it was nothing and then they laughed together at the fact that there was no explanation.

This desert doesn't look like anything I've seen, she said.

Get used to it. Keith's hand was riding the wind above the rearview mirror. Hot, he said.

They had not passed another car in half an hour.

I'm surprised, Charlotte said. I'm surprised your father even had you baptized, inside a church and everything.

It's weird, he said, but that was a long time ago, you know, he's changed since then. Now he always says it was one of his biggest mistakes, baptizing me, that things would have turned out better, I would have. Been luckier or something.

You're doing all right, she said.

Cursed from the start, he says I was. When I was little, did I tell you about that?

What? she said.

When I was little he used to put me on a leash, fifty feet long, so I wouldn't run away. He really walked then, miles and miles, and he hardly spoke to me, he forgot me, he just pulled on the rope if my leash went tight.

That's not true, Charlotte said.

Why don't we talk about your father? he said.

There's nothing wrong with my father. There's nothing to talk about. She took Keith's hand and put it back on her neck. Think he'll miss you? she said.

He'll find me. He follows me. You'll see how it happens. Sometimes it takes a while, but he always does. Want me to drive?

Not yet, she said.

Ahead, the gold car floated above the highway, then descended as they came closer to where it was parked. Charlotte slowed down as they passed.

Back up, Keith said, just pass by again.

She stopped, put the car in reverse, and drove slowly backward, alongside the other car. It was a gold Continental, silver and rusted scratches along the side, one fin crushed, the taillight long shattered.

Park behind it, Keith said.

Why?

I want to see if I can tell what went wrong.

There was no wind when she stood on the highway, and the sun did not feel like it would ever stop. When she slammed the door she saw a sparrow caught between the bumper and the corner of the car; its broken neck was twisted so its head looked out, its eyes burned away.

Charlotte hurried to catch up with Keith, who had already reached the other car. He pointed out the date written in yellow chalk on the rear window, left there by the police. The car had been there two days and would probably be towed soon. She touched the chalk numbers and the glass was hot. The tip of her finger came away yellow.

The springs were rusted and the hinges full of sand, but the hood finally opened. Charlotte stood next to Keith, looking down into the wheels and belts and tubes.

That's power, Keith said. Giant. The fan got loose. See how it cut everything up in here?

How bad is it? she said.

They had not heard the car door open, but it slammed shut, almost bringing the hood down on their heads. They could not see around the hood and they stood still, listening.

Hello? Keith said. He stepped around the car and Charlotte followed him. The car was empty. They carefully went around to the other side and still they saw nothing.

There's someone in my car, Keith said, and just then the man climbed out, looked at them, then took a couple steps closer. He tottered a little on his cowboy boots, and even with them he was not much taller than Charlotte. The seams of his jeans were ripped on the outside, halfway up to his knees; the shadow from his cap hid his face and one long tail of hair curled along his back, bleached at the tip. He walked a slow circle around them, looking them up and down, before he spoke.

Thieves, he said.

We didn't steal anything, Keith said.

And why not? I wouldn't of hesitated. He was nervous, his hands jerked up from the elbows. You took the keys out of your ignition, he said, or else I'd be gone by now. Lucky.

Keith began to move and the man put up a hand.

I've got a gun, he said.

Charlotte prayed for another car to pass, but none came. She smelled the asphalt, the tar in the road. She leaned into Keith and he leaned back; she could not tell who was shaking. The light flickered as if thin clouds were crossing beneath the sun, moving too fast to be seen.

I need a ride, the man said. I'm not asking.

We don't have any money, Keith said. Hardly any.

Did I ask for your money? No, I didn't—and that's because I didn't need it, if you know what I mean. I need a ride.

He turned his hat around backward, then brought the brim to the front again. When the sunlight hit his face they saw how young he was; his face did not fit his words.

What I could do, he said, is I could just take your keys

and leave you here, if that was my style. I could take one of you, even, and leave the other one here. The thing is, now I've seen you and talked to you and everything. He pulled up his shirt and scratched at the skin of his stomach. Where you headed?

We're not sure, Keith said.

I don't care, really. From here you can only be going one place, and from there I can catch a bus. Let's get after it.

Charlotte gave the keys to Keith and the man stayed behind them as they walked to the car.

Back seat's mine, he said.

You're not bringing anything with you? Charlotte said.

What? he said, looking around him. Just get in the car.

They left the gold Continental behind them, marooned and abandoned. Soon it was gone, out of sight, and they drove on in silence. Charlotte looked back at the man. She tried to fold the map against the hot blast through the windows.

You can call me Texas, he said.

From there? said Keith.

Never been there. Not at all. He leaned forward, his head close between the two of them. What'll this thing do? he said.

One sixty, Keith said. One seventy-five.

Shit. You can't get this thing to two hundred? Man, I promise you my car didn't stop there. I see why you wanted to steal it.

Don't see how you can stand to leave it behind, Keith said. If it's so hot.

I can afford to leave it behind—let's put it that way. Texas sat back again and Charlotte turned to watch him.

Making you nervous? he said.

No, she said. Should I be scared? Are you some kind of bad man? You're a highwayman, that's what you are.

Texas laughed, then stopped himself. Don't try any tricks, he said. Don't try and butter me up.

How old are you? she said.

Twenty-two, he said. Two-two. Surprised?

A rabbit shot out of the sage and just cleared the front of the car, disappearing into the desert on the other side.

Don't try and avoid them, Texas said. That's where you get into trouble. Just take them right out.

I'm not stupid, Keith said.

No one here's stupid, Texas said. No one said anyone was stupid.

Charlotte tried the radio. Nothing would come in.

How about you? Texas said. How old are you?

Nineteen, she said.

He clapped his hands together. A teenager! We're in the same generation then, isn't that right? Is that how that works?

I'm twenty-seven, Keith said.

You're thinking I'm trash, Texas said. Aren't you?

I didn't say that.

I'm not asking you, he said to Keith.

I wasn't even thinking about you, Charlotte said.

Texas spit out the window, then wiped his mouth. I hate this, he said. You two are all acting like some kind of crime victims and you're just giving me a ride.

Not exactly, Keith said.

I'll tell you what, he said. I'll tell you something so you know you can trust me. That gold car back there, it wasn't my car. It was abandoned already when I found it.

So what were you doing out there? Keith said.

That, well, that I can't tell you. Let's say I'm not at liberty to tell you that.

Mysterious, Charlotte said.

Texas took something out of his pocket. He flicked a switch and there was the sound of static, a garbled word, before he turned it off.

You two got any extra batteries? he said. He stuck his head out the window and looked at the sky. It'll hold, he said.

Where are you from? Charlotte said.

I'll tell you what, Texas said. I noticed you all aren't wearing any rings.

We're not married, said Keith.

Why buy the cow when you can get the milk for free? Texas laughed.

Watch your mouth, Keith said.

There's one thing we don't want to forget here, Texas said, and that's who it is that has the gun. Do you have a gun? I don't think so—I hope I would of seen it by now if you did. So, he said. You two are just driving, unmarried, no idea where you're going. I like that. I like it. Regular lovebirds.

Could you be quiet for a while? Keith said. I'm trying to drive.

Just talking, Texas said. That's all we're doing here. Talking. And you're driving real well, I have to say. You are driving well.

If you say everything once, that will be enough, Keith said.

Jesus, said Texas. And that was a compliment, too.

They drove on in silence for a time. The sun was going down sideways, leaving shadows that made it seem the desert was full of skeletons, strewn with bones.

Well, Texas said, I hope it works out for you two, I really do, you know, sometimes I wish I could settle down like that, one girl and everything, but there's just always someplace else I have to be. As he spoke, he finished one of their water jugs and started on another. He told them he had to go see his cousin in Stockton, that his cousin knew someone and all they had to do was hold two hundred pounds of cocaine for a week, cut it with something, then give it to five guys who were waiting. Simple. All he, Texas, had to do was be the backup, to make sure everything went right.

They drove south, down along the edge of the test site; the highway skirts those places all across Nevada, the gates rising up to keep you out of where people figure how to kill each other, what will cause the least pain and the most destruction. Radiation seeps through the fences down there, it searches for water and animals, for people.

In the dusk they passed a dead coyote, its fur matted with blood; another coyote chased off the ravens. It barked at the car, unafraid.

That's its mate, Texas said. They mate for life. Go back there and I'll put it out of its misery.

No, Charlotte said.

Don't worry, said Keith.

One bullet. Texas laughed. I was joking!

We're almost out of gas, Keith said.

There's a truck stop up here. You fill it up and I'll stay in the car with your girlfriend. Try anything, tell anyone, and I can't promise what won't happen.

What? Charlotte said.

At the truck stop Texas did not stay in the car. He circled it, pacing, opening and closing his hands, jerking his head from side to side. A man with a camper looked over and Texas stared him down. He waved at Keith to hurry; he held up his hand like a gun.

Finally they were on the highway again. The sun was down and the low clouds cleared. The stars descended, closer, hanging their constellations low over the desert. It was quiet, only the sound of the engine, the tires on the road beneath them.

You awake back there, Tex? Keith said.

Texas, he said. And what were you planning if I wasn't?

Nothing.

Who has the gun here? Texas said.

I haven't seen the gun, Charlotte said.

You don't really want to see it, really. Trust me. If you see it you'll know things aren't going right and they're probably going to get worse.

His voice was different, his words seemed harder and his threats truer in the darkness; being able to see his face had taken something out of his words in the daylight. Headlights from the other direction shone ten miles away, were lost around curves, returned, and were gone in an instant.

You, Texas said to Keith, leaning forward to put a hand on his shoulder. You really keep your cool. I'm impressed how you do that.

Thanks, said Keith. Thanks a lot.

I hate this, Texas said. I really do. I like you two, it's just that I'm desperate—I have to get to Stockton and everything.

First they saw the jets at Nellis Air Force base, the lights coming in to land, taking off, so close together, defying collisions; then a phosphorescence in the sky slowly came down and into focus.

There it is, Texas said. Sin city. That is it.

Somewhere a searchlight was spinning, calling people in, cutting through the night. Charlotte read the neon. Stardust. Riviera. Circus Circus.

I can see it, Texas said to her, you've probably always wanted to be a showgirl, wear a glittery bra and all those feathers on your butt. I can see it. I really can.

Shut up, Keith said.

We're almost there, cowboy. Why blow it now?

Turn here? said Keith.

No, we're going downtown. That's where the bus station is. Believe it or not, I'm actually going to leave you two lovebirds.

The windows were still down, but the air was not cool enough to be refreshing. WORLD FAMOUS, the sign above the Palomino said, TOTALLY NUDE.

Next block, Texas said. Here's good. He took off his cap, raked his hair back, then put the cap on again. Opening the door, he had one foot in the street before he spoke.

I forgot your money.

What? Charlotte said.

I'm just kidding, he said.

On the sidewalk, everyone seemed to be walking crooked or with a limp. They all walked alone, with their hands in their pockets, staring into the car as they passed.

Remember that, Texas said. I didn't take it even though I

could of, you know. Later. He stood up, laughing, and slammed the door.

Clapping his hands, still laughing to himself, he walked toward the bus station with one thumb hooked in his belt loop. The entrance to the station was under construction; the bill of his cap kept him from seeing the blade of a parked bulldozer — it caught him right on the top of his head. He stopped, took off his hat, and looked up at the blade, then turned to see if they had been watching. Rubbing his head, he scowled and spun away.

What a case, Keith said. What a loser.

I didn't hear you say that to his face, Charlotte said.

There's lots of things I don't say to people with guns.

I never believed there was a gun, she said.

Right.

Harmless, she said.

The three of them moved as if they were on the moon, so slowly they seemed to be floating through a dream. One woman came out the bottom of the wooden box and went sideways, like a crab, along the floor. She was barefoot, and so was the other woman, who stood yawning, one hip cocked up and then the other, looking away. From time to time she skipped a few feet forward with one arm up in the air, sweeping the other as if she were displaying something, asking for approval.

It had taken Keith a moment to understand what was happening. He had seen the act before, upstairs on the stage in the casino, but then the magician was in a tuxedo and the women were in sequined vests and tights. Now the magician wasn't even wearing his toupee; he smoked cigarette after cigarette, moving so slowly in sandals, shorts and a sweatshirt.

Again! he said. All right now, focus this time. Focus!

Keith sat on a folding chair against the wall and he let it all pass him by. It was hard to believe the sun was still shining outside, above the ground, though an hour before he had been working, squinting through the windshield, driving the airport shuttle bus for the casino. This was his third week and it was already a routine. After work this afternoon, he'd gone through an Employees Only door he hadn't noticed before; he kept following the stairs down until he found himself here, in a huge cavern that lay under the casino. In some places the fluorescent lights couldn't decide whether to stay on or off, and the ceiling dropped low and rose up again—it was impossible to tell how far the whole thing stretched.

The magician kept talking, his assistants moving in slow motion. All the performers were down here, men and women arguing in Italian, Korean and Spanish, carrying ladders, hangers full of costumes. Acrobats stood in the corner, clapping off their timing. Keith missed the smell of salt and sagebrush, the oil on his hands, the sound of engines, but at least now he always knew where Charlotte was. A woman passed with two long, silver knives in her hands; uninflated balloons hung from her mouth—red, blue, orange and yellow along her chin. Above, airducts, pipes and tubes snaked over and under each other, carrying water and air and waste, bringing it all in and taking it away, never stopping.

Stay sideways, stay sideways! the magician said. Don't turn your back now. He looked in Keith's direction, a look that was partly nervous and partly angry.

Do you actually want me in the box? the woman said. Do I have to climb in it now? I know what to do.

Now with the hands! The magician turned to the other woman. Your hands now, draw their attention with your hands, look like you know there's nothing going on over there. You're counting this off in your head, right?

Keith leaned back and wondered what his father was doing, where he was, if he was getting closer. Johnson would hate all this, and the thought, turned over and over, was almost enough, by itself, to make Keith like it. He smiled at the magician. His father disliked Charlotte, also, and that dislike had the same effect—it made Keith resolute.

I warn you, Johnson had told him, what you'll get there is plenty more pain than pleasure.

All he knew was he had to be near her, to try to hold on. He missed her now; her words itched at his ears when they were apart. At first she'd been slowed by the city, unable to both walk down the street and watch where she was going, but now she could make her way. She was starting to like it under the lights. He saw how everything here was more exciting to her because it had been forbidden; this was no place for a Mormon, there was no telling what would happen, and now they were here together.

You supposed to be down here?

Keith looked up, into the man's face. I'm an employee here, he said.

That's obvious from your stupid clothes, but I don't know if that means you can be down here. Not that I care either way. He smiled, squeezing his nose between thumb and forefinger. I'm Harrison, he said.

When he turned, Keith saw a long rod, like a thick riding crop, sticking up out of his back pocket. He was stocky, in tight jeans and a t-shirt. He looked back, waiting, and Keith stood up and went after him.

You might know me as Renard, Harrison said. The Man Who Talks with Animals.

Haven't seen your show, Keith said.

Well, that's too bad. It's the only one you don't want to miss. You sure you don't know me?

They kept walking, under steel girders, around pillars of cinder blocks. Somewhere a tiger roared, a woman screamed.

A person could get lost down here, Harrison said. They could flat out disappear. If I was going to murder someone I'd do it here, that's for sure.

Nice to know, Keith said.

Harrison turned on a light, over a row of cages that held small animals. A rabbit, two dogs, an iguana on the end.

So you talk with the animals, Keith said.

It sure looks that way. Harrison laughed. You haven't worked here long, he said, but I've seen you around. You really don't know the city.

Not really.

It's a hard place to get ahead, I want to tell you, to keep things straight. Gambling or drugs is usually what happens.

That won't happen to me, Keith said.

Everyone working in Vegas is on the make, Harrison said. You can't trust a soul. Drugs is how I handle it, but I cut out the middleman and deal a little on the side. Got a guy who goes down to L.A. for me and buys it in bulk, little guy that thinks he's hard.

Named Texas? Keith said.

No. Rick or something—some guy who used to work security at the Tropicana. All those security guards are so sure they're badasses.

Keith nodded. He saw two fans, in square openings in the ceiling, and they were still, their blades not moving at all. Quick figures went in and out of doors in a wall on the edge of the darkness. Harrison opened a cage and took the rabbit's ears in his fist, squeezing tighter and tighter; Keith waited for him to lift the rabbit, but he did not do it. Somewhere there was a clapping of hands, a screeching that did not sound human. It seemed to Keith that the casino above, all the people, the weight of the slot machines and all those coins, might collapse through the ceiling at any moment.

So what do you think? Harrison said.

About what?

What I've been talking about for the last ten minutes.

I don't want anything.

Well, don't think you can gamble your way out of this town.

I sure don't, Keith said.

It's just that I don't trust this guy I got. He'll lose it one of these days and then I'll need someone new. Trust me. Harrison reached out and hit Keith's shoulder with a fake punch. How's that little girl of yours? he said.

What?

She's a sweet little thing, that's for certain. You're surprised I've seen her? Oh yes, I know more about you than you think.

Why? Keith said.

What?

Why is that?

Harrison just walked further down the line of cages. He turned on another light and the chimpanzee clapped again, running to the door of his cage as it was unlocked.

Rufus, Harrison said, taking the chimp's hand and leading him out. A short chain dragged from his ankle.

The tigers in the next cage were sleeping. Keith had never been so close to tigers and he was surprised they were so small, so scrawny. Their fur was patchy; in some places the skin showed through.

A man in a leotard, an acrobat, came around the corner, gave them the finger, then turned and walked away.

Son of a bitch, Harrison said. Those prima donnas, they want my animals out of here, as if fresh air wouldn't kill these pussies! They'd freeze to death if the mercury went below fifty. As he spoke he poked the tigers with the blunt end of his stick, through the bars of the cage. Rufus had hold of a tiger's tail and was twisting it.

Do you have to do that? Keith said.

This is my business, Harrison said. You have something to say to me about it? On top of everything else you have the health code people—as if people don't have animals in their own homes, you know, for company and everything. He was still poking at the tigers, but they had managed to roll over and crawl to the other side of the narrow cage, just out of his reach.

I don't trust you, Keith said.

Good! Harrison smiled. There's hope for you yet—maybe you're smarter than you look. That's how you have to do it, all right; Rufus, here, for example, has been my partner for six years, and do I trust him? Hell, no. A chimp's five times stronger than a man, you know, strong as five men. That's why I got this cattle prod, and I got two, so one's always charging, so I have enough juice.

He waved the prod like a wand and Rufus sat down, put his hands atop his head and closed his eyes. His feet were clenching and unclenching. Harrison laughed. He slapped his belly, then pulled back the sleeve of his shirt and flexed his bicep.

Tell me the truth, he said. Do I look forty-five to you?

I have to go, Keith said.

I'll see you again, I'm sure. Come back down if you change your mind. Either way.

Keith went one direction, then the other, walking quickly and then jogging. He looked back once and Harrison was turned away. Rufus was leaping into the air, trying to grab a bare lightbulb, his chain trailing, weighing him down.

Keith finally found an unlocked door and kept climbing upward; he felt fresh air, a draft, on his face, and he leapt three stairs at a time, his palms slapping the walls. When he opened the door at the top, when he could see through the brightness, he was surprised to find himself on the parking terrace. It was the second level, so he could see down into the trailer park, Circus Land, behind the casino, and he could see their trailer, surrounded, in the middle. He did not want to go back down the stairs, back inside, so he followed the spiral to the bottom. A car honked and slid close by, forcing him to the wall.

Maybe they would find something cheaper, off the strip, if they ever got settled, and maybe they would find jobs in the same place or match their schedules a little better. Now he hardly saw Charlotte. He wondered if it was possible that anyone could ever settle in Las Vegas.

His car did not look right standing still, parked outside the trailer; he ran his hand along the hood as he passed it. Inside, it was too hot to breathe. He opened all the windows as wide as they'd go, then he turned on the fan. Charlotte was not there, and she had left no note. He let his pants fall to the floor, then undid the top buttons of his shirt and pulled it over his head. He hung it on the back of his chair, next to Charlotte's extra uniform.

Acid resistant, flame retardant, she'd laughed, reading the labels. If there's ever a fire we'll just pull on our uniforms and we'll be totally safe.

He sat down on the bed wearing only his underwear, then rolled over, onto his back. It was so hot at night it was impossible to sleep—the rare times Charlotte was there it added to the frustration, all his muscles tangling and tightening on each other, his jaw clenched all night. He had waited so long to share a bed with her, to sleep by her side, and it had not turned out to be so easy. Still, he could bear the physical side; it was the other, his need to be closer and closer, for her to need him, that was growing. He was not used to that. She was up to something strange and true and he had to be close.

I need you, she'd told him. I just don't know why. Not yet.

Nothing should ever be forced, he believed. Sometimes it was enough just to feel her watching him. A spider walked all the way across the ceiling of the trailer. Keith knew he would not sleep.

He felt like himself in his own clothes, invisible. In his uniform, people expected him to be able to answer their questions. He locked up the trailer and started toward the strip, walking through the dusk and coming in the back of the casino. At the buffet the line stretched down the hallway; security guards watched the doors, keeping the street people from finding a cheap meal. Keith nodded to the guards and kept moving. When he reached the gambling pit he waved to the dealers, but they also ignored him, they did not recognize him out of uniform.

Ropes were strung above the pit and clowns hung from them, rag dolls as big as men. Above them, the acrobats were in the middle of a show and colored lights, stars and rainbows, were projected on the ceiling. The heads of elephants, tigers and giraffes stuck out from the walls and the Horse-A-Round Bar spun its slow carousel circles.

Keith was lost in the sound of the machines, the cheap song the organist was playing for the acrobats. He went up the stairs, to the midway, past all the games where the balls were blown too big to fit in the hoops, the milk jugs tilted slightly away to make winning almost impossible. The children were taken just as their parents, gambling below, were, at the same time and with the same foolish innocence.

None of the gamblers even looked up. The acrobats flipped above, holding each other by the ankles, their hair so stiff it didn't even move when they were upside down. Keith had seen the acrobats before; he'd seen the magic act, the bike tricks, dog tricks, the woman who threw knives. The show was finishing. One by one the acrobats fell down into the net, bouncing high again, the trapeze swinging empty.

He went back downstairs, outside and across the alley. On the street the giant clown loomed, all lighted now, its huge lollipop hypnotizing everyone below. Keith went into Slots-A-Fun and ordered a beer—here it was cheapest. Drunks slept with their heads atop blinking video poker machines, all along the bar. He paid for his beer and headed back outside.

You could be the next big winner, a disembodied voice said, broadcast over the sidewalk. Come on in and try your luck! It could change your life. You could be the next big winner! It repeated itself again and again.

People stood drinking under the lights, pigeons clustered

around spilled popcorn, the air heavy and hot and still. He kept moving, not looking anyone in the face, just sensing which way they leaned and going the other. People carried cocktails, blue drinks in plastic cups. Everyone wore the pink fanny packs the casino gave out free, held together with cheap hooks that thieves had to love.

This is all something I needed to see, Charlotte had told him.

Across the street there was a marriage chapel; they all boasted which celebrities had been wed inside, as if that was assurance of a successful union. He passed the long mirrored wall of the Riviera as people tried to hand him flyers. Two missionaries went by and he held out his beer, then pretended he was going to follow them. They looked back, afraid, picking up their pace.

Don't believe them when they say it's free, someone said, standing outside Caesars Palace.

Keith went in, passing a muscular centurion with a brass breastplate, sandals, hair like Samson's. The lighting was not so harsh here, the machines seemed quieter. There were no children, and that made it seem less sinister. Here they only promised luxury, not innocence.

In her shorts and black fishnet stockings she looked like a different person, though he would never mistake her.

I want some change, he said, sneaking up behind.

More of the same for you, Charlotte said. She turned and pulled him down to kiss him.

He took hold of her cart and pretended he was going to push it away.

I'd have security on you like that, she said, and besides, it's wider than all the doors.

You've already tried it, he said, laughing.

Maybe. She kissed him again. Another hour. She pushed her cart toward an old man who was calling for quarters.

Keith set his empty bottle on the bar, but he did not order another; here, it would cost three times as much. The cocktail waitresses came and went. They wore short togas and cones hidden inside their hair, false braids wound around them. He watched Charlotte with her cart, five hundred pounds of metal—they joked about the muscles in her arms and legs. She blew him a kiss and he returned it. One hour and they would be holding onto each other to keep from being lost in the lights and the throng of fools who had pockets wild with coins, swinging heavily with every step, dragging them along. He and Charlotte would make it back to the hot trailer where they would be unable to sleep, where they might run out of words. Keith stared into the roulette wheel, which spun slowly in the mirror. One day it had rained and it was cool inside the trailer and they had sprawled across the sheets without talking. They had just listened to the rain. Now he wondered if it would ever be like that again, why it could not be like that all the time.

Someone had told her that Las
Vegas always looked like it could
be gone in the morning, like it
couldn't be trusted; Charlotte believed it could really only be seen
in the morning. After work sometimes, before the sun had risen, she
would walk to the edge of town
and look all the way across the desert, to the growing light on the horizon. She walked behind the casinos, where it was dirtier, quieter,
more abandoned. Gates led to loading docks, dumpsters, parking lots
full of semi-trailers that held poker

chips or lobsters or money. Once she thought she saw hawks around a dumpster, swooping down, veering in for the kill; when she leaned close against the fence, she saw it was seagulls, that her eyes were playing tricks. She shouted at the birds, she threw stones. Those seagulls had never seen water — they would be frightened by the ocean.

Two men loading a truck looked up when she shouted. She saw the flash of their faces. When they started in her direction she turned and kept walking, not looking back. Above the buildings the iron skeletons hung, the backsides of the huge, colored signs, the framework which held the lights. Vacant lots were covered in paper and broken glass, bent basketball hoops, men sleeping on pieces of cardboard.

She felt as if she were still pushing the cart of change, of coins, her back taut and coiled to force motion. She was trying to find a place where it was silent, but the bells get in your head, the flashing lights have a sound of their own and you carry them inside. It's been years, decades since my hearing was right. Charlotte was working nights like I work nights. Her hair and clothes were full of cigarette smoke, her hands smelled like money, dirty bills, and her fingers tasted like coins no matter how often she washed them.

On a telephone pole a note was stapled, from a mother to her runaway son. I'm here in Vegas for two weeks, it said. Please call, just to talk, we won't force you to come back, we just want to see you and talk to you and tell you we love you as we always have. Charlotte tore it down and put it in her pocket.

The sun rose and far away, at the foothills of the mountains, its light caught the golden Angel Moroni atop the Las Vegas temple. He blew his horn, calling the saints, but he kept a safe distance from the casinos, just keeping them in sight. The temple could not compete in the darkness, as if God would see the night for the sake of the day, as if He could not master the neon hours.

Charlotte had been to the temple; the first week in the city she'd been afraid and felt drawn there, believed it might be closer to where she belonged. She had not asked to borrow the car, and taking it thrilled her. She drove out of the trailer park and beyond the strip, past the cheap motels that were rented an hour or a month at a time, their swimming pools a suspicious shade of green. Her parents would never know about this, they would worry, they would not believe. She felt herself circling, speeding up, funneling down. She passed strip joints and malls and butcher shops, hundreds of condominiums being built, wrecking balls ready to swing.

There was a huge parking lot at the temple, but there were very few cars. On the front of the building, in gilded gold letters two feet high, it said HOLINESS TO THE LORD. THE HOUSE OF THE LORD. She pulled open the heavy glass doors and went inside.

Music was playing so faintly she doubted it was playing at all. She was the only visitor. The people behind the desk, the brothers and sisters, waited for her. She did not want all their attention, she shivered under it, she could not think while they were watching her. They could not know, understand or believe the things she'd seen. She was wrong to come here, but she'd seen that too late. When she signed the visitor's book she just put Las Vegas where it asked for an address.

Can I help you? one of the sisters said.

I doubt it, Charlotte said.

She turned away from the long desk and walked toward the paintings and pamphlets, the plaques on the walls. There wasn't much room for visitors here; this temple was all business—doors led to secret rooms for marriages, blessings, baptisms for both living and dead.

Are you all right? one of the brothers said.

I'm beyond that, she said, swaying back and forth in front of the paintings. Brigham Young hung next to Moses, as always; the young Joseph Smith was talking to an angel. The man still stood next to Charlotte and she could tell he was about to speak again. As he began, she put her hand over her mouth and escaped into the restroom. Her eyes in the mirror frightened her and she knew if she waited long someone would follow her, they would ask what was the matter and try to help her.

She went through the room, past the desk so fast they had no time to stop her. A man and woman stood in the doorway as she climbed into the car, as she laid rubber in the parking lot, out the gate; the back of the car fishtailed, swinging onto the road, and she accelerated toward the strip, back to iniquity and the temples of Mammon.

No, she had not forgotten, and yes, she believed and was hungry for more signs, she needed more; it was just that there was so much going on in Vegas it was hard to concentrate, impossible to know where to look. She was frightened, not afraid.

Now she walked in the dawn, watching the sky. Some men called to her from a pickup truck; she ignored them and they slowly drove on. She did not want to talk to anyone, she did not want to answer any questions. Sometimes she felt someone was watching her, following her, that they had been for a long time, and she did not dislike it. She didn't want to shake them, but only to surprise them, to surprise herself. Yes, she must have been wondering where I was, what I was doing. I was thinking of her, coiling around myself, preparing my old body for her touch. She was not ready for me then, not that I would have turned her away. What she did down in Vegas she had to do. No doubt she felt me close, knew I was after her.

Girls looked up from the sidewalk, watching her from the colored flyers, holding their breasts in their hands and pursing their lips. Charlotte picked one up and leafed through it. Cartoon stars covered the girls' nipples, hearts and firecrackers were airbrushed between their legs. Every single one had a phone number—Asian girls hardly smiling in front of faded wallpaper, goosebumps on their arms; girls rolled in pink feathers; girls wearing dog collars and leather hoods, their tongues pierced by steel rings.

Charlotte had never imagined so much skin before she'd moved here, and it wasn't just the flyers. It was the showgirls in the casinos, the cocktail waitresses, even the uniform she had to wear. Reaching down, she touched her thigh at the hemline, not even halfway to her knee.

There were telephone numbers for private room dancers, totally nude, black girls and white girls who danced together, who wanted to come to your hotel. On the back were advertisements for all the brothels just outside of the city limits. Turkish baths, Swedish massages, girls who preferred older men. She folded the whole thing and put it in her pocket.

Even out of uniform she recognized the others who had worked all night, returning from the casinos bleary-eyed and free. The construction workers weren't even out yet; they were at home fast asleep or filling their thermoses, trying to find misplaced hammers. Charlotte walked past the frames of the last houses, to the place where empty plots were drawn out across the desert, waiting for people who were already traveling to fill them. There was nothing in the sky except the jets at the Air Force base; they had none of the grace of hawks or eagles, they had no relation to the wind. If she could see one hawk she would know things were improving. She tried to see through the thin clouds and she wondered if this was praying, if this would count.

In the book at the temple she had only written Las Vegas next to her name and still they had found her. She'd been taking a nap, wearing nothing but a t-shirt and underpants. When she opened the door of the trailer, the two missionaries were standing there, smiling at her.

I'm Elder Larsen, one said. We'd like to share what we believe. He was blond and pimply and looked like every boy in her high school. We'd like to tell you about our church, he said.

That's my church, too, Charlotte said.

You're a member?

I know it's true, she said. Of course I am.

An active member? he said.

In my way, she said. I've been moving around a lot. Did you want to come inside?

She pulled on a pair of shorts as they looked away, at the ceiling of the trailer. Elder González was from Nicaragua and he did not say one word.

It's funny there are missionaries here, she said.

We're needed here, Elder Larsen said. Did you know we have chapels in some of the larger casinos?

Very functional, she said.

We're the most feared men in Vegas, he said, trying to joke. People lock their doors when they see us coming.

I like it here, she said, and they smiled at her like they were waiting for the truth. She sat down so close to Elder Larsen that their thighs touched. It made him nervous; he stammered and shifted but there was nowhere to go. Her stockings lay on the floor like braided wire, like the nets that came up full of fish.

I'm here for a reason, she said, and they had no answer for that. She wanted to tell them that she'd seen signs, but that was pride and it might slow her down, go before a fall.

What do you do here? Elder Larsen said.

Live. Like anyone else, I guess. She could not tell them the truth and it was exciting to lie to them. Part of what she did was lie, she wanted to say, that was what she did here.

Do you live alone?

I live with a man, she said.

Is he a member?

Oh no. She laughed. I don't think he'd want to talk to you, though. She felt their eyes on her as she lifted her feet off the floor, flexed her calves, pointed her toes. She was happy to find the boys seemed so strange to her, so young. They had been up since five in the morning, praying. They had ironed their shirts, brushed their teeth, shined their shoes. Sweat shone on their foreheads, but they were slow to take off their jackets. Their ties were tight.

Are there still miracles? she said.

Now?

Yes.

If God once performed miracles, then He must still. He doesn't change.

Is that a yes or a no? she said.

You're familiar with the gospel? he said.

Of course I am.

Well, there's your answer.

Charlotte leaned her face closer to his. Do you think I'm bad? she said. Why or why not?

Elder Larsen was trying to answer when the door slapped open. Keith just stood there, wearing his cap with the clown on it, his black pants with the crease and flare, the pale pink shirt of his uniform. He stood there and looked at them.

What? he said. Did someone ask you to come here?

No, Elder Larsen said. But we were invited inside, sir.

Charlotte laughed out loud. Next to Keith the missionaries seemed girlish, too sweet-smelling and clean. Still, she wanted him to shout at them and he did not shout. She wanted him to hit them, to hurt them a little, and he let them go. There was a clatter of their bicycles outside, chains and sprockets, and then silence.

Why would I be threatened by those boys? he'd said. Get serious. You're the one who let them inside.

He was too resigned for her now, sometimes, too passive. She wanted to see him in action, trying to have his way with things, with her. She wondered if he was afraid of her but she did not want to ask if that was it — she was not anxious to hear the answer. She needed him, but now, as she walked, she was waiting until she knew he'd gone to work, so the trailer would be empty when she returned. She was too tired and wound up to talk with him, to be crowded together in the trailer and recount the details of her night. She wanted to be alone, hidden, to sleep while everyone else was working, to pay them back that way. When Keith returned she would be ready for him. She'd be the one who was calm and rested and clean.

She had spent all night listening to the change-counting machine. She would explain to him how it sounded, like a butterfly with metal wings. She'd tell him that every single person, every man who bought a roll of quarters, made the same joke about punching someone with it in his fist. The other girls spoke Spanish, they called her Blanca, they called her, Pecosa, for her freckles. She understood enough to know they were making fun of her, and she did not care. She tried not to see herself in the mirrors, as a part of all this, caught inside. Lecherous old men tilted their heads to look at her legs through their bifocals. One held on to her shirt so she could not get away.

The elevator, he said, as if she would understand.

Let me go, she said.

Just looking for a place to put it.

Keep looking, she said.

Now she was coming back up the strip, the lights pale in the early morning. The colors were all washed out and there was something in her that liked it, there was a way in which it all felt familiar. Almost the only people on the street were the very old, who never slept, who needed vigorous walks to escape death in the morning. As the city rose from the desert at nightfall, it sank a little as the sun extinguished the lights. Charlotte wondered if she'd ever go back to a world where lights were shut off, where everyone slept at the same time; she was beginning to understand why people were afraid of the dark.

Someone honked at her. She looked up and saw Keith pass in the van, the stupid clown painted on the side. She was safe now, the trailer was empty, though later he would ask what she'd been doing. Nothing, she'd say. Unwinding. She stopped and watched two little girls in a parked convertible. They were dancing, standing up and shaking their nonexistent hips, holding their t-shirts out in two points from their chests.

Jesus Christ, Superstar, they sang, who in the hell do you think you are?

She smiled at them and they broke down laughing, slapping each other's hands. She knew she was in Las Vegas for a reason; she was convinced of it. Deep down she believed it all and still she was frightened. She knew there was no such thing as pretending to sin, no false temptation.

Yes, they had their arguments. They would wrangle through the hours their schedules overlapped, whispering as if someone outside was trying to listen. Keith tried to pace, but there was nowhere to go in the trailer.

What are we doing here? he would ask.

If I'm late again I'll lose my job, she told him. Not that I care.

We need the money, he said, if we're ever going to get out of here.

Out of here, Charlotte said.

That's right. Everything here is changing too fast.

Did you expect them to stand still?

You're after something, he said. I've seen it for a long time. You know I know that.

I can't tell you.

Can't or won't?

I'll tell you when I have it, she said.

Keith would open the door, look out, then close it again. He would repeat himself. What are we doing here?

I'm having fun, she would say. Aren't you having fun? She wanted to see his temper, she wanted to see the danger she believed he'd promised. Sometimes she wondered if she'd underestimated, misunderstood him somehow.

Now she was in the middle of a split shift; she sat at the bar in Caesars Palace, swinging her legs. Her feet did not reach the floor. She had three hours and she wanted to talk to Keith but she did not want to wake him. She considered going quietly, just lying next to him and listening to him breathe.

Employees' discount, the bartender said, pushing her money away as he handed her the grapefruit juice. They don't pay us enough that we can afford to drink here.

The change signs were blinking everywhere. She watched another change girl trying to get her cart around a row of wheelchairs parked in front of slot machines. The old people just smoked and played and had no idea where they were; their nurses tried to beat the keno machine, so they could retire forever, grow old themselves.

He'll never do it, said a man at the bar.

On the television there was a strongman contest, fat men throwing tires for distance, trying to lift the backs of cars off the ground. When they grimaced the camera focused in on their square, white teeth.

Sometimes Charlotte felt she was sharper now, more perceptive than ever before. Still, she had her doubts; the more time passed in Las Vegas, the harder it seemed to believe in the messages she'd received, the more difficult it was to remember them. She could not tell how much she'd forgotten. She could not get far enough outside to tell what she was doing now.

I lose the same amount of money every night, a man was saying. That's how it is, unless I'm feeling lucky, in which case I lose more.

The other men at the bar were arguing about the Hoover Dam. Farther away, a crowd of conventioneers slapped each other's backs, throwing drinks down their throats, their ties loosened into necklaces. Charlotte thought of the missionaries earlier in the night, how they had come to find her in the casino, how they stood nervously watching everything around them, trying to talk with her. They said they could help her if she'd only listen. They told her someone had slashed their bicycles' tires and she only laughed, told them not to come crying to her.

The men all swiveled on their stools as the showgirl came up to the bar. She sat next to Charlotte and Charlotte could not believe how little she was wearing, walking around the casino. The skirt of the dress was just glass beads and the rest was covered in silver sequins; it was cut high all the way above her hips and the back was sheer, showing the whole curve of her spine. Silver shells cupped her breasts. Her black hair reflected light from all directions.

How you doing, Jamie? The bartender knew what she wanted before she said a word. He brought two cocktails and she drank the first one fast.

I'm doing, she said. Hard at work here.

Sirens were going and a jackpot was paying out somewhere back in the rows of machines. That sound always makes everyone else feed in their quarters a little faster, try a little harder. Charlotte saw the showgirl watching her in the mirror behind the bar. The men were still arguing about the Hoover Dam, their voices rising, disputing whether or not there were workers entombed in the cement.

They died to make the desert bloom, one said. That's on the plaque.

I came to Vegas to party, said another. Not talk about this.

Right, said the third man, but just because people died on the project, it doesn't mean they're buried in there. Come on! What do you girls think?

Never been there, Charlotte said.

At least it would be fast, one man said. Probably. I always thought it would be worst if you were caught under a fallen tree or pinned beneath a steering wheel or something.

I've spent some of the best times of my life pinned under a steering wheel, Jamie said.

Now this girl here, the man said. She loves to party!

Jamie just turned away, toward Charlotte. There was silver in her hair, on the skin of her face, caught on her cheekbones. She crushed ice between her teeth.

You're not from here, she said. What's your name?

Charlotte.

That's your real name?

Yes.

Like the spider, then. I like that. You spinning a web?

No, Charlotte said.

What are you drinking? she said, then called for a gin and tonic and a grapefruit juice. Sure that's all the drink you want?

Yes. I don't drink.

Grapefruit juice. An excellent choice. Have to sin to get saved, you know. Jamie leaned closer. Kiss me, she said.

What?

You heard what I said.

Thirsty, Charlotte said. The lights and mirrors were spinning her eyes around. She held on to the bar with both hands. Suddenly it seemed impossible that she would work all night.

A person can't help sinning, she said.

Jamie laughed. Isn't that what I just said?

We're going to sin no matter what, Charlotte said. The best we can do is avoid the most obvious ones.

Those are some of the best ones, said Jamie. You've just got a stick up your ass. Just because you're afraid to kiss me.

126

I'm not afraid. I just don't want to.

What does your boyfriend kiss like?

He races cars, Charlotte said.

That's my kind of kisser. Jamie kept waving for more drinks. She put her hand on top of Charlotte's hand.

Charlotte reached for the bowl of peanuts, the bowl of pretzels; they both made her thirsty.

Where you from? Jamie said. She didn't wait for the answer. I can't remember how I got here, she said, and I can't imagine ever leaving. That fool was right—I do love to party.

You like it here?

I like to see what happens.

Show us a few kicks, a man said, and Jamie ignored him. Her earrings were long tangles of rhinestones, trading light with the sequins, the glass beads of her dress. Charlotte reached out and touched a strand. She moved closer, as if all the lights were warm. Jamie spun like the sun.

An hour after every show, she said. It's in my contract. Mingling out here in the casino.

Your dress is like a chandelier, Charlotte said.

Same idea, she said. She leaned forward all at once and kissed Charlotte, hard, holding a hand behind her neck so she could not pull away.

Cool it down, ladies, the bartender said. Cool it down.

Was that so bad? Jamie said.

No, said Charlotte. I don't know.

Is that how your boyfriend kisses?

We do it all, she said. He can do everything.

I'm sure he can. Jamie kicked her high-heeled shoes onto the floor and Charlotte did the same, swinging her foot close. They were the same size.

When I was a girl, Jamie said, I practiced kissing on my arm.

What I want, Charlotte said.

Say the word.

I want to try it on. Your dress, the costume.

I was hoping you'd say something like that, Jamie said.

Where you going, beautiful? a man said, calling after them.

Inside the bathroom, everything was chrome and marble, mirrors on every wall, ten sinks or more, all connected.

I don't know, Charlotte said.

You do know. Jamie was already halfway out of her dress. She turned on a faucet and splashed water on her face, her throat.

Slowly, Charlotte stripped down to her bra and underwear. Shivering, blushing, she folded her uniform and stacked it on the sink.

It all has to come off, Jamie said. All of it. She spun Charlotte like a little girl and unhooked her bra. Small-town girls, she said. I love it, I love to watch you, to see what happens when you're thrown into this. She hooked her thumbs at Charlotte's hips and bent down, taking the underpants with her. Nice freckles, she said.

A woman came out of one of the stalls and hurried past, staring at the floor. She left without washing her hands.

There, Jamie said. Here we are.

Charlotte could not close her eyes. She tried to cover herself with her hands and she saw how Jamie didn't even seem to notice her own nakedness. Her smooth skin had no marks on it, pale and full like something out of nature, something that couldn't belong here, where they were together. Charlotte shivered; she wondered if Jamie was going to kiss her again. Jamie took perfume and cosmetics from a tray on the sink. She shielded Charlotte's eyes from the hairspray, pinned up her hair so a few curls hung loose. She leaned close and their breasts touched, giving way to each other, and the way it felt made Charlotte want to pull away. The sink behind her was cold against her skin. There was nowhere to go.

Aren't you going to get dressed? she said.

We'll get to that, Jamie said. First we have to get you set up here.

The dress was heavier than it looked. A third silver sea-
shell, one she hadn't seen before, settled between her legs. The
tights were too long, and she felt Jamie's hand high up on her
thighs, gathering the material there, folding it over.

The beads cover more than you think, Jamie said.

You put something in my drink, said Charlotte.

I wouldn't do a thing like that. That would be boring. What
do you want, an excuse? Look in the mirror.

Everything was turned around and Charlotte could not
believe that it was her, covered only by the silver shells, the
glass beads, her hair piled up and the loose curls brushing her
shoulders. She spun to see the skin of her back, then stood
with her feet apart, so the strands of glass swung between her
thighs. She leaned forward, following the reflection all the way
down her throat, between her breasts.

Perfect, just perfect. Jamie was putting on the clothes
Charlotte had taken off. When they traded shoes they were
almost the same height.

Now, Jamie said. Miss Beautiful Spider. You can't tell me
you don't want to wear it home.

You'll need it back.

Not as much as I need to see you wear it home.

They moved through the casino, in a wide arc around the
bar. People were saying things to them, but Charlotte did not
listen, she just held on to Jamie's hand.

Don't you think this is funny? Jamie said. I do.

On the street, a man was calling free spin, free spin, free
spin. Charlotte felt a little unsteady. People sped up as they
passed her, swerving by, coming so close. None of the cars
were driving straight and everywhere the lights were chasing
each other, changing color. Charlotte was thinking of a bird
that had flown into the casino, a pigeon that could not find its
way back out. It circled and circled around the gold statues,
along the ceiling, too quick for the security guards, even the
busboy from the restaurant. Finally they had caught it with a

fishing net and took it back outside. Charlotte held on to Jamie's hand. Two men were yelling back and forth, trying to have a conversation from different sides of the street.

This is it, Charlotte said when they reached Circus Circus.

Boyfriend's home?

Should be.

Bet you don't dare kiss me here, Jamie said.

Charlotte felt the glass beads all over her skin when she leaned her face to Jamie's. She kissed her. Their teeth touched.

Good night, Jamie said. It's truly been a pleasure.

For a moment Charlotte could not believe she'd been left there. She watched Jamie go, then walked down the alley, toward Circus Land, the trailer park. Behind her, someone whistled.

She opened the door of the trailer, then stood for a moment in the darkness. She heard Keith roll over, the boxspring beneath him, the blankets dragged across.

Aren't you supposed to be at work? He turned on the small light next to the bed and squinted across at her. Is that you?

It's me, she said. What do you think? She whirled all the way around, stumbling a little, the beads slapping the metal kitchen cabinets. She could not see him well and she wanted to see his face, his reaction. She turned on another light.

Are you drunk? he said.

No, I'm not drunk. You know that. Watch me. She danced so everything on the dress was shaking. She kicked one leg up on the counter and rolled her hips, her hands on the shells that covered her breasts. Keith turned over, he turned his face to the wall. She let the shoulder straps fall down along her arms and danced harder; she kicked off her shoes and climbed onto the bed, shaking over him, the dress hanging from her waist and the straps dragging their hooks along the skin of his back.

Turn over, she said. What are you afraid of?

Why are you acting like this? he said.

It doesn't help to think, she said. I should know. It's you—why are you acting like this?

I'm the same, he said. You're the one who's changing.

He would not look at her. She stepped down from the bed and pulled the dress all the way off. She turned on every light in the trailer, then returned to stand next to the bed.

Isn't this what you wanted? she said. What you've been waiting for? When she tried to reach under the covers he fought her hand off and pushed it back at her. Standing naked, she began to feel cold under the wind from the fan. She began to feel angry.

Look at me, she said.

Put on some clothes, Keith said. This isn't part of it.

He lay still, his head buried in the pillow. He lay like that, in the silence, for a long time. When he finally looked up, Charlotte was gone. He had not heard her put on any clothes, though he had not been watching. The dress lay on the floor, collapsed in on itself.

Standing, he walked to the open door and called her name. He knew there would be no reply. It was possible she was close by, naked in the shadows, watching him, but he was certain she was far away already, that the distance was increasing.

He dressed, then went outside. He passed through the other trailers, the lighted windows and sounds of radios, televisions, air conditioners. He was not exactly searching for Charlotte, as he did not know what else he could say to her, if he had the words to calm her or bring her back. He just had to get out of the trailer.

When he went into Circus Circus time sped up; everything jumped at his eyes and ears, colors and noise and cigarette smoke. People shuffled by as if hypnotized. Keith walked right into the middle of the gambling pit and turned a slow circle. On his second revolution he saw her, sitting upstairs at the Horse-A-Round Bar. He recognized her from behind, as the whole thing spun away from him, hiding her again. Moving slowly, he went for the stairs, trying to decide what to say, wondering if he would follow when she tried to get away.

The floor pulled sideways when he stepped into the bar. He walked against its turning until he found her.

Come sit by me, she said. Pull up a horse.

Those aren't your clothes, he said.

Whose do you think they are? Charlotte's? Jamie laughed. You're in her web now, aren't you?

Keith took the drink she handed him, but he did not sit down. He looked below, into the slot machines, across to the midway, children throwing darts at balloons.

She's a very nice girl, Jamie said.

She is, he said.

Very nice. Jamie took his arm, sat him down. How is she in the sack, anyway? she said. I wonder.

That's not it, he said.

What? Getting laid?

That's never solved anything.

How little you know, she said.

As the bar turned, Keith looked out over the stage. The knife-thrower was just finishing her act; she stood to one side, her head thrown back as she swallowed a sword with a snake for a handle. Next to her, her husband ate a ball of fire, then spit it toward the ceiling.

That's not how it is. We're more like brother and sister, Keith said, and immediately wished he had lied.

She doesn't put out, I take it.

I didn't say that.

I don't think she prefers men, Jamie said.

That's not true.

Whose dress do you think that was? Jamie finished her drink and spun it along the top of the bar. Anyway, she said. I've heard some pretty hot things about you.

You probably heard wrong, he said.

I'm going to the ladies' room, she said. Wait for me. I'm not even close to through with you.

He watched her go, then hurried, ducking low, struggling to find the way out of the bar, impatiently waiting for a door to line up with the stationary floor of the midway. Shielding his face, he went through the noise of the games, the floor beneath him now a little more dependable.

Free toss, a girl said, holding out a rubber ball. He kept moving, down the short flight of stairs and across the front of the empty stage, past the sign that said NEXT SHOWTIME 11:30. He hit the button for the elevator and as he waited a security guard came up behind him.

Can't go down there, he said.

I'm an employee. Keith showed his wallet, his identification, but the guard just shook his head.

I have to see Harrison, Keith said. The animal trainer. I have some business with him.

Why didn't you say so? the guard said. I know what's going on around here—don't have to treat me like an idiot. You need a key for this elevator, anyway. Didn't you know that? He took one from his pocket and stuck it into the wall. Think you're so smart, he said.

It was a huge elevator, square, built to carry props and animals. Keith hit the lowest button he could find and he closed his eyes and tried to catch his breath as the whole thing descended. After a minute it hit the bottom, shuddering and settling. The door opened.

Two jugglers were arguing; one held two bowling pins and the other shook a frying pan in the air. Keith went around them, nervously, trying to look like he knew where he was going. They hardly noticed him. He stepped into the shadows as a midget rode by on a tiny bicycle. Keith passed a pile of barbells, towers of round weights stacked atop one another. He listened for the animals and he kept moving, peeking around corners before he turned them. In one room a bald man looked up at him and smiled; he had tattoos across his face, all over his skull, and he looked like he'd been in a fire, as if all his skin had been burned and could only heal halfway.

Keith was lucky—there was no one there, Harrison was gone. NO TRESPASSING, KEEP OUT, PRIVATE PROPERTY, the signs said. When he turned on the lights the small animals froze and looked up like he was going to kill them. There were locks on some of the cages, but if he came back he could bring wire cutters. He did not know where he could set them loose, if the animals could survive in the desert. He flipped on another light, then flipped it back off when he saw the tigers were sleeping. It would not be easy to get them out; he had no idea how to get them to follow him.

A piece of apple hit him in the chest, and other pieces of fruit fell around his feet. Rufus screamed. Keith stepped behind a pillar and excrement hit the wall, thrown through the cage. He waited until the chimpanzee had run out of ammunition, then opened the door to the rabbit's cage. First it tried to bite him, but he managed to pull it out and put its feet against his chest. It scratched him as he petted it, it was terrified, its eyes open wide, and he stroked its ears until it calmed down.

I knew it, Harrison said.

Keith hid the rabbit inside his jacket at the sound. He turned around and saw Harrison standing there in his stocking feet, holding his boots in his hands.

Didn't hear you coming, Keith said.

Damn right you didn't. Have to sneak around now just to keep people from fucking with my animals. I'm staying, no matter what—you people better get used to that idea.

I came to see you.

It's you! Harrison said, leaning closer. Still, this sneaking around. You could lose your job for just being down here, you know that. He unlocked Rufus's cage and brought the chimp out. The things I could do to you, he said. I could set Rufus on you for one thing; I could do that.

Keith tried to zip up his jacket, to shift the rabbit so it was better hidden. He watched as Harrison stuck a tiny spoon into a film canister and took a snort up each nostril. He shook his head, holding his nose, then licked his fingers.

Wasn't I friendly enough to you? he said. What was it?

I said I didn't trust you, Keith said.

Right! And now you want to talk business. Mutual distrust, that's right. I could use your help, you know.

I need a little more time.

He who hesitates, Harrison said. He looked around the pillar as an enormous woman walked by, her huge legs barely able to move her weight. Freaks, he said. They've got a show in here now, you know, and they're going to find out what anyone knows—freaks scare the hell out of kids. You know what kids want to see? Animals is what they want to see.

You're right, Keith said.

Fat women, he said. Man. They're fun to ride, but you don't want to be seen on them, know what I mean?

No, Keith said. I sure don't.

You need more money is what it is. That's what's brought you back to me. Money. We haven't even talked money. I could give you enough that you could do whatever you wanted, even get out of this town, if you can't keep up.

Maybe that's not it, Keith said.

Yes, you've got a woman on your hands. That's trouble. Tell you what—two people who meet someplace else and come to Vegas always go their separate ways; people who get together here and try to leave, that doesn't work either. He tipped his cattle prod toward the floor and Rufus lay flat, covering his face with his hands. A fluorescent light came to life down the hall. Harrison laughed.

Don't, Keith said.

Vegas makes a person mean, he said.

What if, Keith said, what if two people start off here and don't leave?

Never happen. Listen—everyone has their troubles. You're a funny guy, you know, but don't act like I don't know where you're coming from.

You know where I'm going?

Harrison laughed. You see! That's exactly what I mean—

coming up with some shit like that. He looked back down the hall, where the freaks were gathering. These people, he said. I swear to God.

It's something, Keith said.

Don't try and trick me, now.

Keith tried to hold the rabbit still. He stood in front of the cage so Harrison wouldn't see it was empty.

Think about it, Harrison said. I give you two days. Right now you can amscray. I got a show in half an hour.

What are you looking at? the fat lady said. Keith just kept walking, trying to get away before Harrison realized the rabbit was missing. This time he found the stairs more quickly; he opened the first door and stepped out into the parking lot behind the casino.

There was a terrible screaming outside, women screaming, and he ran toward the sound, toward the pool; when he looked through the bars he saw it was some kind of cheerleading squad, illuminated, screaming under the lights. Girls in bikinis stood on boys' shoulders and the boys walked across the shallow end that way, showing off, throwing the girls up in the air. They screamed and screamed.

Keith turned and walked away, opening his coat to give the rabbit some air. Halfway to the trailer he passed a small man carrying a bag of groceries; by his shiny chin he recognized him as the fire-eater.

How's it going? he said. Marry a woman who can throw a knife, I always say, and you find yourself doing all the chores. Haw!

Keith knew if he went searching it would only get worse, that the people would only turn stranger and more dangerous as the hours progressed. He wanted to go somewhere else, anyplace he hadn't seen before, where he knew no one and no one knew him. Only he would need Charlotte, and where was she now? How could she stand it in the midst of these people?

There were lights on in the trailer; he could not remember if he'd turned them off. She was not inside and he knew he'd never sleep. He could take a shower, but he'd never feel clean. He closed the door behind him and set the rabbit down. When he took a step, glass beads broke under his feet, the dress where she'd left it on the floor. Sitting on the bed, he turned off all the lights. The rabbit sneezed in the darkness.

Keith had been glad they'd ended up in Vegas because he had figured that was what Charlotte needed to see, what she was looking for; he didn't think it would turn out to be what she liked. He had had the natural desire to get her dirty, to sully her and bring her down a little, but now he was unhappy with what he was left holding. He lay down in the darkness and listened as the rabbit inspected every corner of the trailer. Charlotte was out there, somewhere in the city, and he knew his father was moving, coming closer, no doubt; he knew that, at that moment—closer than either one of them, just a couple hundred yards away—Harrison was onstage, talking to the animals, terrifying them into responding.

I went after them. Should I have
let them go? Some might say those
two were simply in love, finding
their way, and some might question
my need or right to interfere. I'll
let those questions stand for now —
as if I should apologize, as if I
couldn't appeal to fate and have
my justification granted. Fate is a
cheap excuse, one I don't need. I
went after her. I threw myself off a
pinnacle in hope that the angels
would catch me and of course she
was falling, too, we're all falling, all
the time; when our velocity is the

same, this falling can be so hard to realize, almost impossible to remember. As if my mind could keep up with my heart! I don't know what I was going to do when I found them. I had nothing to say to her, I only wanted to see her, to see how she was doing and to see if I could tell how soon she was coming back to me.

The other residents of the trailer park opened their doors and windows to watch as I drove out. They just watched, they did not wave. I pulled my whole house behind me, the stationwagon straining with the weight.

Don't get your hopes up, I called out the window.

It did not take me long to get underway; if I took all the vacation days the Stateline owes me I would never work again. First I drove through Wendover, across town one time, back again. The dogs were chasing each other in circles around Anita's house and Johnson was sleeping in the yard, flat on his stomach as if he were kissing the ground. The horses watched him with murderous eyes, their heads stretched over the fence. There was no real need for me to talk to Anita; I turned and the trailer followed in an arc behind me.

A policeman switched on his siren, then back off, waving as a kind of joke, curious about what I was doing. I drove under Wendover Will and the metal cowboy waved to me with the assurance that he would wait, that he would not let things spin too far off-center in my absence. I left him there against the sky.

I was driving by instinct, almost by scent; it did not matter that I'd been told where they were, that I was armed with facts and guesses and hypothetical outcomes. A feather hung from my rearview mirror, a hawk's feather from Charlotte's hair; her photograph was propped up on the dashboard, looking back at me. We left Wendover behind. We went through the hills, into the sun.

We came down out of the hills into the desert, where the land resists, where it quickly gives towns over to ghosts. There is no relief for the eye in shadows, in dark colors, in heavy foliage. I drove through it, watching her, watching the needle of the temperature gauge as it climbed across the dashboard. Nothing is soft in the desert, nothing—shards of rock, spines and needles of cacti, the fangs of snakes and the tails of scorpions, the brightness of the sun—the sand just broken glass, after all, multiplying everything, sharpening it still. The flowers can only bloom at night; they have no choice.

The seat next to me was covered in books, and in the back I'd gathered strands of tangled barbed wire, rolls of duct tape, sharpened sticks and razors, propane torches, anchors, coils of rope. Behind me, the trailer went serpentine, rising and falling around corners. Inside, all the furniture was screwed down or lashed in place, pots and pans swinging loosely from hooks, all things prepared for movement, either to resist it or to play along. I thought of everything there, of the chairs and the table where Charlotte had often sat, the light through the window showing the blue veins in her arms, forking all the way to the ends of her fingers, making the curve of her thumb.

There were cirrus clouds above, strangely made of ice; two thousand feet up, tails and sheets of rain would never reach the ground. A car passed in the opposite direction, headed toward Wendover, and I just lifted a finger from my steering wheel to return the man's wave. People are always on the move, not because they're dissatisfied with where they are, that's clear— the problem is with what they are, who they are, and that's something so few ever know. I at least know who I am, that I'm wretched, yes, yet I can see all the angles and I don't fake anything. This is not to say I'm satisfied with myself—that goes against everything I hold sacred. If I were a proud man I'd be more selective about what I tell you; if I weren't innocent I'd have nothing to say.

The car was hot, almost overheating. It was inevitable. I'm not the kind of fool to turn my radiator into a geyser. Pulling all that weight under the hot sun was too much for my car; I pulled over and turned off the ignition. It's a stupid cowboy who runs his horse into the ground, who runs it to death. It's all discretion in the desert. I would let the car cool down and then I would give it a drink.

There were gallon jugs of water on the floor of the front seat. You can't have too much. I've drunk water from a radiator many times, all grit and rust, and I won't do it again. I drained one, reached for another, then opened the door. Most men my age have to piss every half hour, but I'm not like that, I'm a desert rat, always parched. The water never gets down that far. Yes, my own body disgusts me sometimes, withered, gnarled and knotted, all dried out, but it has served. It will continue to serve.

I reached under the seat and took the pistol I keep there; I put it in my belt, under my shirt. I opened the door of my trailer and everything was perfect, in its place. I locked the door, walked around the whole thing, then felt the gun, the keys in my pocket, and turned away, into the hot smell of the sagebrush. The heat came on the wind, the air pushing down on the earth, a pressure that's always there, perhaps even more when we can't feel it.

The desert, out on the highway, is no place to stay with your car. Everyone is a danger there, everyone is between things, no matter how definite, and there's no certainty how they'll act or respond. That's why I left my car and trailer there, planning to return when things had cooled down. I headed up an incline, trying to gain some elevation so I would see anyone before they saw me, so they would not know where I was.

They say if you spend enough time in the desert the sand and wind will polish you smooth, take off all the gnarls and rough edges. It is a brightness where it seems nothing could hide, but then the heat unfolds some places and suddenly folds others away. It is all mirrors, the sisters of those in the casinos, expanding inward and outward at once, concealing and revealing—at least seeming to reveal. In the heat things never develop but unfold, untangle, turn back on themselves, ever recombinant and tangling again, new folds bringing previously separate things into contact. I believe everything's had to happen this way in order for it to turn out right. Vertebrae showed through the sand, sand tailed out behind sagebrush. I looked for gila monsters, I stopped and listened for the rattles, for any slither. The desert teaches you the trick of quiet.

At the top of the rise I found the cave. Lizards ran across hot, flat stones, disappearing into shadows. The mouth of the cave was unmarked by footprints, unlittered by empty beer cans. It was dark inside and I sat down in the dust where the air was cool. I breathed it in. I could hear the squeaking of rodents, mice in their burrows somewhere behind my head.

When my eyes adjusted I saw the drawings, pictograms and petroglyphs, on the wall across from me. There were sheep and deer, what looked like a mastodon; there was a figure with wide shoulders, short arms and no legs at all, as if it was rising, floating on air. It was good to know that someone, some day long ago, had used the cave as I used it now, had found shelter. I closed my eyes and sat there for a long time. I may have slept.

One night before my departure, I saw Anita at the Stateline, drinking by herself at the bar, looking my way.

Where you been? she said. She was wearing her necklace of all the snakes' rattles. What you been up to? She took my hands and turned them over. Any hair on your palms?

Same old, I said, and ordered a couple shots. I had just finished dealing for the night.

It took me a while to turn the conversation my way, to turn it to Charlotte. Anita said she'd heard from Charlotte's parents, that they were worried. Anita didn't tell them what she suspected, that Charlotte was in Vegas. She thought Vegas would do Charlotte some good.

It's impossible to know why people do things, I said. I surprise myself all the time.

At least your delusions used to be more interesting, she said.

We all do our best, I said.

Anita told me three of her horses had turned on another

one in the night, that they had kicked in its head and she'd found it halfway through the fence in the morning, trying to escape. She walked across the yard and shot it, still wearing her nightgown. It had no eyes left to see her do it.

It's like keeping killers in your house, I said.

They're all right, she said. They sort themselves out.

We had a few more drinks. A pathetic procession of senior citizens were trying to get a conga line going through the slot machines. It had probably been fifty years since most of them had been up that late.

What about Charlotte? I said.

That little Mormon fool, she said. They'll have her ass in Vegas, but that's about right, it'll fix her.

I just smiled along as Anita went on about Charlotte. Seeing someone fall is equally pleasant for some as it is unpleasant for them to watch a sinner straighten out and get religion. The unrighteous have a righteousness all their own.

I nodded and had another drink. When I left, Anita tried to get me to go home with her, as if that was what I was waiting for, as if I covet a return to her bed.

Where's Johnson? I said.

Don't know, she said. He's been talking about going walkabout.

What?

Like those guys in Australia, she said. The old ones.

I see, I said.

I'm getting lonely, she said.

I told her I've been lonely every day of my life.

Something in the paper got him going, she said. Johnson. Something down south.

It was actually the days I did not see Johnson that I began to worry; it made his lurking seem more likely, more ominous. Nights in my trailer I'd awaken and hear my dog's breathing in the darkness. It took me a moment to remember he was gone, and then I would know someone was inside with me. Every time I turned on the light I would find myself alone. I'd go outside, barefoot, in my underwear, and there was no one there.

In the daytime, also, things were not right. Little things— I'd fill a glass of water and if I left it for a moment it would be almost empty when I returned, before I took a drink. It all made me doubt my memory, a thing I cannot afford to doubt. I had to believe otherwise, to trust myself.

First I crisscrossed my trailer with fishing line, I covered the floor with flour before I went to work; I detected no intruders, things disappeared and new ones took their place, things I did not believe I possessed, that had to have been placed there. Books of matches from places I'd never been, lighters shaped like women—put a thumb to their breasts and their tongues rise in flames.

Early one morning, before sunset, I climbed to the top of the ridge that overlooks Wendover. I went past the painted words—SLEIGHT OF HAND, KENO KING, JACKPOT—and the numbers, climbing higher and higher. Below, grown men played with model airplanes six feet long, flying them from a short runway along the airstrip. They flew over me and I shielded the lenses of my binoculars so they would not reflect the sunrise and give me away. I looked down from the ridge. No one went in or out of my trailer; no one even went near it. An arrow of stones pointed to my front door, though, it seemed to, and there were scratches on the rocks that could be from the legs of a tripod for a telescope or even a gun. I did not know. Smaller words were painted on the stones around me, under my feet, a record of the illicit acts performed on that ground. No, I did not expect to find an easy explanation; I would have been disappointed if I had found one. I backed away from the ridge, wondering who in the town had seen my silhouette, wondering who was behind me or hiding in the rocks nearby.

Some say you cannot run away from your problems, that they follow and rise up again. I'm not one who believes that.

You can trick your luck, you can lose it as a way of turning it around. I wanted to give it time, to let the whole town work itself out, and I had to go after my love; I did not know how the two things were connected, only that they were.

When I was on the ridge I could hear the engines of the cars out on the salt flats, I could see the roostertails left behind but not the cars themselves. I thought about the words Charlotte had seen there, and I thought maybe the angels had done it, God's messengers, that they riddled us because they love confusion or because they have trouble making sense.

If anything, I found the way things were turning—all I couldn't understand—encouraging, as a sign of my involvement. Still, in those days I did not know who to trust. I suspected that the boys had turned against me, that they had seen and misunderstood what happened with Charlotte that last night on the flats. She pulled away from me in delay, not denial; I felt the hesitation. Anyone who's waiting for an apology better get comfortable.

The sun had fallen a little while I had my eyes closed; when I opened them it lit up the wall of the cave, the pictograms and the petroglyphs. Standing, I rubbed at the pictures and they came off against my fingers, just charcoal and chalk. They might have been weeks old, perhaps even months, but I would not grant them years.

I stepped out of the cave and looked out over the desert. It was late afternoon and the sun was still blinding, incessant. Out by my trailer and car another car slowed down; I was relieved when it kept going. I looked out the other way, away from the road, and I saw him coming through the heat, walking across the sand. I could not avoid him now; I started down from the cave; I set out to meet him. I did not call out. There was no sound and the wind had died. We were walking straight at each other, cutting the distance in half, in half again. I drank from the jug hooked over my thumb, resting on my arm as I tipped it up, still walking, my other arm holding my pistol out straight and level.

I was twenty feet away when I understood, and still I pulled the trigger. The heat had made it seem as if it were walking, but it was only a scarecrow, set up for target practice, riddled by the bullets of others. A tear in the sack of its head gave it a leering, laughing mouth; cardboard and straw spilled from its pants leg. I felt good, it had felt right, but it was stupid to shoot, to make that noise. I was a mile from the highway and I turned a slow circle, holding my pistol out, anxious all at once and I could not trust my eyes. The air would not settle around me.

God organized, but did not create us, for we are as old as He. So the Mormons believe. I was pleased to know that, also reassured to read that miraculous power did not disappear after the biblical days, that it is among us. Of course it's among us! How would we ever let it escape? What would we do without it? It's amazing to me the things people will believe. What they call miracles are usually only misunderstandings; a lack of facts coupled with a faulty interpretation based on the desire to believe, the wish to be surprised.

Yes, if anyone could bring miracles into the daylight, if anyone could organize miracles it would be the Mormons. They are an organizing people—they like to make sense and straighten things. They track down their ancestors to posthumously baptize them, save their souls; they have all the names, everyone's, safe and dry in caves where the temperature and humidity never change; they store enough food in their basements, cans and cans, to outlast any apocalypse.

The car had cooled down and the sun paled slightly in the late afternoon. I drove south, hardly seeing a town. Joshua trees stood tall in the desert; cows and everything else hid behind them. I anticipated the cattleguards before I passed over them, corrugations that can trap a hoof, that reverberate through your bones. Sometimes they passed under with a surprising smoothness, they turned out to be only painted on. Who knows why that fools the cows.

The Mormons are so organized they have three levels of heaven and plenty of distinctions inside them. Celestial, Terrestrial, Telestial Kingdoms. Don't worry, we'll do all right—even the lowest level is better than anything we can imagine, and you don't even have to be a Mormon to get there. Even I have hope, even a fool like Texas, that car-jacker, will be all right up there. It is a nice thought, I admit, seeing Charlotte, being together with her forever in the Celestial Kingdom. It would take some sacrifice—I would have to convert, we would have to marry—but we would share the highest of heavens, all weightless and dressed in white, surrounded by fountains. We could have celestial children, never ceasing. Our skin would be perfectly smooth.

People believe that. I'd like to think there are chances we could do better right here, if we worked, if we put our minds to it, our hearts. My mind is tricky and I know my heart will not be organized. All organization is born of anxiety and fear, after all, of nervousness. They hope the system will be tight enough that there will be no reason to fear anything, either from without or the more dangerous things within. I don't trust it. I want to see what I am. I want to find out what we have here.

As if I could change the things that happened. I went after her. Her photograph watched me from the dashboard as I drove. Past her, thin clouds failed to gather, Indians used billboards to try to sell me cheap tobacco and illegal fireworks, watering troughs sat under windmills, the tanks shot dry, sieves of bulletholes. In the desert there are shell casings everywhere, twenty-five feet from every sign and historical marker. People shoot cacti, ignorant that the plants are their elders. I've seen joshua trees mutilated—slashed, broken, partially uprooted. There is no respect for age, not even in the dry air of the desert, the preserver, the love of librarians.

I hoped to get there before midnight; the incident with the scarecrow had slowed me down. I was surrounded by nothing, surrounded by space, but it did not bother me. They call agoraphobia fear of open spaces, but actually it's the fear of the agora, the fear of the marketplace—the desert has nothing to do with commerce, it forces you into solitude. It's no miracle gambling would spring out of this landscape; it is a form of commerce where all agreements are forgotten. No one has more friends, no one is more alone than the winner.

It is a miracle that anything thrives out there—yet I must admit that all things strike me as miraculous. The circling of vultures, the spacing of the cacti and cows, the bones in my fingers, the truth in everything I have to say. We are all spinning around the sun, a ball of fire falling through the sky. What if the world was to spin loose? Is it happening now? Would it make any difference? What would loose be? As if a world that is spinning could be set still, measured and organized.

These people would have it so. In the early days, before Brigham Young took over, Joseph Smith sensed all this, he felt the spinning and movement in all things. He used stones to find gold and treasures buried in the ground. He could feel it down there, he could see through the ground. This was before he was a prophet. Once he promised a whole chest of gold, buried with a feather, and when they dug they found only the feather—yet they trusted him, he had the power of words. He said the gold had gone down; he promised the heat of the summer caused treasure chests to rise nearer the earth's surface. Try and settle that down now—those ideas won't be organized.

The sun grew hotter even as it paled. No doubt treasures were just inches below the sands of the desert, ready to be discovered, eager to be had. Charlotte was all I wanted and I was getting closer. I drove on, watching every ripple of air, looking for Johnson out in the desert; the false alarm was reason for greater alertness, not the other way around. The first violence justifies all paranoia. I felt under the front seat—I checked again and again to be sure my pistol was there, that it was loaded and ready. I worried, glancing in my rearview mirror, wondering if someone had gotten into my trailer and was hiding there, if I was carrying a parasite. Every fold in the air hid something, every buckle of the earth.

The last time I saw Johnson in the Stateline, he was telling me about some people, in a far country, who filled boats with puppets and set them out to sea; this way, the puppets took the blame for what the people themselves had done and thought, all their sins. The puppets were even painted to look like individuals; they worked like a kind of reverse voodoo dolls.

What do you think? he said. What will happen with our sins?

I told him I wasn't so sure I believed in them.

You do, he said.

You don't know my sins, I said.

Some I know so well, he said, it's as if I sinned them myself.

I'll take credit for my sins, I said. Carry them myself and not try and palm them off on anyone, puppet or god.

There were many times I wished Johnson would try something, that he would stray from his words and into action. He was hard to grapple with, and as I drove I did not know where he was, if he was close or moving in the opposite direction.

The front seat of my car was covered in books. I'd been reading all I could on the Mormons, as I figured it might be useful. First, I found a copy of the Book of Mormon, atop a whole stack of them on the counter at Taco Burger. Inside the front cover was a color photograph of the owner and his whole family. They wanted me to have that book; they were sure it would change my life.

The girl who gave it to me, the Mexican girl who sold me a burrito, had tattoos on her hands, blue lines along her fingers. She would not say why, but I knew it had to do with gangs — the whole town, Wendover, was taking a turn that way, falling apart around me. I did not really care. My Book of Mormon was the same, word for word, as the one Charlotte carried. I wanted to think like her, anticipate her moves and, yes, to trick her if it came to that. Perhaps that's a sin in itself, taking someone's beliefs only to use them as weapons against them — yet I also ran the risk of being taken in, of being turned into a believer.

I went past the town of Rachel without a thought, without a suspicion of what was happening there. People argued in cars passing in the opposite direction; they waved as we shot by, ten feet apart. With each car I worried that perhaps Charlotte and Keith were ducking down in the back seat or even that their bodies were folded into the trunk. Still I drove straight, through open range, cows spread far apart, usually in groups of two, at least, keeping each other company.

There are few alive who have lived as long as I have, who could tell you these things and speak from experience. Was it Hermes who delivered messages for the gods? He also spent half his time taking souls to the underworld, so perhaps he carried the messages of the dead back with him. The angels carry messages and even they descend — they're dead themselves, in their way. They like it down there; they have to fly upside down and they hang suspended, teasing the souls below. It's safer there than on the surface, aboveground; remember how the angels were treated by the men of Sodom.

Anita was right, Mormon angels do look like you and me. Stranger still, three of the twelve Mormon apostles were given power over death and they're walking the earth today. When they are thrown into prisons, the prisons cannot hold them; they are cast into furnaces that cannot burn them; they play with the wild beasts sent to rend them limb from limb. They are known as the Three Nephites and I know how they feel, to be so old, to know so much and still to be treated with such condescension. It's especially frustrating when one is only trying to do good, to bring about what is right.

When Charlotte asked the missionaries about the Three Nephites, they told her to pray about it, they gave her no real answer.

Do the Nephites get lost? she asked them. Confused? Do they always travel together? And if they get split up do they recognize each other?

She had too many guns for those boys, she was too far gone. She might as well have levitated or washed their feet. They were not prepared for her questions, and perhaps even then she suspected the answers would bring her to me. I'd tell her the Nephites can feel no pain, only pity, that they cannot be tempted because they are beyond temptation, because they skip right past temptation and straight into action.

My whole house snaked and swooped behind me. The sun was coming down. I passed the remains of a coyote, its fur all matted with blood, then another, more recent, a little farther along. I had adventures that aren't pertinent, that wouldn't shed much light—I had coffee in a brothel, the girls all lined up and watching me, their worn-out skin showing through their clothes; I had a cowboy tell me I wasn't worth kicking the shit out of; I had a man let me know that jackalopes sing with the voices of women and that's why they're called the sirens of the desert.

I learned much in my search for Charlotte. When I saw

what she was after, I realized that I too had felt the same desire, all along. I had sensed this, it was what drew us together, but I had not understood it before. I knew we would hear words meant only for us, we would understand all movement, we would see by spiritual light, all lit from within and all on fire. This is not to say Charlotte does not need physical attention. It would be foolish to neglect our bodies—as if we'd be best advised to take the roofs off our houses so God could more easily snatch us out, gather us to Him! The life of the spirit can be very cold.

I drove behind a car on a trailer, painted to be in a demolition derby. Its headlights were eyes and it had a mouth full of sharp teeth, triangles of scrap metal. DANGER it said across the hood. IMPACT ZONE. I followed it all along the edge of the test site, where the men who work underground hardly do any tests but still practice every day. They don their radiation suits and burrow down in the ground; they hope and dream they'll get permission to blow something up. In the dusk I saw cows out in the desert, standing alone except for their calves; I guess that's one reason to have children, to stave off loneliness, and Lord knows older men than I have been fathers. The painted mouth of the car on the trailer went ahead of me. It taunted and threatened and retreated all the way down into the city of lights.

The man was standing on the seat of the bicycle and the woman was doing a headstand on the handle-bars, scissoring her legs backward and forward, perfectly straight; then she kicked sideways and went right through the bicycle's frame, the triangle of it, and was suddenly behind him, then on his shoulders. They were an Asian couple and they smiled so much, ceaselessly, it seemed they never breathed. They could do their act underwater if the bicycle was heavy enough. They rode around and around, circling the small stage. The organist played in his sleep, the drummer stuck to his high hat and snare. Colored lights swirled on the ceiling above, the slot machines and green felt tables glowed below. Off to one side a whole bar spun around like a carousel.

When the bicyclists finished, music began to play. America the Beautiful. Those terrifying clowns, huge dolls, hung over the gambling pit—it was a nightmare down there and every bit as beautiful. The Circus Circus employees wore bright pink and the dealers looked over their shoulders; they guarded their cards a little more closely because of the midway above, where I was standing. The flash and clumsiness of those dealers was unbearable for me to watch, but I admit the whole scene was familiar, it was not nearly too big for me. No, I'm not ashamed to say I felt at home in the midst of this, that I felt safer and more dangerous than I ever could in the desert. I recognized the energy and took it in, the kind that makes you feel hollow and like you'll never sleep again, that you will be constantly alert. This is the perfect feeling when you are in pursuit.

On the midway, children's faces were painted to look like cats, like pirates. They wandered, whining after their parents; they needed more money, more tickets. I kept my hands deep in my pockets so I would not strangle those children. I stood looking over the pit, lights racing along the tops of machines, and I tried to decide where to begin.

You looking for something? the security guard said.

Who isn't? I said.

Right. He took his walkie-talkie off his belt and held it up toward his face, as if to show it off, to let me know he had it. I'm in charge up here, he said. I'm the head guy.

I can tell that, I said. That's obvious.

A woman walked by carrying a giant stuffed bear—most likely she was an employee, it was all a trick to fool the children, to pinch the parents a little harder. I took the photograph out of my pocket, still in its frame, and held it up to the security guard.

Whoa there, he said, jumping back. Thought you were pulling a gun. Lucky for you you weren't.

Do you know her? I said, watching as he held it close,
watching his expression. You don't know her.

I know her boyfriend, he said. I know who she is.

Where is he?

That I don't know.

I handed him a twenty and he pretended not to take it.

I know who could tell you, I bet—the animal trainer, the
guy who talks to the animals. He's down in the basement,
though, and that's off limits. Real high security down there.

I slipped him another bill and he hooked one finger through
the air over his shoulder. I followed because sometimes you
have to make a little room, a space where chance can have its
play. We went past the darkened stage, down a short ramp,
and stopped at the door of an elevator. He took out a key, put
it in the slot, then hit a button.

I didn't let you in here, he said, clapping a hand over his
badge, where it said his name.

The photograph, I said, I need it back, and he handed it
through the closing doors. The elevator was moving, only very
slowly, not anxious to reach its destination.

When the doors opened I stepped into a world of low ceil-
ings, dim lights and long corridors; there were holes kicked in
walls, water dripping from light sockets, backed-up drains on
the floor. None of this surprised me. I had long suspected
there was a vast network of tunnels under the city, a darkness
to balance the lights above.

I came around a corner and saw the acrobats working on
their bicycles, shining the rims and checking the spokes' tension, talking back and forth in a language beyond Spanish.
They were still smiling. A man in a magician's cape passed; I
cringed when I saw he was carrying a deck of cards. I kept
moving. I felt myself closing in on her now.

The big cats did not look good. They were skinny and tat-

tered and did not seem to notice when I passed by. A chimpanzee lay on its back on the concrete, lethargic, shaking a row of
small cages, his feet in the mesh. He poked at the smaller
animals as if he could prove his relation through cruelty. I kept
out of sight, behind a pillar. Nearby, I heard a man grunting,
his shadow rising and falling along a wall. He was doing
chin-ups on a bar hanging from the ceiling, coughing out numbers, kicking his legs to get the last ones. He jumped down,
stretched his arms out in front of him; he looked them over, all
down their length, turning them to see every side.

You talk to animals? I said.

He turned slowly, like he knew no fear.

Onstage I do, he said. Down here I just teach them to listen.
He kicked at the chimp—it jumped sideways just in time.
What are you looking at? he said.

You, I said. You're the man I came looking for.

What exactly do you want, oldtimer?

In my peripheral vision I saw doors open and close, doors I
had not noticed before because they blended into the walls.
Hallways forked into the darkness.

Must be skeletons all over down here, I said. Frayed strings
in their hands.

Junkie? he said.

Not even close.

Lost a couple dozen snakes, he said, before I gave up.
Cleared up the mice and the rats, but someday someone will
find rooms full of snakes.

Tunnels, I said.

Listen, he said. Even if I had something, even if I was the
kind of guy who would have something, I just don't know—
but, you know, I'm actually not holding right now. I'm all
tapped out.

I'm looking for a guy named Keith, I said. Young guy.

Don't know him.

Keith, I said, he works here. He's a friend of yours, I heard.

All right, whatever. So he works here. He hasn't done any work for me, though, not at all. So what if I've talked to him? That's it.

Where is he? I said.

Hell if I know. Lives back in the trailer park, though, this one here. Slot sixty-four, I think. I think that's right.

I turned to go.

If I'm wrong, he said, don't come asking—that's all I know.

The girl that's with him, I said.

Works at Caesars, he said, pulling on a dog's tail where it stuck through a cage. Pretty little thing.

I found the stairs and took them up into the casino, then went outside and down the alley next to Slots-A-Fun. It was either the noise of the casinos or the heat outside; you escaped one only to be embraced by the other. I put on the visor I'd bought, with its transparent green brim—the light shining through made me look undead, beset by scurvy. I did not want to be recognized, and so I'd bought all new clothes. Sandals, wraparound sunglasses, a red sweatsuit with three white stripes down the arms and legs. It was not easy to get those stripes lined up. Anyone who doubts me, who would have mistaken me for some geriatric tourist, should have seen me later that night. That's all I have to say.

I went down the rows of the trailers, counting up the numbers. Of course I thought it was wonderful that Charlotte lived in a trailer—it was even better that she worked in a casino, after all the ribbing she'd given me. Den of iniquity, she always said. Pit of sin.

I stopped at slot sixty-four. There was no answer to the bell, no answer to my knock. The name on the mailbox was not hers, not his, but this did not surprise me. Slowly, I crept around the side and looked through a window, into the kitchen, dishes stacked in the sink; I waited until my eyes adjusted to the darkness and then I waited a little longer, until I was certain the trailer was empty.

I headed back down the alley, out into the sun. People were

thick in the shadows. All the neon was on and since more light was impossible it only added to the heat. Women passed, fanning themselves with flyers for strip shows. Water would have saved me, but I would find a way down the strip to Caesars if I could avoid thinking about my thirst.

Across the street from Circus Circus, the El Rancho stood, all boarded up. Flames took it in 1960, but it wasn't half the fire of the one at the MGM Grand. That was more recent and I need only close my eyes to bring it all back. It started small, in the deli; later they claimed it was just a kitchen fire. People laughed, they kept gambling as the smoke thickened. It wasn't long before it had convinced them that all they wanted was to lie down and sleep. Ten people were dead in the first minute. The firemen couldn't get above the ninth floor and the column of smoke was a mile high.

It happened at seven in the morning, when this city is weakest. Inside, the burning plastic let out poisonous gases. Poker chips and furniture melted, joined into new shapes, came apart again. People staggered out, coughing and bleeding, they lay on the ground with oxygen masks on their faces—but even they did not want to leave, they wanted to watch the flames. Fluorescent lights exploded from their sockets and the flames were beautiful, climbing themselves, struggling to get higher. Neptune rose up in the lagoon in front; there were flames all above his trident and water would not heed his call.

In windows, people tried to knot sheets together, they hung from ropes that window washers had left behind. It was no use—the fire burned out their sins and more, it boiled the blood right out of their veins. It was a baptism of fire, it was for the spirit and the Holy Ghost went right on in.

I admit I picked through the ashes afterward, I saw the blackened, broken slot machines, the walls scorched where paintings had hung. Yes, the sound of a fire engine stirs me; I never said otherwise.

Everything in Vegas looks better from a distance—that's not specific to the city, only more pronounced. Down the strip

I saw signs for Nudes on Ice, Wayne Newton and other celebrities admitting self-parody or business acumen by playing here at all. A man ran past, panting like a dog, his tongue hanging out. I walked on, under the sign for Ginseng Barbecue—yes, they're after the Asians now, putting out hooks and snares. Further, I saw Caesars, the fountain at the Mirage, the huge Easter Island heads at the Tropicana. There were red, white and blue streamers everywhere and I could not figure them out.

The sidewalk was hot through the soles of my sandals. I went into the Riviera and the air conditioning turned my sweat clammy. I shivered, looking over the expanse of the casino, the mirrors multiplying space, expanding and contracting light, casting indoor mirages. The vastness can make it difficult to believe in the presence of people fifteen feet away. The confusion the mirrors multiply—the sound and lights, people always moving, cocktail waitresses and change carts—is designed to disorient you. People wander in casinos, unable to find an exit, coming across machines they hadn't noticed at first, machines that are no doubt luckier. I am used to the confusion, it is my life, and the advantage is that the outside world is always in slow motion for me. That I would miss something is ridiculous, inconceivable. The eye sees more than the mind can understand, less than the heart knows.

A band was playing, and the saxophone player walked right into the lounge, among the tables. The singer was talking about Ray Charles singing Georgia on My Mind—the singer said he'd been to Georgia and hadn't seen anything like that down there.

What time is it? someone said, and someone else asked if it really mattered.

Was it my business to shout out that Ray Charles is blind? I had my hands full, I was after her, I was surrounded by mirrors.

A descent into the gambling pit of a big casino is a descent into hell, into the world of lies and false hopes, pure artifice. I passed the roulette wheel, the steel ball dancing and rattling, everyone suspecting magnets. I can't stand watching the blackjack dealers in Vegas; they're all flash—I could make them nervous in under ten hands, I could make them lose their jobs before the night was out. I saw the door open, hidden in the mirrors, I saw the pit boss coming between the tables.

You disappeared, he said. We thought something terrible had happened.

I was raptured, I said.

Who did it?

Who do you think?

But you're all right now, he said. Now you're back. Years later.

Straight up in the air, I said.

You've come back.

Yes and no.

You know you always have a job here, he said. No questions.

I've taken a couple steps closer to being human, I said. I appreciate the offer. I'll let you know.

On the way out I passed old women playing four slot machines at once, wearing leather gloves on one hand. They don't really entertain the possibility of winning, they don't actually desire it—yet the act of pulling the slot machine's arm is an affirmation. All the hype provides a cover under which they can be saved from being caught doing nothing or appearing truly hopeless. Yes, desperation is just closer to the surface in Las Vegas; once you learn to recognize it, you see it wherever you go. There are different kinds and I know them all. The strong varieties, where it's always just under the surface, living on the verge of tears, are the desperations I know best. It forces the gamble, it desires the situation where all agreements are off, where what passed for exchange can be set aside, where people can be set free from what they deserve.

Out in the heat, everything seemed more crowded. People jostled against me. Boys walked down the street with their shirts off, glistening, a beer in each hand, never stepping out of anyone's way. Everyone I passed was ready to lose, full of hope; you can always tell a professional gambler by their walk—like they're going to work at a job they don't find too distasteful. It was too hot to breathe. I saw a dog in a car and I wanted to break the window. I wanted to wait for the owner and break him all the way down.

Children ran wild, the wrong direction on the moving walkway at Caesars. The fountains stretched below, the pale blue lights just visible. The valet was wearing a gold helmet with a brush on top; he looked moments from heat prostration.

It was cool inside, elegant. At Caesars things are so classy they turn down the noise of the machines just enough that you can hear the coins falling from even the most paltry jackpots. The dealers wear gold medallions around their necks, they are the property of Caesar. I would have known Charlotte worked there even if I hadn't been told.

Shot of Jack, I told the bartender. Better make it two.

Down the bar, three men were arguing about the dolphins at the Mirage, about the white tigers. On my other side two girls could not stop laughing. The color of gold caught in all the mirrors. The bartender returned.

I have a question for you, I said. I set the photograph down and he just spun it around, didn't even pick it up from the bar. Over his shoulder there was a framed photograph of Evel Knievel in a white jumpsuit, astride a motorcycle.

Yes, he said. She works here. Change girl. She might even be around here someplace. He looked out over the machines. Hold on, he said. Let me see what I can't find out.

I'll have two more, I said.

I have to get out of here, a cocktail waitress was saying. Behind me, I heard screaming in Cantonese, back at the baccarat table. It's not an American game, really; we cannot stand the suspense. For a moment I believed I saw Charlotte in a mirror—it's not like me to be fooled like that. I had a feeling of foreboding, I fought off a sense of worthlessness. In the end you begin to feel the pressure of the mirrors on your internal organs, your lungs and your heart.

Willie Nelson, one man said. Willie said he got stoned on the roof of the White House.

Carter administration? said the other. That'd be about right. Man. Willie. Did you know a woman once said she and Willie had sex for eight hours straight and they did a somersault? You know what he said?

What?

Willie said, I'm not saying it couldn't of happened—I just don't remember it.

They laughed together, punching each other's shoulders.

Hold on, the bartender said to me. We'll get something here yet. Girl's name is Charlotte.

I know that, I said. Keep the drinks coming; I'm starting to feel them now. I looked along the bar and slammed my shot glass down. Once, I said, once Willie drank a whole fifth of whiskey.

That's Willie.

And then, I said, then he beat up three men. Big men.

Willie's tough, one of them said. Even if he's not that big.

And he was singing the whole time he did it, I said, and when he was finished he bought a drink for all the men's wives.

I bet he did at that!

The women wanted to go home with him, I said, but Willie just took one for the road. That's what he did.

That wasn't Willie, one of the men said. That was Jerry Jeff Walker you're talking about.

It was not Jerry Jeff, I said.

How would you know?

Because, I said. I know that because I made the whole stupid thing up.

Drunk, the man said, and I laughed out loud.

A woman sat down next to me. The bartender brought her a drink. In the mirror I saw she was a showgirl, dressed in glass beads, pieces of mirror, a headdress with red and purple feathers that came to a sharp metal point between her eyes. I still wore my green transparent visor; in the mirror, sitting side by side, we looked like two creatures from hell. She took off her helmet and set it on the bar.

So, you're looking for Charlotte. She laughed.

I am.

You her father?

No.

Too bad. That could have been interesting. You must be some kind of highroller, though—no one else could afford to look like that.

It's comfortable, I said. I knew right away she was going to test my patience, but in the end I would find out what I had to know.

You look familiar, she said. I've seen you before.

Lots of people look like me, I said.

You're old, she said.

Thank you. What about Charlotte?

We'll get to that, she said. She was drinking faster than I was, catching up. First I've got to figure you out, figure out how much I can tell you.

Did you know she's a Mormon? I said.

So what? Who isn't? I've been a Mormon myself. Jamie leaned close to me, so close I felt her breath on my ear, on the skin of my neck. Would it surprise you, she said, if I told you I was a man?

No, I said.

Liar, she said, laughing. Any fool could tell I'm not a man.

She picked up my roll of bills, turned them end over end, and set them down again. I wondered what she wanted, if she really knew Charlotte or was after something else. I suspected myself of being too eager to believe.

I saw a lot of her, Jamie said. All of her, in fact. She set down her empty glass, put on her headdress, then stood up.

Where you going? I said.

Don't worry, she said. You're coming, too.

There were six elevators and we got into the first one that opened. It was quiet all at once. The light was steady.

I can't sleep these days, Jamie said.

I said I wouldn't be surprised if you told me you were a man, I said, not that I'd believe it.

Maybe I was her corruptor, she said. Our Charlotte.

I stretched my neck back and looked up into the mirror on the ceiling, where I was hanging suspended, my feet high above and my face squinting down, a monster. I closed my eyes and saw skeletons rattling, dancing, hardly touching the ground. They scattered their bones with the skeletons of animals, mixed everything up.

She led me down a hallway. Somewhere she had been carrying a key to the room. She locked the door behind us and I stood in the darkness, envisioning straps and hooks and metal rings. Jamie did not move right away. I jumped when the lights came on. It was a normal room—a king-sized bed, a table and chairs, a television, a bust of Thoth or Anubis holding some kind of golden shepherd's crook. Jamie opened a cupboard full of mini-bottles and poured us each a drink.

Where is she? I said.

You think I can help you out?

You said you could.

Better than Charlotte, I can, I can promise you that.

I'm sure you're right, I said, but I don't think you understand.

I'm sure I do. How much money do you have?

Usually enough to do whatever I want, I said.

That's all one can hope for. She took my hand and sat me down on the bed, close beside her. Let's talk, she said. She's gone, I think, Charlotte, or she could be in the city still, I don't know, hiding out. It was drugs, he was into them somehow, her boyfriend.

As she spoke she stood up, trying to reach back over her shoulder. I helped her; I pulled her zipper down. I saw the gray in her hair. She could not hide it from me here.

You look so familiar, she said.

I'm not, I said.

That's what it was, she said, some kind of drug trouble. That's why they took off.

You don't know where she is, I said.

Never said I did. I only said I knew her.

I stood up and walked to the window. I pulled back the curtains and saw the lights, the crowds far below. It was night, all of a sudden. Nothing could be more artificial. Charlotte was out there somewhere—I had not lost her scent, I would find her—and behind me Jamie sat on the bed, wearing nothing but her headdress, waiting for me. When the sky exploded I jumped back, my hands over my eyes.

It's the fourth of July, she said. Where you been?

I returned to the window. I stood between the curtain and the pane of glass. Showers of white lights came down, parachutes of blue, gold stars and silver arrows, red hearts. It's hard to remember sometimes that the desert surrounds Las Vegas, that out there it is quiet and dark and dangerous, that there are broken towns where there are no lights and there are no people.

There was not an unbroken pane
of glass in the whole town. Doorways opened into nothing and
staircases stopped halfway, giving
up, or were missing altogether.
The broken-down foundations of
old buildings lay lost and hidden in
the desert, and next to these crum-
bled facades were the newer buildings, their windows shattered and
corners smoothed by sand, their in-
terior walls kicked apart by unknown people. Charlotte stood in
the shadow of a doorway, surrounded by loose bricks, shards of

glass and beer cans as old as she was. She turned her head from side to side, checking for movement. Nearby, an old root cellar had caved in, like a grave into the ground; there were bones in the bottom, but Keith had told her they most likely belonged to a cow that had fallen in and broken its neck or a leg. Across the street, rusted saws and old tools hung on a wall, wooden pulleys and long curved scythes, so old it was impossible to tell if they were for carpentry, mining, or torture.

Through the doorway behind her, someone had started a painting on the stone wall and left it unfinished. Three figures with wide shoulders and triangular bodies and one line below, meant to suggest the ground, as if they were floating through the air, flying.

Lizards moved like sundials, just enough to keep out of the shadows, and the rabbit stayed in one corner of its pen, hidden by the shadow of a tumbleweed. Keith had brought it all the way from Vegas, driven with it on his lap. He'd built the pen of chicken wire found in the ruins; soon, he said, he would set the rabbit free.

Charlotte and Keith stayed in one of the older houses because there was less chance of infestation, no hollowness to the walls, no attics for the packrats to fill with nests. They had been in the ghost town for two weeks. They hung their food from the ceiling, in mesh bags thrown over exposed beams, out of reach of the mice.

Keith? she said.

She did not know where they had gone. Stepping out into the street, she let the sun catch on her skin. It was quiet and still. The town was built up on a rise, hidden below a ridge, surrounded by boulders, mine shafts everywhere. At night, in the darkness, she would listen to the wind and guess at the sounds. Keith would reach out and she'd pull away at the touch of his cold fingertips. She listened for the snakes close by, polishing the stone walls, hunting mice.

Standing still made her itch and so she would wander, among the ruins, out into the desert. She went slowly at first;

the day before she'd come upon an old coyote trap—she tickled its jaws with a stick before springing it. She searched the skies, looking for hawks, staring into the sun and then recovering herself. In Vegas people had planted trees, but here there was nothing like that, here there was no cover beneath bells and horns, the calls of dealers, no lights to hide the night or to sharpen it. The sun was as quiet as the moon and all its reflections had the same voice, twisting every day to make it alike. She'd heard it said that boredom only visits the boring, but this was not boredom—it was impatience, constant attention and anticipation. Patience can take a lifetime to learn. It has taken mine.

At night she could not see the lights of Las Vegas, but she could feel them from the south, bright and burning cool. She felt as if she had failed, down there—she had set out to sin, held herself amid all she'd ever been warned against, and she'd found no depth; it was as if she had misunderstood, and sin was shallow, nothing but surfaces. The nature of Las Vegas, not what it held, had surprised her.

Her shadow was lost straight beneath her, buried in the ground. The sun burned the air away from her. When she looked up she saw them. Keith was on the stilts and Texas was leaning close, whispering encouragement, then stepping back and straightening his hair as if he knew he was being watched.

The stilts were six feet tall and made of cow bones lashed together; their ends were sharp so they left almost no mark on the ground. Texas walked backward, shouting up at Keith, clapping his hands. One stilt was hung up in some sagebrush. There was no wind and it did not seem likely Keith could stand if there was. Charlotte turned and walked the other way, down along the ridge, before they noticed her.

Some days they would practice with the stilts, some days other things. Sometimes they ran through the circles of drainage pipes left out in the desert, they climbed through the old mining machines—elevators and powerhouses, tangles of cable—and leapt over the shafts that opened cold and suddenly, straight to the hot center of the earth. Charlotte kept walking. She heard the sound of wings in the desert but could see nothing.

They were training, Texas said, because they didn't want anyone to run them down. Charlotte suspected all the training was his way of keeping Keith occupied, so Keith would not have the time or energy to question what he was asked to do at night, what he was being paid for. It had surprised her Keith went along with the plan, that she had allowed herself to be convinced; then again, it seemed more than a coincidence that they should find themselves with Texas again.

Looking back, she saw Keith tip over, tumbling down from the stilts, and Texas helping him to his feet and then hoisting him up again.

Texas had been in Stockton the whole time they were in Vegas. He'd been delivering drugs, saving money for what they were all doing now. Early on he'd made a point of showing them all the money, hundred-dollar bills in thick stacks. Even among all the people in Vegas, after months of changes, she had recognized him right away, holding out a hundred and asking for silver dollars. He needed to talk to her, he said, and to Keith, and when she told him Keith would be down to Caesars later he said he'd wait. It's important, he told her, don't doubt it. Important. Despite how hard she believed she'd become, how much she'd learned since the drive from Wendover, still he unnerved her.

There were bones everywhere in the desert; gravity and time couldn't hold, they slipped, lost their purchase. The edges of objects could not be trusted. Charlotte kept walking, toward the ridge where she could look over the valley and all the way to town.

Texas had told her he knew it all along, that he'd come looking for them. Destiny, he said, and she wondered if he was right—there must have been some reason they'd stopped to see the car, that they had met him on the highway and were now brought together again.

Wasn't chance, he told her. The three of us are all tangled up. Plain tangled.

Now, he acted like the ghost town was his domain, strutting back and forth in his worn leather vest, standing atop the walls of the ruins and pissing down. Some nights he just listened to his weather radio—anxious about what was next, though the weather never changed—and some nights he broke windows and kicked holes in the walls with his pointed boots.

Far away, the highway fell down, flattened out, then climbed again, empty. Charlotte's binoculars were hot against the sockets of her eyes. She focused and the two circles became one, her vision straightened. Joshua trees rose up, growing at a certain elevation, and the low mountains rolled around the town of Rachel. It was five miles away and she watched people walking from trailer to trailer, dogs sniffing each other, cars kicking up dust before they found the blacktop of the highway. She stayed low, as if someone could see her, as if her silhouette could hold together and remain visible through miles of heat. She watched the people carefully, because she suspected there was a reason Texas had brought them here, outside of this town.

When she turned she could not believe what she saw in the sky. She looked through her binoculars, but then the cow disappeared. It was over the horizon, tipped onto its back, swimming in the air, its long, thin legs stretched to walk across the firmament. Charlotte tried to climb higher, to gain some elevation, but then she lost it and the sky was clear.

She walked fifty feet and when she looked up she saw the bodies in the sky. The two of them looked like they were falling, headlong, stretched out like they might snap back up into the air and they would never reach the ground. They flew with no struggle, unbound by gravity, cooled by the clouds. At first they seemed to have no legs, then she saw them; she felt her heart grow to crowd everything inside her body. She ran, watching the sky. When they moved, arms and legs would disappear in the heat and then surface again. As she came close, the heat folded them away, then spun them so their legs were the right length and their feet were on the ground.

The surface of the desert was jumping on every side. She shielded her eyes from the sun. Now Texas was standing with the stilts leaning against his shoulders; he swung a hammer out from a length of rope, in a circle around him, passing it from hand to hand behind his back so he would not have to turn around. He let it out and brought it in, swinging it low above the ground but never letting it touch. Keith stood to one side, watching, and Charlotte knew the two of them had no idea what they had been doing, up in the sky, that they were oblivious to their flight. Keith saw her and waved, but she did not get close enough to hear their voices. They may have been calling her name as she turned away.

She came back into the ghost town from a different direction; she passed a furrow in the ground overflowing with rusted cans, twisted wire, license plates smashed and flattened, illegible, then she spooked a jackrabbit out of the sage—it bolted straight, jerking back and forth, disappearing again. In the graveyard all the headstones had been knocked over and now lay flat, like babies' graves. She walked over them, stepping-stones, she tried to pray though her pride was greater than her weakness.

As she walked, I was driving to Vegas, I was swimming in mirrors, I was reading the Book of Mormon to get ahead of her and lay in wait. Yes, I knew when I had found it. I almost tore the page from the book. The Mormons believe God still talks to man, that He lays revelations down. It is not so easy for a woman—no doubt the Mormons fear what women would make of God's words—yet that's what Charlotte wanted.

I learned plenty in Vegas, but I did not know she was in the ghost town until I'd gone back to Wendover and intercepted the letters she sent Anita. My sources are manifold; they multiply.

Charlotte wanted conversation with God, unmediated. Myself, I hear voices and I've never even been baptized; I've seen and felt things I cannot explain. I have never understood if you trade your sins when you are baptized, or if the water just saves your body and your soul needs fire. This is what I suspect.

The Mormons baptize the dead by proxy, they read off the names and let the little children go down under the waters. This way you can be helped up to a higher heaven, you can become a member of the church even if you failed to do so while living. She did it when she was a girl, gasping, going under hundreds of times, prepared to drown if that's what it took. I won't be satisfied until I take you all the way down, Charlotte, through your body and straight into your soul.

They walked along a dry stream
bed, under a line of trees that was
barely making it, dying of thirst.
Between their words there was
only the sound of their footsteps in
the soft sand of the wash. Tonight
even the coyotes were silent.

All this talking could give us
away, Keith said.

We're not that close yet, Texas
said.

They had been shouted at, shot
at, chased by dogs. They had come
close enough to houses that they
heard kettles whistling, children's
voices.

You wouldn't shoot a dog, Keith said.

I wouldn't have to shoot it. With his free hand Texas brought out a knife, cut the air, then put it back away somewhere. That'll quiet a dog right down, he said. Right down.

I see the fields, Keith said. I think.

How did you two meet? said Texas.

What?

You and Charlotte.

We just did.

You know lots about women?

Some.

Enough? Texas said.

I guess so.

Liar. Like you couldn't always learn more.

Headlights shone along the highway, a mile distant, and the two men instantly dropped to their stomachs and lay flat, lower than the height of the sage.

You think you're something, Texas said. You think you're pretty tough. I wanted you on this job because I thought you could keep your cool. Maybe I was wrong.

They waited awhile longer, then stood up and walked again.

If you don't like the way I'm doing things, Keith said, you could have found someone else. Still can. Anytime. It's not like I need this.

Yes you do, Texas said. And remember, even if I didn't have the money I'd still have the gun. Tell you what, though—let's cut the bullshit. He reached out and clapped Keith on the back. We're friends, after all, aren't we?

Don't threaten me, Keith said.

It's just you're in on the secret now. It's not like I could let you out. Texas laughed. Know what I was thinking? One night you and me could hit one of these cathouses, these chicken ranches, you know.

What?

I know you're all set up and everything, but variety, man, that's all I'm saying.

I don't need those places, Keith said. Why would you think I'd want to go to those places? Think you know something?

Easy, easy there. Forget it. It's just, three or four different girls in a night—can you imagine?

No, I can't.

Exactly, Texas said. I'm sure you can't.

They came to the first field and kept walking, careful to stay on the hard edges around the border, not to leave any sign that they had been there. The syncopated sound of the sprinklers, the birdies on the irrigation line, started slowly and rose up as they walked closer. Keith smelled the water in the air; even at night it evaporated before it could do much good. There was not enough moonlight to show the purple in the alfalfa's flowers, not enough to give them away. A dog barked and they froze, waiting a full minute before they moved.

Keith took the radio, gave Texas the hammer and line, then helped him up onto the stilts. He stepped back and watched Texas start into the field, a slow step at a time, lifting the ends of the stilts high so they would not betray that anyone had been there.

Texas looked back once, swaying a little. Stay low, he hissed. The shadows.

When he knelt down he could smell the dirt, dark soil somehow mixed with the sand. It was clear to Keith by the way Texas moved that whatever he was doing it was not out of kindness. He tried not to think about, to wonder, what purpose all this could possibly serve. His job was only to watch for trouble—Texas did all the work, but he taught Keith how to do it so he would have a backup. Mostly Texas needed the car. And even though Keith was the lookout, he was never trusted with the gun.

Out in the field Texas climbed carefully down from the stilts and leaned them against his body. He took out the hammer, tied to the rope, and began swinging it around in a circle, letting it out, passing it smoothly behind his back, thirty feet out and then he brought it down low, circling clockwise, breaking the stalks of the alfalfa and bringing it all down flat and perfect. He was always trying longer lengths of rope, larger circles, overlapping them and making new formations.

Keith heard wings, above in the darkness. The kiss-kissing of the sprinklers, the sound of rain circling, retreating and returning, wound the muscles of his neck, the nerves, tighter and tighter. As he watched Texas climb back onto the stilts he tried to think of Charlotte; they had come out of Vegas together and he couldn't imagine anything stronger trying to pull them apart. He thought he heard someone whispering and then it was gone and there was only the water, the slight wind, the low whistle of the rope as Texas swung it again.

Charlotte came back just in time, the light on inside the cab so her head was illuminated and seemed disembodied, wearing a halo as it came down the highway. They loaded the car in silence. She moved over to let Keith drive, and then they were back on their way toward the ghost town.

I'm sorry, Texas said from the back seat. I been thinking on it—I feel bad about the way I acted when we first met, when you gave me a ride down to Vegas.

We didn't give you a ride, Keith said. You took it.

I felt bad about the way I acted to you, Texas said to Charlotte.

It didn't show, she said.

I mean I just hadn't spent that much time around women back then, he said.

And now you have? she said.

Is it some kind of hidden charm? Texas said. The kind you have? It's hard to see it sometimes.

After the turnoff, they hid the stilts in the culvert, then drove without the headlights, climbing through the darkness. They parked the car, brushed away its tracks with tumbleweeds, and did their best to disguise their own footprints. The night winds usually wiped the ground clean. In the dusk, two clothesline posts faced each other like sinister crosses; abandoned, disconnected, they weren't easy to recognize.

Texas tried to light the fire in the ruin of a square building that had no roof. The fool cursed the matches, rearranged the kindling, muttered about newspaper. Finally Charlotte took the matches from him. She leaned over the small flames and coaxed them on with her soft, hot breath. Rising, the fire reached for her, then reflected off the four walls; the windows were covered so the flames could not be seen from outside.

Those boots are shot, Charlotte said.

They're lucky, Texas said.

You like them because they make you taller, she said, but they must be impossible to walk in.

My father had a growth spurt when he was twenty-five. He shot up another four inches.

There's hope yet, Keith said, boiling water on the Coleman stove.

What kind of thing is that to say? Aren't we all friends here?

I'm here because you're paying me, Keith said.

Fuck you.

Tell me why we're here, Keith said. Why we're doing this.

That's part of the deal. No explanations.

We're a kind of friends, Charlotte said. That's what I would call it.

These people, Texas said. I could really give a flying fuck what other people think, but these people here have something on me, at least they think they do. Man, I don't want to talk about all this, I don't know how you got me started, except that I really do owe you, you know, I feel bad about how we met and everything. That's why I'm doing you this favor.

This isn't exactly a favor, Keith said. I've seen real favors before.

Texas just moved closer to where Charlotte was sitting, watching the fire.

You weren't scared back here, all alone?

Why? she said.

Not at all?

No.

Three circles, he said. Each bigger than the last.

Congratulations, she said.

When there's nothing to look at, you know, people just make things up. They make it up, not that there's not weird shit out there. I mean the nuclear testing, the herds of bald sheep. You think I always looked like this?

I don't know, she said.

I have. That was a joke. But out here you got the secret Air Force base, all those planes you can't even see, and that's why they got all these sightings now and everything. Who knows? Anything's possible, I guess. Texas reached to take the bowl Keith held out for him. You cut up the hot dogs and everything in here, he said. Perfect.

Could we have a little quiet now? Keith said. He sat down next to Charlotte.

Man, I don't want to be mixing up your thoughts, Texas said. I'll just concentrate on this food for a minute here.

Sparks climbed and disappeared, straight into cinders. Texas could not let the silence last.

What's after this? he said. We'll worry about that later. A guy like me finds the action wherever he is. Just a couple more weeks and, believe me, you'll be paid for every day.

I'm so tired of this, Keith said. You probably don't even have a brother in Stockton, you're such a liar.

A cousin.

Not even that.

He's half-Mexican, Texas said, but he's still my cousin. What's the matter with you? You want more money?

I want an explanation. Why are we doing this?

Sure you don't want more money?

Fuck the money.

Texas stood up and walked away. After a while he returned and added a few sticks of wood to the fire.

If you really want to know, he said, then you'll have to let me start from the beginning.

All right, said Keith. Begin, then.

It was the babies.

The babies? Charlotte said.

My mother's, Texas said. There were four of them, all in the space of six years. This was all before I was born. There was no reason they died. They just stopped breathing.

Crib death, said Charlotte.

Exactly. It started there, with the babies.

So what's the problem? Keith said. If no one knows what happened. Did someone think something different?

It was the new guy, the new D.A. in Lincoln County. He dug up the records a couple years ago. He's the one who thought it all up, who made everyone believe it. Texas turned his face away from the fire; his voice was uneven.

You're from that town down there, Charlotte said. Rachel. Aren't you? Your mother lives there.

So what was the matter with them, then? Keith said.

What? said Texas, turning back. It never went to trial, he said, she never confessed or anything, but a lot of people believed it.

Well, Keith said. It sounds like something was going on, somewhere. Can't blame them.

Texas threw some pebbles into the fire, then some others over his shoulder, rattling against the ruined walls. Charlotte stood and sat closer. She put her arm around him.

I can't believe this, Keith said. I mean of course I don't believe the story, but even more I can't believe that you could believe it, Charlotte. He's tricking you—that's all he ever does, I know it, tries to make you think things that aren't true.

Keith, she said, but it did not slow him. He went out through the blanket that hung over the door and she could not see or hear him anymore.

He's got more of a temper than I thought at first, Texas said.

It'll pass, she said.

That's not a thing my mother could ever do, he said, but my father believed it. He's the one who really lost it; he didn't stand behind her even when a bullet came right through the house.

The fire settled in on itself. Charlotte shifted her weight, about to stand, but Texas began talking again, to keep her there.

He told her everything that night, he opened himself up and showed her. It was simply because he had to tell someone, that there were reasons he'd done people wrong, broken laws, hoarded money—all this was for his mother. He needed Charlotte to understand this. And I know the crop circles were his way of settling with his father, who also lived in Rachel, with his mother, who had come to believe what people said about her. When you take on one conspiracy, others will be drawn to you, gather in your head and multiply, more and more far-fetched. The man's judgment on his wife spawned other beliefs—he came to speak of cattle found mutilated, as if they'd been used in scientific experiments; he tore sheetrock from the walls of his own house, searching for he knew not what; he hung maps and marked them with clusters of colored pins. Sightings. Yes, Texas wanted to play his father for a fool, that was all, to hear his mother's laughter, to help her forget.

Charlotte knew he was waiting for her to say something. She did not understand how far she'd been taken in, not yet, though she was right to believe. It followed all that had happened and was part of everything to come. Finally she stood and arched her back, stretching. When she reached to pat his shoulder he took hold of her hand, but it slipped away.

Don't get any ideas, he said. I don't have any interest in you at all, not like that. You're Keith's girl, for all I care.

The dress was dark red and it was
long. The lace at the hem would
drag through the desert unless
Charlotte wore high heels. Keith
had bought it for her and now, late
at night, it hung across the window, its silhouette both curtain and
ghost. The breeze brought it into
the room, then took it back out.
Lace came up into ruffles on the
front of the dress, it followed the
square of the collar, circled the
arms. The skirt hung in loose
pleats—they caught the breeze and
the moonlight, they folded shadows
away.

He had given her the dress because he wanted her to have it, he wanted to see her in it. Also because he believed she was unhappy; he thought perhaps she missed going to church. Stretching, he pulled the wool blanket sideways, then reached out to be sure she was still covered. She was a little surprised he'd brought up church again, but she knew he was trying to bring her back a little, that he worried about how she had changed and the direction she was headed. His bare leg touched hers, then pulled away. Too much had happened, and she knew better than to try to go backward; still, going to church did not have to be that way.

Even if I did want to go, she said, Texas wouldn't like it.

I don't care if he doesn't like it.

The day before, Keith had discovered that the rabbit was missing, that its pen was empty. He'd blamed Texas and Texas had denied it, told him he had bigger things to worry about.

The stupid thing could of given us away, he said, but just because I'm not soft like you doesn't mean I set the fucker loose. It's better off, anyway, more than likely.

Keith just stared into the empty pen. Well, he said, finally, I guess you're right about that.

Takes a big man, Texas said. Takes a big man to admit I'm right.

Charlotte listened to the mice on the floor, coming and going. Not even the bats bothered her now. One hit the dress and fell back out the window. When Keith first gave her the dress, that afternoon, she was so surprised that she didn't know how to react at first, what to say. Her fingers had trouble with the buttons when she went in to try it on. Keith just whistled when she spun back into the street, the skirt kicking out around her.

You like sissies, she said. I suspected it all along.

Nothing wrong, Texas had said, nothing wrong with wanting your woman to look like a woman. It was a risk, though; he was not happy that Keith had gone to Tonopah to buy it. It draws attention, he said. Men buying dresses. People wonder, you know. Stupid. We can't afford it, not now.

It was only days before that Texas had fallen off the stilts while practicing. He'd broken his arm and wouldn't go to the hospital for fear of giving himself away. He ate aspirin by the handful and still it hurt him. The battery ran out on his weather radio, also, which made things even worse. He asked Keith for the car keys and only let him keep them after Keith convinced him what good friends the two of them were. Texas said he would trust him a little while longer. He needed Keith now, more than before. Keith had done only one circle, but it had gone all right.

I don't like the way he watches you. Keith rolled over to face her through the darkness. When you're not looking.

It's nothing, she said.

He used to be scared to ask me a question and now he bosses me around. He thinks I care about his money and his gun. You know how he talks now, like the three of us are going to head out someplace after this. Together. God.

Texas had been asking a lot more questions. About their plans, where they were from, where they wanted to go. Mostly they made it all up; even if they knew the answers they would have kept them from him.

I think we'll be found out pretty soon, Keith said. I think people know we're here.

Not too much longer, she said. He said we're almost done.

It's different with us, Keith said, with him always around and everything, always needing our attention.

Outside she could hear the clicking of Texas's gun as he practiced. He was saving bullets and said they were too loud, anyway. He'd already shot all the old signs, shot the trough dry where they used to bathe. Finally it was quiet again and she listened to see if Keith was asleep.

God, Keith said. He gives me the creeps. Talking like me, dressing like me—it was you who cut his hair like that.

Take it as a compliment, she said. What's bothering you?

Nothing, he said.

I heard something, Charlotte said. There's someone outside.

He swung his legs sideways and sat on the edge of the cot, then took out the half-petrified ax handle they kept underneath. He stood and took a step to the door.

Either it's him or it's someone else, he said, and she lay alone in the room, listening as the dress whispered in the window. She thought of Texas, how lonely he must be and how sad, trying to make things right. She knew how it was to turn over the same thoughts again and again, how slow the world, how frustrating.

Nothing, Keith said, returning. No one. He did not sit down on the cot again or climb under the blankets. He stood still in the middle of the room. All right, he said.

What?

I'll tell you what it is. He rubbed his arms, shivering a little.

Get back under the blanket, she said. It's cold.

I saw, he said. I saw my father. I took your binoculars to be sure and it was him.

What does he want?

I don't care what he wants, Keith said. Maybe he read about the circles, maybe he just figured out where I was. He always does. It's a miracle he didn't find us in Vegas.

What if he had?

I'm just tired of it.

Did he walk all the way down here?

I don't know. I doubt it. Keith tossed the ax handle under the cot and the clatter made Charlotte jump. Slowly, he lay down again.

Thank you for the dress, she said.

Keith had stood for a long time, watching his father that afternoon. Johnson disappeared in the heat, then emerged again; he was out on the edges of the alfalfa fields, pacing slowly with the wire hanger in his hand, the dowsing rod, wearing the highway reflectors over his eyes to shield them from the sun. It was strange for Keith to see Johnson out there with the circles, unsettling to be part of something that could trick him.

These boys are haunted by their fathers, that's clear; I've watched it all and I like to think I've stood in for them, been sensitive to what they needed. Yes, I've helped them grow. I've helped them on their way.

Charlotte did not know what they had to fear from Johnson, though those we don't know are rarely so dangerous as those we do. She did know that the space was collapsing around the ghost town, that she felt she was being watched and it wasn't just Texas. The morning before, cows and calves had wandered through the ruins, waking them all, frightening them. Texas, half-asleep, took a shot at a calf—they were fortunate he had missed.

I thought we were all done for, he'd said.

Charlotte thought she saw someone at the window, behind the dress, but she didn't want to be wrong again.

Do you think we should have done something some other way? Keith said.

She did not answer. She'd thought he was asleep.

I know where he keeps the money, he said. I think we should take it and go.

Leave him here?

We'd leave him something.

It's not fair to him, Charlotte said. He said we're almost done. He needs you now, with his arm and everything.

The dress swung a little in the breeze, letting in just enough moonlight to show the painting on the wall, the people flying above the horizon. The dress came down and they were gone again.

He did say we're almost done, she said.

Your sympathy is too much, Keith said. I'm not waiting on that fool.

When we do go, she said, I choose this time.

You'll want to go back to Vegas. I can't do that.

You could, she said.

I can't leave here without you, I know that. I love you. That's all that matters.

It matters, she said, but it's not all that matters.

It's the main thing.

Maybe I will go to church, she said. There's a wardhouse in Ash Springs, I think.

If it'll make you happy.

His hand brushed against her leg, under the covers, and she pulled away.

I'm not dumb enough to try anything, he said. You know that.

Did you hear someone call my name? she said.

No.

I'm dreaming. She watched the dress turn slightly in the window and she imagined the entrance she'd make if she went to church. She could tell how it fit her by the expressions on Keith's and Texas's faces when she tried it on. She wanted to wear a dress like that in heaven, red, with sandals on her feet, ribbons in her hair.

She managed to sit up without waking Keith. She waited, but he did not stir. Slowly, silently, she made her way outside. Bats sliced around her and she went on, trailing one hand along the old stone walls. She stood in the doorway of the building where Texas slept until she heard his breathing, saw the dark shape of his body on the floor.

She took a step inside and his arm shot out, swinging something at her. She leapt back, just out of his reach.

It's me, she said.

What the hell?

She stepped closer, kneeling next to where he'd been sleeping. All she wanted was to say she'd been thinking of him, of his mother, that she understood, that she wanted things to turn out right. That she knew he was lonely. She tried to kiss his cheek and in the darkness he turned and gave her his lips. He took hold of her wrist, tightly, and she touched his neck to let him know, to calm him. At first she tried to hold him, like a boy, like a little brother, she thought that would help, and then she felt his hands inside her shirt, along her spine.

His fingers were nervous, they trembled and fought themselves around her buttons. He whispered her name but it did not come out right. He pulled her clothes away until she had none left and her skin was everywhere, scratched by the burrs in the wool blanket, under his hands, pressed beneath the rivets of his clothing. He was more afraid than she was, he was uncertain, trembling. She felt the weight of his ribs, their cage, every bone coming down on her; she could feel nothing but sorry for him, a tenderness turned inside out.

When it was over, she stared across the dirt floor, squinting at the shapes her clothes made against the far wall. She was surprised that she was not sorry it had happened.

It was all right, Texas said. Didn't you think it was all right?

Fine, she said. She knew he believed this was what she'd been doing with Keith all along. It was all right, she said, but it won't ever happen again.

I know that, he said, but you don't have to ruin everything by saying it right away like that.

The rain could be smelled, all
the night before, though it never
reached the ground, and the thunder came like a voice that needed
no lightning. Charlotte woke early.
The sunlight shone in through the
square of the window.

Keith slept in rasping, uneven
breaths with his face pressed
into the metal edge of the cot; the
nerves at his temples jerked
through a dream. She took one corner of the blanket and worked it
under his head, then, slowly, she
stood and took her pants from their

hook, her shoes in her other hand; she went to the doorway and stood in the slant of sunlight, trying to take some of its warmth. She felt it coming on—her movements followed no choices but arose out of themselves.

In the shadows of the ghost town a mist still lingered, evaporating where the sun caught it, elsewhere settling along broken rooftops, sliding out of doors and windows. There was no sound. She turned quickly and still no one was there. Stepping along the wall, she wondered what had happened to all the birds, where the lizards were hiding this morning. The window was empty, and her hand traced the empty space which had once held glass. She looked inside and Keith was sleeping just as she'd left him.

Turning away, she walked down what was left of the street. She looked in through windows, she went into buildings, past piles of broken glass and twisted wire, tin cans, the sole of a shoe. There were can openers everywhere, blunt and rusted, as if to lack one would mean starvation; there were ten for every ghost left behind. The only remnants of furniture were those that would not burn—metal cabinets, the abandoned bases of kerosene lanterns.

When she got to the building where Texas slept, she took off her shoes, then stepped inside. He was asleep, along one wall, and she went carefully past him, into the two small back rooms, making sure he had not hid it from her. She heard the wings of one bird outside, along the wall, and then they were gone. Back in the front room, she watched Texas sleeping. She leaned down, then knelt even closer. He was sleeping so quietly that she suspected he was faking it.

Tex, she said, whispering, but still he did not open his eyes. She wanted to see under the blanket; she lifted one edge, one corner. She half-expected to find him sleeping with the dress, just holding it tight against him. It was not here, and she knew something was wrong, or at least unexpected, which meant it could be right. She stood and went back outside.

She wandered in and out of the buildings, climbed down

into sunken foundations and fruit cellars, kicked through trash and bones and weeds. A shutter fell from a window when she brushed against it. She stood still, waiting for the sound to settle. Nothing followed.

One building was different than the others, lower and longer, a kind of stable. For mules, she imagined—it was usually mules when people were mining. Texas said it was silver, though hard to get at and never very much. She lifted the door to one side, it was only leaning there, and stepped into the darkness. She could just make out the pieces of stalls, most of the wood broken out to feed the fires of a different time.

Inside there was only one shadow that was moving, and by that movement she knew her search was over. Most anything the wind could move it had blown down by now, persistent, it would blow everything away if given the time, wear it all down. She looked for the light, the source of the shadows. The dress was hanging high up in one corner, underneath a hole in the roof and glowing in the light that funneled through. The red twisted like flames and the fabric folded and slid across itself, levitating.

Charlotte jumped, but she could not reach it. Finally she found a half-rusted washtub to stand on. She pulled the dress down and, coughing in the dust kicked up, she held it tightly against her as she made her way back outside.

Something in the night had changed the dress. She laid it down, then held it close again. The quiet closed in on her, it tightened down. Her eyes would not be still, they were searching for what was missing, the pieces of fabric that had been cut away, the red loop cut straight from the hem, circles from the arms. Yet all the lace was still there, it was just that everything was smaller, even the zipper had been cut down or shrunk somehow, the waist invisibly gathered so now the dress could only be worn by a girl of four or five.

Charlotte went into the stable again, holding the dress tightly, as if someone might try to snatch it from her. It was so hard to read this, and she could find no footprints in the thick dust except her own. There was no note or message, no letters scratched into the rough walls. She knelt down under where the dress had hung, in a patch of light on the floor, and all there was was the straight line left by a lizard's tail. Above, the pale sky wheeled past, across the ragged hole, the roof bowed and the shingles like paper. She wondered who could have lowered the dress from above, who was light enough to stand on those shingles without crashing through, without landing where she now stood.

Yes, I would like to claim the dress; no, I cannot claim it.

Outside, she smelled salt, though not the spray of the ocean. She turned and looked at the fragile slope of the roof, then she lay down flat on her back, spreading the fabric along her body, staring into the sky. At last it had come to her, another one, though not one she could understand. Not yet. The earth was restless beneath her. She had not seen a bird all morning and suddenly, all at once, they flocked past, all kinds mixed together. She turned her head sideways and saw a cluster of jackrabbits flash by. A cloud shot past. She closed her eyes tight and listened, praying for more. When she opened her eyes, Keith was there.

I was afraid you were gone, he said.

Here I am.

What is it? he said.

She handed him the dress and he did not notice the change. He turned it all around. She lay flat, watching him.

Strange weather, he said, looking away, scratching his teeth with a fingernail.

It's the exact same dress, she said. It feels the same, it even smells the same, it's in the same proportions.

It is, he said.

It's a sign, said Charlotte.

What?

It's smaller, she said. It's a girl's dress now.

He held it up again and looked at it, then looked at her, the size of her body. He swung it closer.

Yesterday, she said. You remember how it fit me.

I'll get you another one. It was a mistake, some kind of switch or something.

It was more than that.

He took her by the shoulders and pulled her up so she was sitting. It was then she felt how the wind had changed. She lifted the dress and when they looked past it they saw what was happening with the sky. One side was dark and moving closer; they could not see through it. Sand and dust started coming on the wind, everything thickening.

Hurry, Keith said, and she followed, crawling toward the shelter of a solitary stone wall. The last twenty feet before they reached it, everything was sliding sideways. The earth itself was trembling, reeling. Charlotte crawled with her arm through the dress, ripping the fabric a little, so she would not lose it, so it would not be pulled away. The sand stung her arms and legs, sharp like glass and everywhere at once, only slowed by her body and then continuing onward.

There was one empty window above them, the rest of the foundation poking up here and there. Charlotte looked through it and saw tumbleweeds twenty feet in the air, never touching down. She could withstand this. She welcomed it. Rubbing her eyes, she sat back down next to Keith, their backs against the wall. They did not have long to wait.

She wondered how high the sand and dust could reach, how wide; it was impossible to believe it could end, that its edges could be imagined. A hawk or eagle could be caught inside, tumbling blind, uncertain which way was up. All the elements were in commotion, and she knew that was a sign of the coming end and also of renewal. Next to her, a lizard sought shelter, pressing itself hard against where the wall met the ground, digging with its front claws. Three rattlesnakes twisted close by, intertwined, searching for a seam, any niche of refuge. In the last days all enmity between animals would cease and all people would agree and get along. She held tightly onto Keith.

Her eyes were closed, her face buried in the dress. She had seen how things could be set up, how people could fake a miracle like the crop circles, but she did not understand who stood to gain by the dress. She had hoped to wear it to church and now it would not fit her and perhaps it meant that she herself was somehow unfit. Even if some person had set all these things up, would that make them any less of a sign, less of a miracle? What would compel someone to do these things if not some kind of possession?

She prayed and she listened for her thoughts, for the answers. She opened her eyes and saw dust and sand coming in solid squares through windows, then shattering and circling, wheeling the walls, searching for cracks to escape again. Nothing on earth wanted to stop moving; it wanted to outspin all that supported it.

Yet she was not sorry when the sand began to thin. She was not afraid to see the end, but she knew there was still work to do, and she knew sometimes little storms will come first, as if checking the area for what's rolling in behind them. When she stood up, the sun looked like it had spent itself, just visible through the dust and sand. Somewhere she could hear what sounded like Texas crying. Things slowly settled and a quiet came down, the dust and sand in drifts along walls, dampening all sound.

She was still holding the dress, full of grit. They found that the faces of their watches had been sandblasted, so cloudy the hands could not be seen. They came upon Texas shaking sand from his radio, cursing, holding the plastic case against his ear.

III. THE TERRESTRIAL KINGDOM

Believe me, we are living in a
world where people murder dogs,
where they risk everything in the
hope of getting more, where they
find joy in hurting each other, in
settling scores. Wings cannot save
you from it, but I have no fear, I
have no lack of pride, I know the
inside of love.

I stood in the shadow of Wendover Will, the neon giant, man of
metal. This is the place, he always
says. He creaks like the tin man; he
has no heart. During the day he
looks a little weary, all his un-

lighted tubes, faded paint, wires hanging here and there. I whispered her name to him, I scratched it into the sand in his shadow, casting pathetic spells. Leaning, I looked up at the metal tassels on his holster, the huge, stiff bandana around his neck, the gigantic hat tipped back. I whispered low to him so no one else would hear. I dream he will pull himself loose and crush everything in our way.

The sun bakes the earth, dries it out, turns it all to tinder. It won't ever rain. I had a gallon jug of water in my hand, faintly tasting sour milk every time I took a drink. Will has no answer for the sun, his metal body holds the heat, the machines of his organs grind and choke. His voice is the sound of his one arm moving, the heat that emanates from his body, the promise he signifies. This is the place, you'll want no other—yet every satisfaction harbors its itches, every beginning carries its end. I was there, I am here; I have all the words for you. I am laying them down only to bring you closer.

All the time I was talking I did not miss a thing, I took it all in. I stood watching the people in the hot glass walkway that connects the Stateline to the Silver Smith, the casino across the street. The people looked across at Will, down at the cars passing beneath them. Lowriders cruised between the five or six casinos, turned and passed again with their dark, tinted windows. The cars stopped only to check with the boys—my boys, grown six inches in the time I was gone, who once hung on my words and now pretend not to know me—or the young Indians who gather around the public phones across the street from where I was standing. I live like this. Fools abound.

I could smell the salt and sage, though there was no breeze. Up on the ridge I saw a silhouette, the figure of a horse, and then it was gone. Yes, one of Anita's horses finally got loose; it hangs around the edges of town, acting like no one can catch it, daring and taunting, when the fact is no one wants to catch it. The police warned her they'd shoot it, but she doesn't care. Every now and then it will take a run through the center of town.

A man walked toward me and I recognized him, I sized him up. A local, a family man, from the Utah side of the border.

You, I said. You're the owner of Taco Burger.

How did you know?

Picked up a Book of Mormon there, I said. Photo of your family pasted in the front. Pretty little girls.

Thank you, he said, stepping into Will's shadow. Did you read it? People do take them, but I always wonder.

Yes, I said. Very interesting.

Didn't get your name.

I don't go out much in the daylight, I said. I work in the casino.

Did you get to the end?

What?

Of the book.

Not yet.

Well, he said. See that you do. There's a surprise for you at the end.

He turned and I watched him go, walking like a man with many children, who had provided tabernacles for plenty of souls and was not through yet. I'd read every last word, of course, searching for clues, hoping for leverage on Charlotte, but that man did not need to know. At the end you are asked to look into your heart, to ask if these things are true. They count on people surprising themselves, being disconcerted, but I know my heart well. Where else could I go, where would I find myself?

I let the devil pass by and I caught my breath, I checked my watch; my break was over. As I found my balance I crossed Will's shadow and the sun went straight through me.

The casino's door swung open and the air conditioning took me in. I passed the Cadillac, shining, surrounded by its velvet ropes. Mike the bartender snapped a rag in my direction. In a mirror I saw one of the restaurant's waitresses close behind me, mimicking the way I walk. All the other girls were laughing. I let it go, I feel no ill will, I carry the knowledge that I could give them what their husbands, what their boyfriends cannot. After my return from Vegas, from the desert, the heart of Nevada, I understood again how a town like Wendover cannot hurt me, how I can overpower anything that might challenge me here.

I moved through the slot machines, the lights and bells, the cold cigarette smoke. I unlocked my chips and brought them out, brushed the green felt of my table. People lose their money faster in the heat, when it's hot outside. Don't ask me why. They gamble recklessly, as if they want to get it over with so they can go take their chances with the sun. I tore the cellophane from a new deck of cards, then fanned and shuffled them before my new victims. No, I do not know arthritis. I take these fools over twenty-one before they know what's happened; they're already busted and they want another card. They don't realize how cruelly I could cheat them, how many years it takes to learn the sense of movements under these lights.

Between hands, I noticed Anita sitting at the bar, watching me. I'd seen her a few times since my return and more often than not she was alone, trying to rekindle something that never burned that well. I will not believe she and Charlotte share blood; Anita must have married into the family. I pray that's true.

Anita crossed the casino. She stood behind me, waiting. Every time I see her now I am stricken—I often look back and cannot believe where I've been. Redeem me.

One minute, I told my players. I turned to her.

I'm lonely, she said.

Don't, I said. No one will ever learn that loneliness is not an appeal that works on me; my own overshadows all, I can summon no empathy.

All he does is talk and talk, she said. You know what I mean. I could wait for you down at your trailer.

I'm an old man, I said. My players were beginning to stack

their chips, considering moving to another table. One look in their direction quieted them down.

He wants to see you, she was saying. Johnson. I don't know why.

I'm working, I said.

He's boring, she said, taking hold of my arm. He repeats himself all the time now. You never did that.

Yes, I said. You don't remember. You never could.

I dealt a new hand. When dogs are through mating they're still stuck together for a time; they turn in opposite directions and look away, a little ashamed. That's how it was with her and Johnson. The best thing is to ignore it, not to stare.

You would not believe the money I made for the Stateline in that short time. Take my word. At the next break I had a couple hours. I knew I should eat something but had the feeling I wouldn't be able to keep it down. I unclipped my bow tie to get some air. A boy stood just outside the door. I suspect them of whoring now, like the pretty boys in Vegas.

Working all night? he said. I have something that'll keep you up.

I take something for that, I said. Coffee.

It was seven at night and the temperature still hadn't returned to double digits. It was as bright as noon. The boys still stood across the street, everyone right where I'd left them. Yes. When I say Charlotte felt things coming on I know of what I speak. I know what it is to anticipate, believe me. I crossed Will's shadow. I looked up and I saw her.

She was filling the tank of that sad little hot rod. I walked to within twenty feet of her. I just stood there without saying a word. I smelled the gas from the pumps, saw where it joined with the sun to bend the air. I was close enough to see the freckles across the bridge of her nose. Engines popped in the heat, still burning oil, unable to cool down. I did not know what to say. My heart had my tongue. I wanted to take hold of her right there.

She only half-looked at me; in my direction, not in my eyes. It wasn't that she ignored me, it was worse—a faint acknowledgment, as if she did not even hold any spite or much thought for me at all, as if we were standing farther away than we actually were, a greater distance. Keith came around the car with a jug of water in one hand, a bag of pretzels in the other. I knew it was him only because he was with her; I would not have remembered his face. He turned his head back and forth, the fear of being followed, and still he did not see me. I knew if I could just get Charlotte to look at me, to look me in the eyes like she had before, that I could let her know where to go, where I would follow and find her.

The whole night before they had been sneaking around the ghost town, packing what few things they had into the car. They did not even whisper; they stayed low under the bats, they waited silently for clouds to uncover the moon. They had taken off before sunrise, the headlights on high beam, sand kicking out behind. Sagebrush rasped under the car, the tires spun and caught again, pots and pans jumped around the back seat.

Texas was awake as soon as the car started. He had run out after them, shouting and waving his gun, then he took off in another direction, across the desert, hoping to cut them off where the road doubled back.

He'll fall down a mineshaft, Keith said. Or shoot himself in the foot.

Drive, she said.

They turned and angled back and Texas was there, in the middle of the road, holding the gun straight out and level. They veered off into the sage, they went around him. He did not fire. Charlotte looked back and saw him trying to run through the dust and sand they kicked up. He fired five times, straight up in the air.

The car jumped a little, then settled on the highway. They did not talk. They passed Rachel, full of trailers, Texas's parents, all the believers. Smoke rose from the hood after a couple miles and Keith pulled over, climbed out swearing. He popped the hood, then threw a mouse nest, all on fire, onto the highway. The mother mouse bolted into the desert, smoking, and Keith kicked the nest apart before he slammed the hood down.

Charlotte decided, as they had agreed, and she surprised him by pointing north, not south toward Vegas. Still, they did not dare an entirely new path; they went up through Ely, over the pass, across the wastelands. She had not let him take the money. They had enough to get by for a while—after all, Texas had been paying them, he had covered all the expenses.

The sun turned hotter, catching in the windshield where it had been pitted by the sandstorm. As they got farther away, Keith began to smile. He sang along with the radio, singing like he had Charlotte to himself again.

You don't actually feel bad about this, do you? he said. You feel sorry for him, don't you? Texas. He laughed at the name.

Shut up, she said.

They went on, the radio losing its channel, the highway empty. Clouds cast shadows miles across, settling and shifting along the floor of the desert.

Antelope, he said. At least you could look.

They had only stopped in Wendover because they were out of gas. They had never planned to stay here. As they pulled away again, under the cowboy clown, all the pawnshops, the cheap motels, they saw me standing there, watching them go.

I can't believe I stood still. It was patience, a show of will, the right thing to do at that time. I wanted to throw myself under the wheels of the car, force them to acknowledge me. I knew there would be time. As if Charlotte could avoid returning to me, as if she really ran untethered.

There is a joy in moving this old body around; no one else knows it, no one touches my skin. I crossed away from the casinos, under the overpass, planning and plotting, not paying attention to where I was going.

In the yard at Anita's house a few stakes remained, bent; there was no wire in sight. The dogs slid out of the shadows to whine and circle my legs. The horses watched me with their ears pulled back, one side of their corral all rebuilt. Anita appeared, intercepted me before I reached the house. She reached out, trying to get her hand in my pocket.

It's that cast on his leg, she said. Plaster burns. It's like wrestling with someone who's wearing a sandpaper suit.

Any snakes? I said, looking out over the yard.

I wish, she said.

The horses seemed to be looking past, behind me, but I did not turn around. I held Anita's hands to keep them away.

It's him I came to see, I said.

It was dark in the house. I thought Johnson was asleep, but when he reached for the rifle I stepped back, looking for cover. He used it to pull himself upright, then, as a cane; he shook my hand without saying a word and sat back down. His cast ran all the way from his thigh to his ankle. He'd been sleeping outside when the horse had escaped. It would have trampled him to death if he hadn't rolled under the truck. Now he stayed inside, watching the windows, the rifle always within reach. His hair was tangled, his jumpsuit full of wrinkles, his toes filthy where they stuck out of the cast.

You going to shoot me? I said.

He coughed. I can't stand being in here with these cats, he said. I've got a fucking hairball myself. When I was a boy my mother gave me a litter of seven kittens to drown.

Some mother, Anita said.

Only I didn't drown them. I killed each one a different way.

I could smell Johnson from where I was standing. I'm not above getting a kick out of someone else's discomfort. I took it all in and both he and Anita seemed older to me, stooped, little humps rising between their shoulderblades. Look at me here—I stand up straight, I stand erect.

How pathetic you turned out to be, I said. Doesn't seem so long ago you came strutting into this town full of threats for me.

I never threatened you, he said.

All the animals stayed out of his reach. Some were half-shaved, fur growing back in patches after Anita's attempts to save them from the heat. Johnson scratched at his scalp. He watched the windows. On the wall behind him was a poster of a gorilla holding a kitten.

That horse, he said. You hear it kicked apart a telephone booth, destroyed someone's car?

Why did you want to see me? I said.

Is that what she told you? Well I guess I just wanted to see how you're doing.

You're looking at it, I said.

I used to think I knew what you wanted, but now I'm not so certain. You're deeper than I gave you credit for.

I appreciate it, I said, but I still think you're a fool.

We're not going to trade compliments, I take it.

You killed my dog.

I was out of town, he said, hardly listening. Not so long ago. Didn't miss you; wasn't here myself. See your son?

You worried about his little girlfriend? he said.

What? I said.

Well, I don't know where they've been, to be honest, but I'll find that son of a bitch once I get mended a little. Did I tell you where I was? Down around Rachel. He said that was where he was, that there was something going on down there with the crop circles, but he wasn't sure it was energy from the earth.

What else could it be? I said.

What was strange was everyone assumed those things were coming from above, he said, not below, which is the obvious thing to me.

I saw how his words had lost their power over Anita. She stood behind him, yawning. A cat came out from under the couch, a lizard's tail dangling from its mouth. Johnson kicked at it with his good leg.

What I did find, he said, was a real deep vein of uranium. I could feel it down there. Did I tell you they charged me with trespassing? It was me told them the circles were similar to old tapestries, ancient mosaics, and from that they decided I'd go to the trouble to set them up. Imagine. Man, I've had it, I'm withering away, out of touch with the ground. Can't sleep outside unless Anita stands over me with the gun.

You can feel the energy from the earth, I said. So you say.

You know it, he said. Through the soles of my feet. Whole body, if I'm lying out flat.

I heard of a woman, I said, who claimed her organs were made of copper. Said so her whole life and when she died they cut her open and her heart and lungs and everything were just like everyone else's.

So? Johnson said.

So talk is cheap, I said, and it's so easy to be full of it.

Yes, I realize it's a federal offense. On my breaks I would go out and usually the boys just shook their heads—they had nothing for me. The casino security guards had started chasing them off; when I tried talking them down they said the boys made the patrons nervous, that I knew very well they didn't make the policy. Rarely, the boys would have a letter for me and I hurried it into my pocket, dealt for hours in a dream, with the weight of the envelope against my thigh. I did not tear it open until I was safely back in my trailer.

Anita told me about it. She could not understand why her mail was being stolen, why it was eventually returned. They took it all and I gave them back what I didn't need. I believe they returned it; I paid them well. Anita said she hadn't missed anything. She said it wasn't like she got checks in the mail.

Charlotte's handwriting was turning harder, away from its girlish loops. Once I had her address I still did not go after her. I waited, reading to see what I could find out, what purchase I might need. It was delicate, not subtle, what I had to do, and I was hoping not to put myself at risk—not that I wouldn't do whatever was necessary.

Yes, I knew where Charlotte was before he ever came through the door of the Stateline, before he ever found me. It was late, early, after midnight, and I had an envelope in my pocket, unread words from Charlotte, words she'd strung together only days before. It seems we've come so far and all I want is to be clear, to be plain. Believe me, I wouldn't take you all this way for a tragedy. She had held that letter in her hands, licked the envelope with her tongue.

That night I had a terrible headache. They'd brought in a fifties band and all they knew were surfing songs. All the gamblers were pushing walkers, wearing hearing aids. The few people playing blackjack had tried me and preferred their chances with the other dealers. I'm always asked to train the new dealers and I always say there's only so much that can be taught. I say you have to let the fools believe they can win, help them to believe it.

My eyes were turned inward, what with the headache, the surf songs, the letter in my pocket; he'd sat down at my table before I saw him coming. When he took off his straw cowboy hat his hair was all flattened in the shape of its crown.

You old enough to gamble? I said.

Get serious.

When I take your money I'll keep it, I said.

He read my name off the tag, then told me his was Sloan.

Got better ways to make money, he said, just feel a little lucky tonight.

Desperate? I said. He didn't answer. Small talk can soften a player, that I've learned. As I shuffled I asked him where he was from.

I'm on the move, he said, always on the move.

A man after my own heart.

You move around a lot?

Not physically, I said. Watch out now—I never give up the big score.

So I guess this is where I'm from, he said. Right now.

I expected him to play recklessly, but he did not; he didn't bet much, he didn't lose much. He stared at the money on the table as I swept it away, the chips I gathered in. I let him have a small hand, to pass the time, and then another player joined the game and Sloan was quiet. It was a woman I'd dealt to before, a suspicious player, a card-counter, nothing to fear. There was a jackpot somewhere, the clatter of coins at a slot machine, fools rushing past, in that direction. I won three straight hands and the woman left us alone again.

Want to double down? I said.

Nothing doing, said Sloan. You think I'm stupid? Nothing doing.

We'll see, I said.

Listen. He moved a little closer. If you let me win a few big hands, you know, we could split the difference later.

There are microphones in here, I said. Cameras.

I didn't know, he said, looking around.

I'm just kidding.

We could do it.

I wasn't really kidding, I said. I let him win another hand, watching him closely, all his movements, wondering if he would do.

I'm trying to get some things going here in town, he said. Out on the street, you know.

What makes you think I'm in need of money? I said. That I want more than I already have? I've got plenty, and I'm old. More than I'll ever spend.

So do I, he said. Not on me. He stood up. Not quite as lucky as I thought tonight.

Funny how that works, I said.

All through the rest of my shift he was sitting at the bar, looking over his shoulder at me, scribbling on napkins and shoving them in his pocket, going outside and then returning. When I got off, he tried to buy me a drink and I just walked by. I took a double and kept walking, telling Mike I'd return the glass on my next shift.

Right, he said.

The boys didn't even notice me as I walked past. Gallons of coffee spun through my body, tightening the corners and curves. The sun was long gone, though its heat remained and its rise was only an hour away. At the Silver Smith, a Kenny Rogers impersonator was playing three shows a night. Jets took off and landed out on the airstrip, following the path of the Enola Gay. With every step I felt the weight of the envelope against my thigh, the words carrying Charlotte's voice.

Even in the summer it can get so slow during the week that as I walk home the police will follow me and I'll turn, light a match or piss in the gutter, shuffle off like I'm up to something exciting and forbidden. That night I looked back and there was not even the police. I finished my drink, then went down the slope to the trailer park. My neighbor watched me pass from behind his window; only his eyes moved. The hum and clank of air conditioners surrounded me as I checked my car, under my trailer, around the other side. There was no one there.

Inside, I was also alone. Things had not exactly returned to normal in my trailer, though the heat did slow them down. I held my hands under hot water, covered them in lotion and then put on the rubber gloves before I allowed myself to get out the letter. I can tell you that the back of the cupboard is false, that there is a space there, where I hide the other letters, the photograph, the hawk's feather that was once tangled in Charlotte's hair. I read through the other letters first. Some are from Las Vegas, all the way back; these I found soon after Anita mentioned them, sneaking into her house while Johnson slept on the couch. All the animals conspired with me, silent so as not to wake him.

Once I saw what it might hold, I paid the boys to rob Anita's mailbox. Charlotte wrote to her because Anita was the only member of her family she was still in contact with. The relation did not seem enough to justify the correspondence.

The letter had no curlicues or smiley-faces—it was all business. I read a sentence, looked at the photograph, then read the next. Yes, I knew there was another reason that she wrote; finally she had asked about me, wondering if Anita had seen much of me. I had her now. She'd been thinking of me all along.

Trembling, I took the letters, the photograph, the feather, with me as I climbed into my slanted bed. I lay with the sheet of paper over my face in the darkness, and I wish I could tell it better, be plainer, show myself. Should I say that I grew up far away from here? That when I was a baby I had an uncle who carried me through a barnyard and introduced me to all the animals? What good can that do me now? How would it help you to know it?

I was dreaming of horses running inside houses, kicking furniture apart, chasing me down hallways, up stairs, smashing china and tearing curtains in their teeth. Their hooves made the furniture jump, their haunches broke windows and cracked the glass of pictures hung in narrow hallways, frames knocked from walls. I escaped up a ladder, into an attic, and there in the darkness someone took hold of me; as we wrestled I heard the horse below, its hooves on the walls, trying to reach me. I could not turn the person over, could not see the face. Just before I awakened I felt the wings, hooking out behind the shoulders.

Shadows fluttered on the ceiling, the walls of my trailer—

wings, the wings of birds outside. In the silence, as the dream turned over, I heard my car door slam shut. I could not stand right away, I had to wait for the blood to return to my feet. When I heard the knock on my door I lurched up, caught my balance on the counter, then hid Charlotte's letters, the photograph.

I opened the door and Sloan was standing there. I pulled off my gloves, turning them inside out, before I spoke. I never neglect to show hospitality to strangers, for some have entertained angels unawares.

How did you find me?

Followed you last night.

Pretty good, I said. Slept in my car?

Yes. Can I come in?

No. I blocked his way. I stepped outside. It was almost noon; there was not a shadow in the world.

All right, he said. You can be whatever way you want, you know. What it is is I got a proposition for you.

Another one?

This one's different. I just need a little money, and then I'll pay you back double. You said you're rich.

I said I had more than enough for my needs. None of it's here. Why would I trust you?

Here's the deal, he said, nervous. He told me he'd been down south a ways, working some kind of scam, bankrolling it. Two people were working for him; he said their names, but I already knew, I had suspected from the beginning.

Take your money? I said.

This isn't about that. They left before we were done, you know. Bailed out.

Sounds like you have a legitimate complaint, I said.

You can't never let someone think they got something over you, he said. I lost my money some other ways; I promise you'll get yours back, though, and then some—there'll be plenty of green to spread around.

You can keep your voice down, I said. I don't care about the money.

They left me to do it alone, he said. Man, I had no lookout and sure enough they set the dogs on me. The fucking dogs.

He took off his jacket and showed me the scars and stitches along his arms. The whole time I was watching him, listening, I was wondering how he could be of use, if he was the tool I needed.

Shot the first one, he was saying, but then a whole pack of those fuckers took me down.

What makes you think I'll back you? I said.

It wouldn't take much, he said. Not much at all.

But you believe I'll give it to you.

Not really, he said.

One thing, I said, is I'd have to trust you. You'd have to cut this business with the phony name, for starters.

I go by Texas, he said. People call me that.

Sure they do.

They do.

That's what I'll call you, then, Texas.

What?

That's what I'll call you, I said.

I shook the poor fool's hand, knowing that he expected he'd be searching alone—as if money could come without strings and complications. It almost hurt me to bring him in that way, not to give him a chance.

There were already gangs involved, of course, who decided what came and went in Wendover. I doubt they even took Texas that seriously, but he believed they did. They told him they wanted to talk, that they wanted to make a deal, that there were things he could teach them. Then they took him to a house and beat him, tied him down, burned him with their cigarettes. No doubt it was half in fun.

I'm only dealing with friends from here on out, he said.

You and I, I said. We're not friends.

But I can trust you.

Whatever.

Those guys, he said, if those guys really wanted to talk, they could of learned something from me, you know, if they weren't so far up themselves. I could get that town under control in less than a week, but why? Like I'd go back there — four days and I had my fill. Can't even believe people live there.

Careful, I said. Don't forget who you're talking to.

Can't we go any faster?

All the windows were open — it was hot, turbulent, inside the car. Dry. Outside, the flats, smoothed by the wind, were probably going soft now, losing their crust. White, they outran us on every side, spreading to surround us. Texas hadn't slept all night and he winced every time he moved, with every bump. He reached to touch the feather hanging from the mirror. I slapped his hand away.

I was talking about how the two states, Utah and Nevada, need each other, how they lean, and he was paying no attention at all, just looking out the window, picking at the whiskers on his neck and flicking them against the dashboard when he got one.

But I can trust you, he said to me.

This whole time we were moving east, he and I, toward the promised land. As if it was a coincidence that we were there, as if we're supposed to be surprised when two people meet each other. No, that's not shocking to me.

The knees of his pants were worn shiny. His coat hung carefully above the back window, his shirt inside; he'd taken it off so he wouldn't sweat on it, he said. When he stretched, his hairless chest bent outward and his ribs were like wings trapped inside his skin. There was a welt along one cheek, from the night before, round burns all up and down his arms, and still the toothed scars from the dogs, stitches crossing each other, loose ends frayed, the thread all that held him together.

Watching him, I knew if I played it right I could get him to do exactly what I wanted.

Let's not even talk about trust, I said. We share an objective. That's enough for now.

And you don't care about the money.

Just for kicks, I said. That's right.

You're crazy.

Maybe, but compared to what? You might be able to use it to help you.

What? he said.

Watch and learn, I said. I'll move real slow.

He pulled a gun from somewhere and spun it around like he'd spent some time practicing in front of a mirror.

Easy, I said.

Scare you, rich man?

No, I said. Listen, you fool. I have my reasons for doing this, don't doubt it. I have to keep my heart going.

My car threatened to overheat, the flats multiplied the sun, there was not a living thing in sight.

They told me they were going to Idaho, Texas said.

I'd believed we were done with that argument, but apparently we weren't.

Now why, I said, would they do that?

They're from there.

That's what they told you, I said, but I doubt it very much. Let's just say I have a feeling.

You never even met them.

You can trust me, I said. Or you can walk. I slowed down, steering the car onto the shoulder of the highway.

Now you're talking about trust, he said.

I laughed, accelerated back into the lane. I'm your sugar daddy, let's face it. Five days, I said, and if we don't find them we'll head into Idaho and I'll do anything you say, even give you the car and let you search alone—but as long as we're in Salt Lake you're going to listen and follow. I'll find them for you, tell you what to do, then mostly I'm going to watch. I want you to feel good about it, don't you worry. I reached inside my shirt and handed him the photograph, still in its frame.

He held it close to his face, then farther away. I wanted to snatch it back out of his hands for the careless way he held it.

Could be her, he said, but she's a lot older now, you know.

Just don't act like you have any grasp of what I know.

He held the photograph close to his face. No, he said. Actually I don't think this is her at all. Looks a little like her, though.

Believe me, I said. It's her. Or don't believe me—doesn't really matter to me.

At least I want to see what you're going to do, he said. We'll see what happens after that.

No, I said. There's not going to be any anticipation. No mystery. You'll follow me.

How old are you?

Older than you think, I said. Stronger, too.

I knew exactly where Charlotte was; the letters were hidden under my seat, up in the springs, held in the coils, the address memorized a hundred different ways. All I wanted was to play on her belief, her expectation of miracles—and in every turn it can still be said I was the means, I was an instrument, that perhaps the will was not entirely my own.

I want to be plain. Yes, I've done my part, stood behind happenings that seem beyond explanation; yet there were occurrences, even signs—the messages on the flats, the red dress—that arose free of my hands, from powers I do not know. Believe me, I'd like to take credit for them. I cannot. There is plenty I don't understand, and I find comfort in this— what could be more disappointing than to find our limited understanding is correct, is all there is? I count on things I do not know, I stand amid unknown powers and try my influence. I do not know what is center and what is periphery, yet I suspect it is a question of will, of initiative. If I am wrong, do not hesitate to strike me down. I only ask who can match me, who has had more practice? While some strengths atrophy, others accumulate. I've heard of mortals who wrestled angels until dawn. I am unafraid.

We drove on, east, climbing slightly out of the flats. The back of the station wagon was loaded with the things we might need: baling wire and barbed wire, duct tape and charcoal and a shovel, ropes, anchors, old branding irons, a pitchfork with a broken handle. A car passed us, one passenger asleep, the pillow half out the window. A loaf of bread sat on the ledge inside the back window. Wonderbread.

Got a metal pin in my wrist, Texas said. From that fall. He took a tiny magnet from his pocket and stuck it there against his skin.

You carry that thing around just to show off?

He had been telling me all about making the crop circles. He swung his arm out straight, turning all the way around, telling me just how perfect they were.

I laughed to think of Johnson down there, trying to figure it out.

You laughing at me?

No, I said. It all sounds very ingenious.

You would have stayed with me, Texas said. Right?

I told him I never would've been so foolish as to get involved in the first place.

He explained all about the stilts, the ghost town, plenty of other things, things I did not necessarily want to know, like what happened between him and Charlotte. Purity is not my hang-up, though, not purity like that.

So what about this girl? I said.

What about her?

You're in love with her.

I didn't say that, he said.

Didn't say you weren't.

Forget it, he said.

All right. I laughed. You were saying? About the circles.

As time went on, Texas said, it got harder, you know, people were out looking for us and, man, that's when they bailed on me, of course. It was his idea, I'm sure—she wouldn't have left me there. I mean, I'd already broke my arm. So, working by myself, no lookout, you know, twenty guys, a whole posse laid out on their stomachs, waiting for me.

They caught you, I said.

Course they did. They couldn't help but catch me. Texas spit out the window, punched at the dashboard. I had just enough money to cover bail, the fines, after I sent a deputy up to the ghost town, and the whole time in jail was the worst—my mother came to see me and she just cried, couldn't even talk, didn't appreciate what I'd done. That's where they worked on my arm, and I had to pay for that, too. I paid for it. They held me longer than they had to; I paid my bail. And my dad—I could hear him outside in the station, cursing my name. That almost made it all worthwhile.

Everything slid past at an indefinite speed; we could have been going twenty miles an hour or two hundred. Other cars passed us and disappeared like ships on the horizon.

Strange, said Texas. Strange.

Long trenches of water shone along the highway. Here the water was already rising into September, though the heat had not let up. The ends of fenceposts and the top strands of wires showed, pens that could only hold drowned animals.

You're probably wondering, Texas said. You must wonder why we were making the circles.

You and I, I said. We're going to do terrible things together.

What?

Patience, I said.

Well, he said, rolling his window up and then down again. Some people down there around Rachel think there's something going on at the secret Air Force base, that they're keeping aliens out there or something.

A likely story, I said.

The circles were round, he said, like a flying saucer might have set itself down there, landed in the alfalfa.

Or something could be happening under the ground.

What?

Forget it, I said.

My father, Texas said. He believed that stuff.

He must be a fool, your father.

Tell me something I don't know. I was adopted, anyway— my real father could be pretty much anybody.

Don't look at me, I said. I just kept driving, thinking of all these children scarred by their parents. I'm not mistaken when I tell you I could do better. I want my chance.

Bet you never met Keith's dad, I said. Now he's a real piece of work.

What are you talking about? You know him?

No. I caught myself. Forget it, I said. I'm just guessing.

We hit the edge of the Great Salt Lake, where the water looks too heavy for waves. The road was white, covered in salt, and I moved like Gandhi, past the strange spires of Saltair, built by the Mormons to be the Coney Island of the west. Thousands would dance in the pavilion, be bent and twisted by the mirrors of the funhouse, ride the Racer. I told Texas how that rollercoaster was lit on fire, how the whole thing burned down twice. When the two of us passed, those flames were a memory, and water filled the rooms, lapping thickly inside the walls, crowding doorways and reflecting the grand ceiling of the ballroom.

Slow down! Texas said.

Someone had outlined a naked woman in the sand, off to the side of the highway. She was twenty feet tall, moss or plants for pubic hair, broken glass for eyes, nipples of empty bottles, pointed at the sky. We left her behind, Texas turning to watch her go.

Stones formed letters in the desert, only initials and hearts now, foul words and imprecations. I hardly paid attention; I knew we'd moved beyond that. I'd pieced it all together, gath- ered my information and schemed, though I was always certain it would return to its source, to its beginning, that there could be no ending without me.

Cows grazed, sweating in the heat. I checked every vehicle moving in the opposite direction, afraid I'd see Keith's car and I didn't want to lose them, wouldn't let them escape me.

Tell you what, Tex, I said. When we find them, you can do whatever you want with Keith's car.

Texas, he said.

What?

My name is not Tex and I want nothing to do with the car. You think I want to be reminded of all that? I'm doing this so I never have to think about it anymore.

We swung up onto an overpass, swerved around, then descended into the city. Salt Lake was dirtier than I remembered; that was no disappointment. This city held Charlotte, and that was my only concern. She was close. We circled the temple, where people were all dressed up, serene in the heat, eating ice cream. They waited for me to stop at the crosswalk, then looked on in disbelief when I did not.

People always remark on how clean Salt Lake City is, but the truth is it's full of spirits and all the dirt is beyond our vision's range. You cannot get lost in this city, not physically; you can always climb a little, gain enough elevation to see the grid of streets, where you are and where you want to be. This world was ordered, taken under control, so the next one might be focused on and it, too, forced to make sense, bent to the truth.

Charlotte knew this was where it would happen, unfold or unravel.

During the days she walked the city, everywhere, trying to bring it on. Beautiful, all five senses open, she was ready to receive. People walked toward her and she laughed at them as soon as they were past, at the fact that they did not know what she was thinking, what she was up to. She walked along Thirteenth East, the Wasatch Fault beneath her, the underground seam where some day the earthquake would come and shear the city from the mountains.

It was the last sign, the dress, that had led her here, that had brought her back to the land of her childhood. She still kept the dress in their bedroom, hidden between the mattress and boxspring; she'd take it out, hold it against her body, remember when it was her size, when it fit her.

She had told the bishop about the dress, but he had not been interested. He was the bishop of a wardhouse far from where they lived; she did not even tell him her last name. She just wanted to talk some things through, to show where she was and to see if it corresponded in any way with the teachings of the church.

Let's forget the dress for a minute, he'd told her. Why don't you tell me what you've done wrong.

What I think is wrong? she said. Or what I think you'll think is wrong?

It'll be interesting to see the difference, he said. Start with either one.

The whole time they talked she could hear the television and the bishop's children downstairs, his wife with the dishes in the kitchen. He sat watching Charlotte, still wearing his suit from the bank or the insurance office, eager for her words.

I ran away from home, she said. I've lied.

What about boys?

I've lived with a man.

You're no longer a virgin, then.

Yes, she said. No. I mean not with him, I haven't.

We all have our indiscretions, he said.

Do we?

Just testing you, he said. Go on.

She told him about Texas, something she had never even told Keith, something Keith might never need to know.

What else? the bishop said. The world is carnal, but it's bound to get a whole lot worse before it gets better. You still have this boyfriend? Often when we try to lift others up, you know, we get pulled down ourselves.

That's not what I'm doing, she said. That's not what this is about.

Things wouldn't have worked out for the prodigal son if he'd planned on returning, the bishop said. If he'd counted on everyone's forgiveness. The things you've done, they'll be forgiven, all right, but you have to show remorse, you have to try to change.

I had to do those things, she said. Can't you see that? And of course I'm changing—I can't help that.

Easy, he said. Keep your voice down.

Listen, then. She told him about the messages, the stones on the salt flats, the words that came to her.

He leaned close again, his voice low. What else did they ask you to do? Did you want to do these things? How did it make you feel?

She did not answer his questions, she just listened to them multiply. By their heat she could tell he suspected she was onto something true, that he knew this and would not admit it, that he was afraid.

The only thing she could think of was to walk, for she could not sit still and wait for the signs to find her. She was nervous, all wound up. The movement would take her into the midst, it would keep her straight. She walked in the sun while others sought the shadows. Everyone in the city looked familiar, but no doubt they were only cousins or more distant relations of people she'd known when she was a girl. In the city there were no places to run without stopping—not in a straight line, not without circling—there were traffic lights and cars and stop signs everywhere she turned. Trees grew silently underground, lifting and buckling the sidewalks.

The messages would not come the same way twice. There were small signs everywhere—a child crying, a violin case left at the bus stop—but they were never enough, not for long. The wind was unsteady and inadvertent; some days it moved the leaves one at a time, tentatively, so they seemed to be birds. She looked for letters, patterns, words. She walked up the canyons where the snow had long melted and the creeks were bare trickles, where she surprised quail and pheasants by the silence of her footsteps, deer on their hind legs, stretching for leaves, where she disturbed lovers spread out on blankets. She was praying all the time, every step another word.

Down on the west side the Mexicans would watch her from their porches. Gringa! they'd call. Blanca.

Pecosa, she'd call back, and they'd fall down laughing.

It's hard to tell of those early, of those last days in Salt Lake City.

At the temple grounds she was careful not to be slowed by the flowers, she avoided the missionaries at the gates. The way she moved, no one approached her—they could tell she was praying. She went over the bishop's words in her head, and she wandered through the visitor's centers, past dioramas of Mormon mannequins, the women's false faces hidden by bonnets. She tried to touch them and a voice asked her to please step back.

She passed the seagull fountain—only these people would sanctify such a dirty bird—and on toward the tabernacle, its domed roof echoing that of Saltair. She saw the Japanese, listened to the Germans. She saw the pasty-faced pilgrims from Missouri, Illinois, upstate New York—whole white families turned slow circles with crestfallen looks on their faces, seeing at last something that had been imagined for so long. Now, presented with the actual thing, they were disappointed and embarrassed. The temples in their minds were lost forever.

The temple rises up like a theme park castle, its gingerbread spires barely holding the golden angel above the shadows of skyscrapers and car parks. She had been baptized there, many times and for many people, and now she was not sure if she'd ever cross that threshold again. As she stood facing the temple she must have felt me close by, had to know I was watching her, following, close enough to see the freckles on the backs of her ears, the bruise on her heel when her shoe slipped.

It's harder to be inconspicuous in Salt Lake than it is in, say, Vegas—everyone here moves with purpose, with industry. Loiterers stand out, lurkers draw notice. I hid behind dark glasses, a pair of slacks even more ill-fitting than the ones I work in, sky blue, a velour shirt and a cardigan, cheap sandals with white socks. I go into detail to show I was not holding out hope she would discover me.

That day I let her slip away; I knew she was going home, and by that time I knew her movements, where she lived and so much more.

Trying to dodge the missionaries, I found a narrow gap between the thick wall of the temple grounds and the back of the visitor's center, a kind of pathway. No one was watching me. I went down the passage, in the cool shadows, until a space opened up, a tiny courtyard with a shed on one side. Reaching out, I felt the weight of the lock that held the ends of the chain together, that held the doors of the shed closed. I leaned close, I squinted through the aperture and saw two dusty cherubs of plastic or plaster, what looked to be a shepherd standing in the corner with his ear broken off. He leaned on his crook and looked over three tangled rolls of chick-enwire.

Are you lost? she said.

The sister missionary had come up silently behind me. When I turned I saw the look of concern on her face and I knew it was because of my age. Suddenly I thought of the Three Nephites, the Mormon disciples who knew Christ and still walk the earth, two thousand years later, those old men. I asked her if she thought I was one of them.

I don't know, she said. But I think I could tell if you were, maybe. I could feel it.

I don't think I've been here before, I said.

Not many people find their way behind here.

That's not what I meant, I said, though I'm sure you're right about that.

Sir, she said.

Think I'm senile?

Pardon me?

I didn't come here to fuck around, I said.

She led me back down the passage. She pointed out the door to the visitor's center.

Thank you, I said. I'm sorry.

When I opened the door a whole new legion of blond-haired, blue-eyed girls came at me. Charlotte could burn them down, turn them to cinders. Their heads were empty and their hearts were slow. They knew no heat.

Farther in, murals covered the walls, moving chronologically from Nebuchadnezzar's dream all the way to Joseph Smith and the angel Moroni, meeting in the forest—and beyond that, even, to the Mormon pioneers tirelessly bringing their handcarts west. The murals seamlessly brought together old and new; synthesis is the Mormon's strength, that and a surprising flexibility, fortitude. They are a people, a righteous people unto the Lord, not just neighbors who meet on Sundays.

I stopped before the painting of Joseph Smith, a young man, talking to an angel. Above, up a curving walkway, I could hear voices murmuring in all different languages. I knew what was up there and I did not follow, I stayed where I was and tried to recall what I'd learned of Joseph Smith. He talked to angels, he copied down revelations from pieces of parchment that hung in the night sky. Some say it was merely epilepsy, that he caught it from his maternal grandfather, but that old man was struck by a falling tree late in life, that's how the fits started—genetics can't corner Joseph Smith. Other things were going on with him, signs all around him.

The bishop called Charlotte a sign-seeker. That's no compliment, he said. He got out the Doctrine and Covenants and read from the heavy book: He that seeketh signs shall see signs, but not unto salvation . . . faith cometh not by signs, but signs follow those that believe.

Who says I don't believe? she said.

I'm just saying that vision follows faith and not the other way around. Faith can always be improved. Deepen it. Bring your actions into line with it. People who go looking for signs sometimes want to believe so much that they make them up or misunderstand some commonplace thing.

What are you afraid of? she said.

I'm afraid you'll find trouble, the bishop said. Demanding signs from God. Blessed are they that have not seen, and yet have believed—that's what John said.

You have no idea what I'm up to, she told him.

If you keep heading in this direction, the signs you'll be getting are not ones you'll like.

It's not about if I like them, she said. I'm not such a fool as that. Don't threaten me.

I'm only warning you. The bishop leaned forward and touched her knee, tried to look into her eyes.

None of this frightened her; she had no fear. Her wandering had its own logic. Late at night when she walked the streets, the lights were pale, white, promised nothing. She only knew she had to keep moving. She knew it would not be long.

Yes, Charlotte, that bishop said faith comes before signs, that false spirits can lead you astray. Delusions always belong to others; we cannot see our own. It's not so much that we see what we want to see, but that we see what we have to see, in order to survive. It's a little arrogant to believe we have much control or can somehow stand aside to judge, yet more people underestimate than overestimate the power of the will. The amount of energy in the universe does not increase or decrease, it only changes form, and I will pass it through me, I will wreak the change.

Outside, in the temple grounds, I could breathe again. I thought of Texas, back in the motel room, no doubt cleaning his gun or practicing catching quarters off his elbow; I would return to see the coins on the floor, the bruise on his cheek spread into a black eye. I made him promise not to leave that room and the captivity was working on him, just like I'd hoped. I needed him desperate.

Through the plate glass windows of the visitor's center, above, I saw the huge white Christ, the statue pointing at me. Behind me, behind the doors of the temple I will never enter, were the baptismal fonts that look like graves. Everything is a resurrection.

Blessings we won't even understand, someone was saying.

Outside of the gates, out in the streets of the city, I saw people pointing to the apartment where the president of the church was living. The president is the earthly head of the kingdom of God—like Moses, he is the prophet, the translator and revealer. This prophet was Ezra Taft Benson, the thirteenth, and there's no doubt he's dead by the time anyone reads this.

As I looked up at his window I wondered what he was doing up there. Was he praying or fasting, catching his breath in an oxygen tent, sorting his socks, playing solitaire? Was he thinking of the land or the sky, the earth or the heavens? Both, I'd like to believe, that he could hold it all at once, that he stood always receptive to revelation, always listening.

No doubt the prophet could already see what we were going to do—it was playing inside his eyelids, thick on his tongue. I do not know what side he took, if he prayed to hold us back or push us forward, if he implored the powers to turn things the way they went, if he also played a part.

It was possible that he was watching me then, looking down between the dark folds of the curtains, perhaps even that he would recognize me or send someone out to bring me to him. What would he do if he were in my place? Could he imagine such a thing, such love?

By the way she walked I could tell
she missed me. She is beautiful
from a distance and she is dis-
turbing up close. I followed her
through the long, still aisles of li-
braries, her fingers trailing along
the spines of books, I stood close
as she rested her feet in the cool
water of fountains. Leaving her
there, I turned away and cut across
town to reach her house first. She
is wild in my rafters. I wanted her
on top of me, fingertips counting
my ribs, her legs scissoring me in
two.

I scrawled messages to her in the dirt, using a stick, and then I scratched them all out. I thought of putting a king of hearts in her mailbox, but I didn't want to give her any warning.

The house, a duplex, was up in the avenues, on the side of the mountain, at the same height as Moroni, the golden angel atop the temple's spire. In the mornings she'd look out at him, a mile away, check to see that he was still blowing his trumpet, calling the saints. She tried to hear it.

Before I left I walked all the way around the house, memorizing every window and door, the height of the backyard fence. Yes, I carry matches in my pocket. Dogs barked next door and I ignored them as I went through the gate, back up the street. I had watched the house all night, her dark silhouette in the window. Now I knew their schedules, hers and Keith's. Nothing could stop me — I greeted people on the sidewalk, waved to passing cars, talked to children, and the whole time I was thinking about how little everyone knew.

I was circling, coiling and tightening around her. I walked on, planning, and it was not easy to believe the sun straight above was the same one that shone down on Las Vegas. There was no doubt of its heat, though — to see the city like that, no one would ever believe it could snow in winter.

I walked under the eagle gate and then turned up again, toward the Capitol. The mountains crowd you and cut down the size of the sky; they shorten the day and lengthen the night. Slapping the deck of cards in my pocket, I thought of Texas, back in the motel. Three days had passed and he was anxious, warning me my time was almost up, sweet boy. I let him know it would be a mistake to rush anything.

Up by the Capitol I looked out over the city, its trees in straight lines, suburb upon suburb; as Brigham Young promised, the desert has blossomed like the rose. West, I tried to see the lake and the flats beyond. I knew she would realize, finally, that the messages out there were about me, and I'd give her more signs to show her her faith. Oh, Charlotte, despair is the gravest of sins—at least evil has some action, some movement to it and, besides, even the most evil intentions cannot be assured of their success.

I followed her, but I always knew where Keith was. He worked at a car lot, where he couldn't sell what they gave him because he knew too much about cars. He wouldn't even wish them on the sixteen-year-old Mormon boys who came in on their birthdays, leading their fathers.

On his days off she would show him the city. Once they had walked to the This Is the Place Monument and stood, looking down over the valley, the temple, the Capitol, the tall hospital near their house in the avenues.

How do you feel? she said.

Hot, he said. Look, you can see the flats.

She asked him if the cars were racing and he told her he did not know, that he thought maybe the season was over, the flats softening toward winter, the water rising up. She said she'd seen how he looked at his car; she accused him of wanting to be out there.

Charlotte, he said, that was a hundred years ago.

Taking hold of his arm, she turned him toward the monument. All around the base were the trappers, Jesuits, Indian chiefs, all those who blazed trails and were then forced to make way before the saints. High above, atop the monument, Brigham Young stood saying the words, making the promises, shouting to be heard down in the valley, out on the lake, across the salt flats to a border not yet drawn. From his height he can see a long way. He can see me coming out of the casino, Wendover Will waving and taunting him, disputing which place is the place.

I'm related to him, Charlotte said.

Who?

Brigham Young.

We all are, said Keith. Probably. Somehow.

Down below them, across the wide road that came out of the canyon, paving the way of the pioneers, the animals stirred

233

in the zoo, slept as people walked by. Even the elephants looked small, stumbling in the heat, straw on their backs and chains around their ankles.

Two men sat on horses along the base of the statue, shouting through round mouths, letting everyone know that they, the Mormons, had arrived, that they would tame everything, organize and beat it down, turn a profit or die trying. Brigham Young held up one arm, casting judgment over the animals, denying any common ancestry. Charlotte could see the hawks—tiny, dark shapes—resting on perches in a cage fifty feet tall. This was worse than a small cage, really, a hint of space when what they needed was to fly for miles.

I read in the paper, Keith said, where some dogs got into the zoo and killed a bunch of those little deer. Just dogs from the neighborhood, running in a pack.

What's the matter? she said.

Nothing.

You always say that. Tell me.

What else could I want? he said.

Tell me.

I've been true to you, he said. I've stood by you.

You won't collapse on me, she said. Keith.

I just don't want you to forget, he said. I don't want to be left behind.

Charlotte turned to face him. She looked down at the city, up into the sky.

We never had promises before, she said. We can't do it that way—especially not now, when things are so close.

I felt her urgency, because it was also my own. At the end of those days I circled, exhausted, back to the motel. Crossing the parking lot, I saw the tools we'd need through the windows of my car. A pirate and a spaceman stared out at me. Halloween masks, our disguises.

Texas hardly looked up when I came in. I dropped a bag of food on the floor, next to where he was sitting, and he took his time picking it up. All his anxiety was turned inward now—he no longer asked questions, he just waited for my words. I told him just enough to keep him with me; I promised nothing I didn't deliver.

Saw her today, I said. Saw them both, up by the zoo.

Liar, he said. How would you even recognize them?

I know exactly where they are.

Right, he said. You're playing with me.

I shrugged, shuffled a deck of cards. I'm fortunate to be working with you, I said. It's an honor and a pleasure.

All I want, Texas said. All I really want is for them to look in my face. I want to hear what they have to say to me.

Yes, I said. That's not too much to ask.

That's all I want, he said.

We sat for hours without speaking. Texas spread newspaper across the floor and broke down his gun, cleaned it, oiled it, put it back together. I tossed cards like boomerangs, clipping his ear, knocking glasses into the sink, scaring birds outside the window. My mind wandered and I spoke from the dark side of my heart, imagining what we could do to Keith—yes, I envy the time he's spent with Charlotte and I could almost see plastic bags waving their tattered edges from fences down along the Great Salt Lake, the glow of the phosphorescent tailings pond from the mine, the spires of Saltair floating in the heat. I could almost hear the water lapping, circling around us in the darkness of the flooded ballroom at Saltair, waves coming in through the doorway, waves so thick with salt that nothing could sink or drown. I could almost feel the weights we'd attach to Keith, the moment of his descent, bubbles rising to the surface, the strange sense that he was hidden underwater, down by our feet.

What are you talking about? Texas said.

Just daydreaming.

Heartless, he said.

If only you knew, I said. If only I had less of one.

Texas stood and went to the window, staring for a long time, as if he might see them out there. He slid the barrel back and forth along the sill.

Fuck, he said. He said it like a spoiled child, like a little boy. Tomorrow, I told him.

The window was going dark. We were another day closer, closing in, and Charlotte was out there, waiting for us, waiting for it all to happen. She could feel it approaching, deep in her skin. The bishop had accused her of wanting to be exalted and she told him if that was true it was only from within, never from without. He could not grasp that she was most pleased when most uneasy, that she did not want a perfect satisfaction, but only to be close to the powers that would let nothing settle. He told her that even if she was receiving signs, if spirits did visit her, she wouldn't have the power to discern good from evil.

Nothing can lead you astray like a false spirit when you believe you have the power of God, he said. Instead of progress, light and truth, you'll be led backward into darkness, lies, every evil thing. Joseph Smith himself said that.

Are you even listening to me? she said. I'm almost there now, I can feel it coming, and these are the words you have for me?

Yes, Charlotte had sought the other side, dark and forbidden, and instead she had found the darkness was within, that it had its own light. We never so much change as uncover parts of what we already are. The spaces inside stretch like those outside and I'm not even certain I can tell the difference.

On the edge of the trailer park, in someone's yard, ghosts of sheets hang from the branches of a tree. They swing wildly and surprise each other with their edges, collide and finally tangle the fishing line that holds them. They swing together, as if embracing. Beneath them, headstones made of cardboard are covered in misspellings and joke names. It is almost Halloween; this season makes me want to get down on all fours and writhe on the ground. Everything is dying.

Packs of wild dogs now run the backstreets—they haven't attacked anyone, not yet—and Anita's horse still makes its forays into town, each one more dangerous. This is Wendover, the town where I live, the place that gives shape to my days.

These days Charlotte is always before me; she has not faded. Even those looks she gave me in the beginning still reverberate inside, are not spent. The Mormon prophets foresaw trains and automobiles—I have no doubt they saw me coming. They said in the latter days the sea will return to its place in the north and all the continents will become one land again. My paradise will look nothing like that.

All this and I'm not even tired, hardly winded. Rainy days I sit in the library and read sad books, I write this down, I wait to see what the bookmobile will bring me. And when the sky is still and the ground is dry I search for the hawks and I do not despair. I could make better money in Elko perhaps, drag my trailer west and deal cards in the shadow of the polar bear in the Commercial Hotel, but some of us do better on the borders, lost in the edges.

I spend more time drinking in the Stateline now, since that is the first place anyone would look. No one talks to me except the bartenders. I like the sound of others' voices around me when I don't have to respond or take part. It helps.

I see many things, few that surprise me. I heard him come in, but I did not recognize him at first, not even when he sat down next to me at the bar.

Remember me? he said.

Keith's voice was hoarse, beyond a pack-a-day smoker's, as if his vocal cords had been taken out and dragged through glass. The skin of his neck was so badly burned it was difficult for him to turn his head, and his hair was wet like he'd just bathed or escaped a drowning. His skin was white, seared into knots and ridges. His arms and hands were scarred, also, webs between his fingers.

What's wrong with your eyes? I said.

Smoke, he said. I was blind for two weeks. And I couldn't

talk until now. Felt fine until the next day and then it almost strangled me. Burned my throat, my lungs.

I just nodded. I know those burns, only mine come from the inside, the path of these hot words—summoned, they scorch their way out, and I offer them to you.

Come back to race? I said. Can you drive?

Sold my car to pay for the hospital, Keith said. I don't care about that anymore.

What about those angels? said Mike the bartender. Tell some more like you were talking last night.

Which ones? I said. The Mormon ones are the hardest to recognize. No wings, you know. Every time someone has a run of luck I get suspicious.

They take your money?

You know it.

What do they want with money?

I don't know, I said. Maybe they give it to the church.

Machines sang all around us, the infirm and misguided shuffled past, cocktail waitresses came and went. Mike was hanging wineglasses upside down, by their stems, above the bar. I turned back to Keith and asked him what he was doing here.

Came to take my dad back down south.

How?

Bus, he said.

A machine between him and the earth?

I drove him up here, Keith said. I reckon I know how to take him back. This whole area's unlucky.

I saw him wince as he talked. I wondered what his skin looked like, under his clothes.

He warned me, said Keith. My dad did. Said not to go with her, that only harm would come of it, that I wouldn't know what to expect.

If you predict enough things, eventually you'll get one right. Not that it would hurt me to give Johnson a little credit— maybe he was onto something with his ridiculous earth energy, perhaps one day we'll know. As if he could come into my own town and outlast me! And of course Anita still comes by my trailer, wakes me up just to tell me she's lonely. I fear she'll hound me to the end of my days.

Keith showed me he was missing two fingers, that the others swung as if they had no bones. There was a scar right in the middle of his hand. Bullet hole. I put my arm around his shoulders, but did not press down on his skin. I wanted to hear it from him.

The angels only give ten percent, I told Mike, they spend the rest, buy new cars and speedboats, waterskis. They're curious, you know, there's so much they can't remember; they want to understand why we're doing all this.

Aren't you going to ask me what happened? Keith said.

What did happen? I said, pulling him closer, careful of his skin. My sweet boy wanted to talk; he talked to me all night.

Keith had seen him coming, down the street in Salt Lake City. He had stood inside the house, behind the window, and waited for him. He was glad to see him—he welcomed the reckoning and wanted to settle. Texas walked with a mask atop his head, not even pulled down to cover his face.

Texas? I said. No one has a name like that. You're making this up.

You don't have to believe it, Keith said.

Texas looked back and forth as he walked down the street. Children ran past him, holding stick swords aloft. His mouth was moving, whispering; his fingers curled and straightened and curled again.

When Keith opened the door Texas just stood there, looking at him, the gun in one hand.

We were friends, Texas said, finally. We aren't now.

Keith reached out, putting his hand on the barrel of the gun. It went off, the first shot straight through Keith's hand, the second down the hallway and into the kitchen. With his other hand, Keith hit Texas with a punch that took him off the porch and down the stairs, onto the sidewalk. He was knocked unconscious. Two children stopped in the street, watching; Keith did not even notice. He dragged Texas back inside the house, so he wouldn't escape or draw more attention, and called the police. He was so angry he didn't trust himself around the body.

Back outside, he waited for the police car. Children were gathering still, laying their bikes down on the sidewalk, pointing to a spot of blood at the bottom of the stairs.

At first the flames were silent, they hid their smoke. They burned in straight lines and sped up to turn corners; they swerved into designs, stars and letters folding and closing in on each other and themselves. Beautiful, scorching impurity like the holy spirit, drafts ripped through the house, ungluing spiderwebs just before leaving them as cinders. Even the fire marshal could not explain it; he said there was no way the house could have gone up like that, that fast, and all this when the other side of the duplex was hardly burned at all. No one controls fires like that, the marshal said.

Keith ran back into the house. It was late afternoon, a time of day she was never home. Texas knew that; he would never hurt her. The stairs were on fire. Keith used the bedclothes to smother the flames. Crawling to stay beneath the smoke, he dragged her behind him. The doorknob took all the prints off his fingers, it burned the palm of his hand smooth. He set her down on the lawn and when he lifted the blankets Charlotte's body was still smoking.

He forgot Texas was in the house, Keith said, but I don't know if I believe that. Texas did not feel the flames coming for him, and if he did he felt them too late. As if there was any way I could have saved him, as if I don't miss him deeply now, in my way. Yes, people have been left behind, they have sloughed off like the skins of a snake, and where their lives overlapped my own I feel new again, raw and smooth.

Some say angels don't even recognize each other, I told Mike. That's a foolish way to think.

Why the shots didn't wake her, no one knew. It was more

of a miracle that she survived. Keith said she took the fire as a sign, that she refused to see him after that. He said she has scales, gills, webbed fingers like his own, that her eyes won't open all the way. She could not have scarred inside, that I know. No flames can touch her there—they could not match the heat. They would turn back ashamed.

It was a beautiful fire. They said no one could have set it. I am many things—a cheat, a lover, a bitter old man, a liar—but I am no common arsonist. My hands were guided, believe me. Texas went like the tender fool he was, and he went in a good cause.

I still care about her, Keith said, but I'm pretty much past the point where I think that will change anything.

You're right about that, I said. Did she ever mention me?

She hates you, said Keith. You know that.

She may well believe she does, I said.

When feelings are strong that's all that matters; at the heights the polarity switches most easily, the extremes know each other like siblings. Not rivals, but lovers. Yes, she loves me, locked up in her parents' house in Bountiful. She sits in the darkness and she prays and she listens for answers and I have no doubt she hears me from across the flats, the desert, the lake full of salt. It was a sign, that fire, the one she was waiting for.

She knows the truth—that I was there. I said I was a liar, yet I must stand up here, I have to assume my share. Yes, I lit the matches, I led the flames, blessed them and let them loose. They licked, they multiplied. Texas was supposed to get Keith out, Charlotte was not supposed to be there at all. It did not fall out according to my plan, but a higher one. Wings turn inside out and upside down, folding on hinges, closing on my heart. That fire was a long time coming; it smoldered since the day she took the cribbage board from the wall and turned to face me, all challenge.

I am a man who has acknowledged my limitations, reveled in them. That Texas was taken, that the flames found Charlotte—I did not plan these things, but that does not mean they happened for no reason. I was powerful and I was powerless; it was pure volition.

Searching for the birds high above I almost expect to see you there, also; or, letting my gaze drop, I hope to see you climbing up the slope, to me. I won't say the climb is easy for me, but it's not as difficult as some might think. It is the same place where the winds came up the mountains and blew your hair right out of your face—now they reverse direction and come down over my head, carrying my thoughts across the flats.

I had no time to save anyone, even if I had known. I heard no one cry out. Through the window I saw curtains raise themselves and then collapse into nothing, gone. Pieces of furniture floated across rooms, on fire, beautiful, splintering to sparks. Heat rolled carpets and took paint from walls in straight, hot lines. I work in concert with powers I cannot name. The flames needed sustenance; they searched and searched. All I heard were the sirens and I climbed over the fence and walked away; people ran past me, around me, eager to watch the fire.

I light fires in the mountains to keep me warm, to keep me company. Several at once, they purify, they bend signals and words. I fill my notebooks with writing. I carry mirrors and flash messages in Morse code. The sun is cold and cutting.

Perhaps one night I'll come down the mountain, or early in the morning I'll return from work and you'll be asleep in my bed in the trailer and you'll roll over and look at me and I won't care if what Keith said is true, what he said about your face. I'll match you wrinkle for wrinkle and we will play cribbage with the lights dim so you won't have to look at me and I won't have to look at you. And if we do we will see each other as we used to be.

Each day it gets colder on the mountain. I take out a dove on a short lead, as bait; I fear it is too late in the season for the hawks. The dove forgets his lead, tries to fly, falls, forgets and tries again. It bathes in the dust to shed lice from its wings. I check behind myself, nervous, surrounded by fires. I watch the path and I watch the sky. I do not know if you will come from below or if you will come from above. You might come so fast, Charlotte, that I won't realize it until you're standing before me with the dove in your hands. I am ready for this.

ACKNOWLEDGMENTS

This book would not exist if not for the kindness of these people. Thanks to Tina Pohlman, my editor, for her hard work, bravery and insight; to my agent, Leigh Feldman, for her patience and her whip; to Lan Samantha Chang and John L'Heureux, for their careful readings of the manuscript; to the Andersons, the Gurrs, and everyone at the Ucross Foundation and the Stanford Creative Writing Program, for shelter and encouragement; to my many L.D.S. friends (especially Elders Boyack and González of the Provo Mission, winter, 1995), for their faith, generosity and sense of humor.

Special thanks to Ella Vining for bringing me luck and everything else.